Summer's Rage

A Larry Macklin Mystery-Book 14

A. E. Howe

DEDICATION

For members of search and rescue teams everywhere, both
professional and volunteer, human and animal.
Thanks for all you do.

CHAPTER ONE

It was the third week in June, and already I couldn't wait for summer to be over. May had been warmer than usual and June was reaching for new records. Cara and I stood at the front door, trying to prepare ourselves for a new day. My hand hesitated as I reached for the door knob.

"Coward," Cara said.

"I just want to get a few more breaths of cool air before I go out there."

"The high today is only going to be ninety-eight," she said, jabbing me playfully in the back.

"Yeah, same as the humidity."

"You can take it."

Theatrically, I sucked in a deep breath and opened the door. Once we were outside, I gave Cara a quick kiss, then watched with a smile as she pulled out of the driveway and headed for the vet clinic. I was feeling very comfortable in my new role as a married man, and we were both working to keep the newlywed vibe going for as long as we could. There was something deeply satisfying about making someone else happy.

It was Monday and I had a whole new week ahead of me. As I drove to the sheriff's office, I let my mind wander over the dozen active cases that I was currently working and tried to decide which ones took priority. Several of them had the potential to deteriorate quickly.

Number one on the list was a drug-related shooting that had left two people wounded and could easily spiral into a series of retaliatory acts of violence. Next was a child battery case where a non-custodial parent had grabbed her child, leaving some nasty bruises on the ten-year-old's arms and a bad bump on his head when the child struggled and fell down. We were still considering leveling the more serious charge of attempted kidnapping against her. Then there was the man who'd been hit in the head with a beer bottle while walking down the street. This case managed to make its way to number three on the list as it was the sixth similar incident, but the first to result in a serious injury.

When I pulled into the parking lot, I looked around for Darlene's car but didn't see it. That was odd. Darlene Marks was my frequent partner on our most complicated cases and she habitually made it to the office long before the start of our shifts.

As I got out of the car, I noticed Pete Henley, a fellow investigator and my best friend in the department. His ample rear end was sticking out of the passenger side of his unmarked car and there was a large garbage bag at his feet.

"About time you threw out some of that toxic waste," I said.

Pete waved at me with a handful of old receipts and paper cups. "Sarah insisted I do this at work. She didn't want me filling up our cans at home."

"Have you seen Darlene?"

"She's working a traffic accident north of town." He backed out of the car and faced me. "Has she said anything?"

"No, not since we found out that Maxwell is leaving in September."

Charles Maxwell was Calhoun's chief of police. He'd run for sheriff last fall, but my father had prevailed in a surprisingly close election. Everyone knew that Maxwell was bored being the chief of a small-town department, so there'd been no surprise when word got around that he was moving on.

"You saw the ad on her computer?"

"Yeah. The pay is considerably more than what she's getting here."

"Plus she'd get to be the boss."

"There're some minuses that would go along with it. And I don't see Darlene being happy supervising glorified mall cops," I said hopefully.

Calhoun had only about a dozen police officers. Most serious crimes were handled by the sheriff's office, while the police department primarily dealt with traffic violations, parking enforcement and minor crimes within the city.

"She's tough as nails and would make a great chief," Pete said.

"Whose side are you on?" I really didn't want to lose Darlene. She was an excellent investigator and all-around cop.

"You can't hold a person back just 'cause it's good for you."

"Don't go all mature on me."

"Maybe she won't get the job."

"Not likely. She worked for them for several years before coming here. Everyone knows that the only reason she changed jobs was because she didn't have a chance for advancement over there. I'm sure Maxwell will recommend her," I said pessimistically.

"She might not apply."

"I want to ask her about it, but… it seems…"

"Pushy? Nosy? Yep, all of those things. I think this is one of those cases where you're gonna have to let things work themselves out."

"You're a big help," I said, and left him to finish making his car habitable again.

I spent the morning working on the drug shooting. Rousting up drug dealers and junkies before noon had a distinct advantage—they were usually still asleep and easy to find. The only downside was waking and sobering them up enough so that they were able to understand speech and give semi-coherent responses to my questions.

It turned out that the shooters were a couple of rogues who weren't playing by the local rules, so I didn't have any trouble finding people who were willing to rat them out. I even found two people who were more than happy to go on record saying that they'd recognized the shooters at the scene. Now all I had to do was find and arrest the two loose cannons.

I received a couple of good leads, but they were apparently laying low. I drew a blank at the younger perp's grandma's house, though she did admit that they had been there the night before. The girlfriend of the older one said that he'd ditched her and hadn't been around for over a week, but I didn't believe her. One of the witnesses had said that the girlfriend was a junkie and the bad boy was her supplier as well as her boyfriend. The girl was acting much too calm to be out of touch with her source of drugs.

I spent some time watching her place while I called in a pickup order for the two suspects. Finally I headed for lunch, calling Darlene on the way.

"You want to join me?"

"Where?"

"Taco truck?"

"We aren't eating outside in this heat," Darlene objected. "I've been sweating all morning."

"Text me your order and I'll bring it to the office."

Standing in line at the taco truck downtown, I debated whether to broach the subject of the chief's job with Darlene. Part of me just needed to know if it was something I should worry about or not.

Back at the office, I spread the food out in the

conference room where we had comfortable chairs and were less likely to be bothered by anyone or distracted by emails.

"So where's Chief Maxwell going?" I said, slyly approaching the topic while casually munching on my burrito.

"He's taken a job with that security firm your friend works for," she said, causing me to stare.

"Silver Security. You're kidding!"

"I talked with him this weekend. He's taking an upper-level management job. Part liaison with law enforcement and part salesman. The salary is scary big."

It made sense for Maxwell. He'd never been a cop-on-the-beat kind of guy. His wife was a professor at Florida State, and he liked to move in more academic circles. I remembered what my friend, Andrew Reyes, had told me he was making with the same company. He'd tried to talk me into taking a job with them and, occasionally, a little voice inside my head told me I was missing out. But the truth was that, even though it had taken a while, I'd really come to love my job as a criminal investigator.

"So who's going to be the new chief?" I asked nonchalantly.

Darlene set her chicken taco aside and started to say something when my phone went off. I thought about ignoring it, but when I saw that it was from dispatch, I put up a finger and said, "Hold that thought."

I listened for a moment and realized I was going to have to forget my goal of digging into Darlene's future plans. I was needed at the scene of a murder... or possibly a double murder.

"Deputy Sanderson is on the scene and an ambulance is en route," the dispatcher told me.

"You said it might be two murders?" I asked, trying to clarify the situation as I got up and headed for the door.

"It was reported by a young man named Marty Reece. He was pretty hysterical. From what I could tell, a man was killing his wife and Marty's mother hit the man in the head with a piece of wood. Marty said the man was on the ground and unresponsive."

He gave me an address on a road I'd never heard of, which was unusual. I'd lived in Adams County all my life and thought I knew every highway and byway. Then he clarified the location and I understood. It was a private road off of a two-lane highway in the northeast part of the county that was mostly made up of large timber tracts and old hunting plantations. There couldn't be more than one person per thousand acres up there.

With my lights flashing and pushing the engineering of the narrow highway, I pulled onto Byrd Farm Road ten minutes after leaving the office. A large iron gate with "Byrd Farm" expertly welded into the design normally blocked the dirt drive, but it had been left open for first responders.

The land was well maintained. Slightly rolling hills were topped with tall longleaf pines and palmettos, along with the occasional cluster of live oak trees. I turned left as I'd been instructed by dispatch when I saw a forest-green deer stand at the corner where another road teed into the main road. I guessed that the farm covered at least five hundred acres. Probably more.

After maybe a mile, the road opened onto a large, sloping field. A large old farmhouse sat on the top of the hill, surrounded by various barns, smaller cottages and cabins, and a dozen or more cars, trucks and motor homes. An ambulance and one of our patrol cars were parked next to a classic, Florida-style cracker cabin on one edge of the field. Several people were standing outside wearing varying expressions of shock and sadness.

I climbed out of my car and saw two EMTs carrying a stretcher out of the cabin, bearing a man with an oxygen mask on his face. There were gasps and cries of sorrow from the onlookers.

I recognized one of the EMTs and asked, "How is he?"

She looked at me and took a second to answer. "Not good," she finally said, shaking her head. "They'll know more at the hospital. All I can say is that he's alive. For now."

I nodded and headed toward the cabin.

I could hear weeping coming from inside as I stepped onto the small porch. I opened the door and felt the cool air as I walked inside. The living room took up the whole front of the clapboard structure. A woman and a young man were sitting on the couch, holding each other. Deputy Matti Sanderson stood in front of a door at the back of the room. She had her arms crossed and nodded to me as I came in.

"The body's in here," Sandy said, nodding at the door.

The woman on the couch let out a loud sob. I looked at both of them and assumed that the boy was Marty Reece. He looked like he'd calmed down a little since talking with dispatch. He'd raised his head when I came in, but went right back to comforting the woman.

"Hi, Marty," I said in as soothing a tone as I could muster. "How old are you?"

"Seventeen," he said, looking at me with eyes that were red from crying. In his fear and grief, he looked much younger.

"Marty, can you tell me what happened?" I asked gently.

"I came in after... it had happened. But my mom said that Uncle Austin was... hurting Aunt Tracy so she..."

The woman finally looked up at me, her face wet and puffy. "I hit him. I just hit him. He was killing her."

"Your name is?"

"Paula Reece. Tracy is my sister."

"I'm afraid that we're going to have to take some pictures and collect your clothes," I told her, glancing over at Sandy. I was intruding on their grief, but the sooner we collected the clothes the more valuable they'd be as evidence.

"Crime scene are on their way," Sandy told me.

"Are you going to arrest my mom?" Marty asked.

I paused to consider how I could answer that without lying or causing him more distress.

"Not right now. We're going to collect evidence and try

to learn what happened before we arrest anyone. Were you here when it happened?"

"I had stopped to say hi to Cleo. When I came in, Mom was screaming. I ran to the door… It was awful." His voice dropped so low I could barely catch the last word.

I wanted to press him for more details, but I needed to carefully consider how to proceed. If Marty had been on the scene before there were any other witnesses, then his clothes would need to be taken too. I couldn't allow any empathy for the family to interfere with the investigation. It wasn't a good idea to make assumptions about who may or may not have been an innocent bystander. Sometimes the most sympathetic person at a crime scene would turn out to be the bad guy. But I didn't have to be a jerk about it either.

CHAPTER TWO

I took out my phone and called Shantel Williams. I wanted to make sure she was coming with the crime scene unit. Not only was she the head of the unit, but she was also a very compassionate and competent technician.

"We just pulled through the gate. Now if we can just find our way cross country," she said. Shantel didn't care much for the woods.

I stayed on the phone with her until the van pulled up outside the cabin, then I turned back to Marty. "Is your father here?"

He looked around as if he thought I meant "in the room." Then his eyes focused and he shook his head. "No, I'm... They're divorced," he said uncomfortably.

"Do you have any grandparents, uncles or aunts around?"

"Too many."

"Why are you asking him that?" his mother managed between tears.

"He needs someone acting as his guardian," I said, seeing the expression on her face. "Someone other than you. We'll need to separate the two of you for interviews."

I could tell that she wanted to argue with me, but she bit it back and turned to Marty. "Go get your grandpa." Looking back at me, she said, "I haven't talked to his father in years. I don't even know where he is."

Marty started to stand up, but I put my hand out to stop him.

"I'll get your grandfather. What's his name?"

"Bruce Byrd. He's probably out there." Paula pointed toward the door.

At that moment, the door swung open and Shantel came inside, followed by Marcus Brown. Marcus had been working for us part time while he waited to be rehired to a full-time position with the sheriff's office. He'd left the department to work for the Florida Department of Law Enforcement in Tallahassee last fall. The new job honeymoon hadn't lasted long.

I explained to Shantel what had happened, at least as far as I understood it, then I opened the bedroom door and took my first look at where the woman's body lay sprawled on the floor. Her clothes were in disarray, her throat exposed and raw. A blood-covered two-by-four was on the floor beside her.

Deputy Sanderson came up behind me. "I think that guy Byrd tried to get in here earlier. I had to threaten to arrest him for obstructing justice to keep him out."

"Thanks, Sandy." I wasn't surprised. Anyone would want to rush to the aid of their daughter in a situation like this.

I left Shantel and Marcus to start taking photos and videoing the crime scene. Stepping outside, I saw the group still milling in the yard and I didn't have any trouble guessing which of them was Bruce Byrd. A square-built man in his early seventies, with grey hair, a mustache and wearing expensive-looking, day-at-the-lodge-type clothes, was staring at me from ten feet away.

"I want—"

"Bruce Byrd?" I confirmed, interrupting him. I could tell that he wasn't the kind of man who should be allowed to get his wind up.

"I am. I want—"

"I need your help."

His expression made it clear that this wasn't what he'd expected me to say. "With what? My daughter…"

"I need you to take care of your grandson," I said as he joined me on the porch.

"I'm a lawyer and I want to talk to my daughter."

"You know that's not the way it works. She can ask to speak with you. That's her right. But you don't have a right to speak to her. But your grandson *does* need your help."

"His mother…"

"You know that they need to be interviewed separately."

"They don't have to talk to you."

"You're right. But we want to clear this up as quickly as possible for everyone's sake. If this happened the way your daughter says it did, then there's no need to worry or to stonewall us."

"I'm not a criminal lawyer, but I know enough about trauma to know that you can't expect to get all the answers now. I'd like to take them home. We'll come—"

I started to cut him off again, but his eyes narrowed and every muscle in his body tensed up. He leaned in to me and I smelled the whiskey on his breath.

"If you interrupt me one more time, I promise you'll regret it. Let me take her home, and you have my word they'll both come back in a couple of days to give you complete statements."

"I'm not your daughter's enemy, and I don't expect a complete statement right now. However, she needs to give us the broad outline of what happened before I let her go." I stared back at him. "Now, will you help your grandson?"

"Of course I will," he said, taking the opportunity to try to move around me. I put my hand gently on his chest.

"I'll bring him out."

At first, I thought Bruce was going to argue with me, but he managed to choke it back.

I went into the house, thinking that what I really wanted to do was to talk with the boy alone. But that was a big no-no. Underage children needed to have a parent or guardian present during an interview, at least if we wanted it to be admissible in court.

"Your grandfather is outside," I told Marty. The young man got up and followed me to the door, looking back at his mother.

"Mom?"

"Go on. I'll be fine," she told him.

When we stepped out on the porch, the group outside started moving toward us.

"Stay back," I told them, then turned to Bruce. "The first thing we need to do is bag up the clothes he's wearing as evidence."

"But he didn't have anything to do with this," the older man argued.

"He was at the scene alone with his mother. We still don't know exactly what happened. Collecting his clothes will help to make sure we don't regret not having evidence later. Remember, anything we collect could be important in proving your daughter's story," I said softly.

Bruce seemed to mull this over. I glanced at Marty, who looked nervous and embarrassed.

"I take your point," Bruce finally said.

"I'm going to get Marcus, one of our crime scene techs. Take both of them to wherever Marty is staying so he can take these clothes off and get into to some clean ones."

Bruce Byrd nodded solemnly and waited while I rounded up Marcus. I watched as the three of them made their way through the small crowd, then I went back inside.

Paula Reece was standing by the window, staring as her son and father walked away. I explained what was happening and she nodded while wiping her eyes. Then I looked down at the blood on her shirt and jeans.

"We need to take some pictures of you, and bag up your clothes too."

"I understand."

"I'll have Shantel go with you in a minute, but first I'd like to ask you a few questions." As I spoke, I glanced over at Deputy Sanderson to make sure she was listening. Having another set of ears in a situation like this could make a difference.

"I'll tell you what I can." Paula's demeanor had shifted from grief to resignation.

"Who are the victims?"

"My sister Tracy and her husband Austin." She hesitated, then added, "Stokes. Their last name is Stokes."

"Why are you all here?"

"Oh, you mean all of the family? Althea's ninetieth birthday. She wanted us all to meet here."

"Althea?"

"My grandmother, Althea Byrd. She was born here. Not in this house, I mean, but the big one over there." She pointed out the window at the two-story farmhouse. "She wasn't a Byrd then, of course. She married Ryan, my grandfather, in 1944." She stopped. "You don't care about our family history."

"I need to find out as much as I can about what happened here. But, no, I don't need the deep background right now," I said with a small smile. "When did you and Marty get here?"

"Friday evening. We drove up from Tampa."

"Do you know when Tracy and Austin got here?"

"About the same time. They drove over from Valdosta."

"Did you see them before today?"

"Of course, she's my sister. I saw them as soon as they got here."

"Did you all get along?"

"My sister and I are best friends." Paula didn't hesitate to use the present tense.

"And you and her husband?"

"I didn't care much for Austin. He didn't treat Tracy right."

"What do you mean by that?'"

"He was… possessive. You know how some men are. If Tracy and I went shopping, she'd get a dozen texts from him wanting to know where she was and when she was coming home."

"Did she resent it?"

Paula looked thoughtful. "To be fair, she could be as bad as he was. I've seen her get all worked up and text him forty times in half an hour, badgering him. I don't think they were good for each other. On the other hand, I don't know who else would have put up with either of them."

"Did they ever get into physical altercations?"

"I think they probably did, but I never saw any… marks or anything. I saw him grab her a few times, and she's shoved him."

"Tracy never said that he abused her?"

"No. As a matter of fact, most of the time she called him a wimp. In public a few times, she called him names that would have gotten anyone angry. What do you call it? Fighting words."

"How long were they married?"

"Eight years. He's her second husband. I think this was his third marriage."

"Did you ever threaten him?"

"No!" She sounded shocked at the question.

"Did you ever argue with him?"

"I told you, we didn't really get along. I guess I might have argued with him a few times."

"Recently?"

She didn't say anything for several minutes. I allowed the silence to push her to answer. "Yesterday," she whispered.

"Tell me about the argument." Direct questions were usually the best way to get answers, but not always. Sometimes it was better to let the suspect tell their own story in a way that might be even more revealing.

"We all got together at the big house for dinner last night. There was wine and beer. I had a few glasses of wine.

I wasn't counting, but I'm sure Austin had more than a couple of bottles of beer. Tracy had told me that he'd recently lost his job, so when I saw him picking at her, I started asking him about his work, knowing it would make him mad. He called me some names before he stormed out with Tracy. And I might have said something I didn't mean…" She started to cry again.

"What did you say?"

"I told him… I'm not proud of it… I said that I wanted him to crawl off and die." She wiped at her eyes with angry sweeps of her arms.

"Other people heard you?"

"Oh yeah. Everyone there." Her eyes grew wide. "Jesus, they must think I killed him on purpose." Then she seemed to have another thought. "Do you think he'll live?" Paula looked panic-stricken.

"He wasn't dead when they left. I don't have any idea what his condition is now."

"He can't die. Please, God, don't let him die."

"Tell me what happened today," I said calmly, trying to keep her emotions from spinning out of control.

"I came over… I wanted to talk to Tracy. She was mad at me for badgering Austin about losing his job. She'd told me in confidence and then I'd used it to piss him off. At breakfast, she'd given me the silent treatment. I felt bad. Literally, I get bad hangovers. I wasn't feeling well enough to talk to her about it until I got up from a nap." She sighed heavily. "I thought I'd come over here and plead stupid drunk and ask her to forgive me."

"What about Austin?"

"I thought about that too. I decided that, if I saw him, I'd apologize to him too." She saw the look of doubt on my face. "Don't get me wrong, I didn't want to. But I also didn't want this to grow into a big deal between Tracy and me."

"So you headed over here?"

"I… I wasn't exactly headed here. I wasn't quite ready yet. Marty and I were walking to the main house from our camper when Andy came over to talk to us. Then I decided to head on over here."

"Andy?"

"He's the boyfriend of one of my cousin's daughters. If that makes any sense. There's a little clique of younger people camping off by themselves." Talking about her family made Paula grow quiet and her eyes clouded over. I could tell that she was seeing her world with a bold, ugly new line drawn through the middle of it. On one side was the life she'd lived before today and on the other was her future, strange and frightening.

"So after you talked to Andy, you came here..." I prompted.

Slowly, Paula looked at me and her eyes cleared. "That's right. When I got to the door, I could hear banging, like someone was moving furniture around and not being very careful about it."

"Did you hear any voices?"

"No, nothing. I think that's why I wasn't too alarmed. I knocked on the door while I listened to the pounding from inside. When no one answered, I opened the door and called out for Tracy. I thought I might be intruding on... you know. The sound was this steady bump-bump noise, like maybe a bed or something banging against the wall. So I thought about backing out the door and leaving..."

"But you didn't," I prompted.

"No. I... I came in and... I could tell that something bad was happening. I heard... oh..." Paula groaned. "I could hear gurgling and the pounding kept going. I hurried into the bedroom and saw Austin squatting on Tracy's chest, his hands around her throat. He was lifting her off the ground. I... I saw a board lying by the wall and just grabbed it and hit him."

She began to sob again, clearly exhausted. I couldn't question her for much longer without risking a complete breakdown.

I needed to make a decision. Was Paula a danger to

herself or others at this point? Whether or not she had committed a crime wasn't the issue right now; there would be plenty of time to file charges. What I had to decide was whether it was safe for the public to let her remain free. There was good cause for taking her to jail and holding her overnight, but I couldn't see the point. She seemed calm, and as long as she cooperated with Shantel and allowed us to collect her clothes and other evidence, then I felt that the best course of action was to let her remain with her family.

My only qualm was that it would allow her to coordinate her story with Marty's. But even that risk was minor. Few people could do a credible job of fabricating a story with someone else and have it stand up to a good interrogator.

"I'm going to ask you to stay in the county. It will take a while for us to fully investigate the deaths of your sister and her husband. However, in a couple of days, after you've given us a full account of what happened, we'll probably be able to let you go home." *Or charge you with murder*, I thought.

"I understand."

CHAPTER THREE

I called for Shantel and she came out of the bedroom where she'd been taking photographs of the crime scene. After a quick discussion, she escorted Paula to her camper. As they left, Marcus passed by them in the doorway.

"This is one big mess," he said, shaking his head. "That poor kid."

"This is the kind of mess we get into out here in the country. Are you sure you want to come back full time?" I joked.

"Don't even. I get so bored working at FDLE. I mean, it's fine for someone who wants to sit in an office all day, but by two o'clock I can barely keep from falling asleep."

"They have plenty of crime scene techs who go out in the field."

"Those are prize jobs. I might get one in five years… if I'm lucky. No, I never should have let Esther talk me into working in Tallahassee."

"Will you be moving back to Adams County?"

"Nah, she loves her job. It won't be that bad of a commute for me."

"It's kind of a reverse commute."

"Exactly. How many people live in Tallahassee and work

in Calhoun? I won't be battling traffic," he said with a small grin.

"You've always been contrary."

"You, not me." His expression turned serious. "What do you think this is?" He waved his hand in the general direction of the woman's body lying in the other room.

"It's early days. My gut tells me it's exactly what it looks like, though it's hard to be sure since the husband was already on his way to the hospital when I arrived." I shrugged. "Did his hands have her hair, skin and or DNA on them? Where did the blows from the two-by-four land? Do I see Paula as a cold-blooded killer who murdered her sister and then attacked her brother-in-law in order to place the blame on him? That seems like a stretch."

"So what do you want us to focus on?"

"Obviously anything with blood on it that is small enough to be easily transported."

"We've already photographed and videoed the blood spatter."

"Also check anything that has been disturbed for fingerprints. Though it's likely that all of our victims and potential suspects have an excuse for why their fingerprints or DNA would be found in this room. And the DNA would have to be an exact match to mean anything since almost everyone here is related."

I sighed, then heard a soft knock on the door. I opened it to see our coroner, Dr. Darzi, standing on the porch, along with his assistant Ann, who'd recently be promoted from lowly intern.

"You called for the A-Team?" Darzi asked, letting his Indian accent have free rein.

"I called for the A-Team and look what I got," I said, winking at Ann.

"Damn lucky, you are. Things are very busy in Tallahassee," Darzi said, stepping forward. I moved back to let them through.

"Boring as hell," Ann said, *sotto voce.*

"Glad we can provide you with some excitement."

"You'll be happy to hear that we've already done some of your work. Your Deputy Sanderson gave us a heads-up about the situation, so we met the EMTs when they brought the male victim to the hospital and were able to take some scrapings from his fingernails and collected his clothes. I also took some pictures of him."

"Above and beyond," I said, impressed and feeling a little stupid that I hadn't arranged to have that done.

"I always enjoy troubling the surgeons and emergency room doctors," Darzi said with a grin.

"I imagine they were rushing him straight to surgery."

"They had to wait for the neurosurgeon." Darzi shrugged. "In my humble opinion, there was no rush. The man was stable and no amount of surgery was going to make him anything more than an organ donor."

I winced. "Ouch! That's a bit harsh."

"The truth is the truth." While he was blunt with me, I knew that Darzi had as good a bedside manner as any pathologist could. I'd seen him help a number of family members through the worst experience of their lives with a kindness that helped to cushion the horror of the events.

"Come look at what we've got here." I led them to the bedroom. "Did you see where the wounds were on the man's body?"

"The back of his head was crushed in. At least two blows. I'll be able to tell you more when I've had a chance to examine the X-rays."

Darzi's eyes were already intent on the body of the woman on the floor. Tracy was sprawled like a dropped ragdoll. Her tongue was purple and protruding from her lips and dark bruises circled her neck.

As he knelt down beside Tracy, I left the room. There was nothing I could learn watching Darzi and Ann manipulate the body as they checked its temperature and looked for any clues that might be lost in transit. Honestly, I just didn't like seeing the indignities that a corpse at a crime scene had to go through.

Deputy Sanderson had already left to answer another call for service, so I was on my own to conduct any additional interviews. I was standing on the porch trying to decide the best route for questioning a small army of potential witnesses when I saw a familiar shape. I squinted to make sure my eyes weren't deceiving me.

A dark-haired woman in her mid-fifties was walking up from a small cabin toward the main house, followed closely by a deer. Except I knew that it wasn't a deer. It was a Great Dane, one that had been crucially involved in a murder case I'd dealt with last summer. The woman, Bernadette Santos, had been a witness in the case and had adopted Cleo soon after the dust had cleared.

"Bernadette!" I yelled, clumping down the wooden steps and hurrying in her direction. Cleo whipped around at the sound of my voice, though it took Bernadette a couple of moments to realize where the call was coming from.

"Larry," she said, her expression a conflicted mix of pleasure at seeing me and sorrow for her family members. "You must be here for poor Tracy."

Cleo gently tugged at her leash. Unlike Mauser, my father's unruly Great Dane, Cleo had manners. Even when she desperately wanted something, she would ask rather than demand. Bernadette let Cleo go and the fawn-colored giant trotted over to me. She'd stayed with us for a couple of days during her ordeal and now she sniffed my pants and shoes for the familiar smells of Alvin the Pug and Ivy the tabby cat. Then she leaned into me, gently nudging my hand for ear rubs.

Once I'd properly greeted the Queen of the Nile, I looked up at Bernadette, who was in no way offended by my attention to Cleo.

"Are you staying here?" I asked.

"Yes. Tracy was my cousin. How's Paula? I... I don't understand what happened." She reached up to wipe a tear from the corner of her eye and I could see that her hands were shaking a little.

"I'm still trying to make sense of the evidence. You know the investigation will take time. I'm sorry that I can't give you more information right now."

"They're saying that Paula killed Austin."

"I can promise you that, if Paula was trying to protect Tracy or herself, then she won't face any charges."

"Thank you. I know you'll do your best."

"Can we go somewhere and talk? I need to find a room where I can conduct interviews. Talking to everyone present is my top priority right now. If you don't mind, I'll start with you," I said with an encouraging smile.

"No, of course I don't mind. Not that I know much. We can use the dining room up at the big house."

"So you're all here for Althea Byrd's birthday?" I asked as we walked toward the house.

"That's right, she's my grandmother. I'm staying in a little cabin down by the pond. Most of the family lives out of town, but we get together every few years. Of course, Althea insisted on a big do for her ninetieth birthday." Bernadette shook her head. "You'll need to meet Althea. My grandmother is a piece of work." She stopped and looked at me. "You're probably thinking that I'm mighty old to have a grandmother still alive, ninety or not. But Althea was sixteen when she had my father, then Mom and Dad were only nineteen when they had me. I'm the oldest of the cousins."

We'd reached the steps that led up to the porch of the farmhouse. But before we could climb them, the front door opened and a man who was the spitting image of Bruce Byrd, minus the moustache, came out to meet us.

"Dottie, you know better than to bring that dog in the house."

For a moment I thought he was talking about me, then I heard Cleo give a small whine.

"Dad, it's just for a minute while I talk to Deputy Macklin. Isn't Gran upstairs?"

"Yes, but she's all riled up over this... this situation. And if she found out that dog was here, it would just make it worse," he said in a harsh whisper, looking over his shoulder as though he expected someone to come out of the house and attack him.

"Fine," Bernadette said in resignation, then she looked at me. "Would you mind if we sit out here? You can do the rest of the interviews inside."

"Interviews?" the man said suspiciously.

"Larry, this is my father, Owen Byrd. Dad, this is Deputy Macklin. He's an investigator with the sheriff's office. They have to look into the... crimes," Bernadette said. I could tell that she was trying to stand up to him, but like most of us, when talking to a parent it was hard not to feel twelve years old.

"I heard that asshole Austin was killing Tracy, so Paula poleaxed him with a two-by-four. Seems pretty straightforward to me," the man said, challenging me with his eyes.

I walked up the steps until I was on the porch and nose to nose with Owen. I didn't like the man's attitude.

"We will investigate the two crimes until we're satisfied that we know exactly what happened. To that end, I will need to interview everyone who was on the property when the crimes were committed." I used my best tough-guy, film noir voice.

"I think you're overstepping your bounds," he responded, giving back the attitude in full measure.

"Then call our office and complain to the sheriff," I said, handing him my card. "I'm sure my dad would love to talk to you." I tried never to use my familial relationship with the sheriff to push back at someone, but in this case I felt like I needed to make a point.

Owen's face twitched and he ran his hand through his thin grey hair before glancing at the card and slipping it into his shirt pocket. "We'll see about this," was his weak response, then he turned on his heel and tried to maintain some dignity as he went back inside the house.

"Bully for you," Bernadette said, climbing the steps to the porch. Cleo followed, looking subdued. "Dad's not usually like this, but whenever he's around his mother he turns into a little Napoleon. I think he's always competed with Uncle Bruce for their mother's attention."

Bernadette sat down in one of the rocking chairs that decorated the front of the wrap-around porch. I scooted another chair close to hers so that I could face her while we talked. Cleo lowered herself to the deck and flopped onto her side.

"So who all's here?" I asked, taking out my small notebook to write down the names.

"It is quite the group," Bernadette said, starting to count them all off on her fingers. "My grandmother Althea Byrd, my father Owen and my Uncle Bruce. Aunt Debbie. Of course, there was Tracy and Austin. Paula and her son Marty. Then some distant cousins: Ellie and Myron Morgan and their children, Jeanette and the boy… I can't remember his name; Liam Varney and his wife Olivia, and their little son Derrick; and Rochelle and Bridget Roberts. Some boy that Rochelle is dating and, finally, Liam's son by a previous marriage. His name's Cory. Oh, and my mother is staying at my house." Bernadette shook her head. "She can't stand Althea and the feeling is mutual."

"So she hasn't been out here?"

"I didn't say that. She comes out for a couple of hours every day, just to make sure she's not missing anything. The rest of the time she sulks in my house nursing a bottle of vodka." Seeing my expression, she explained, "Mom's not that bad. Althea just gets under her skin. Or maybe it's the fact that Dad can't stand up to his mother and never has."

Bernadette's face darkened. "I'm still trying to wrap my mind around what happened. It's just horrible."

"I know this is hard. But the sooner we can get this figured out, the sooner everyone can begin to heal." I reconsidered this. "Or at least get rid of me so y'all can grieve without an investigator digging around."

Bernadette gave me a small smile. "I'm glad you're here. And I want to help Paula. I'd go talk to her, but I don't know what to say. Besides, Uncle Bruce is probably protecting her like a papa bear."

"Who can blame him for wanting to protect his daughter? What can you tell me about the family?"

"I'll have to go back a ways." Bernadette looked over her shoulder as though worried that someone might be listening. "Althea had three sons. My dad was the oldest. Like I said, she had him when she was only sixteen. Ryan Byrd, my grandfather, was seventeen. His family were big fish in a small pond over in Jefferson county. He'd met my grandmother at a dance in Tallahassee. When he got her pregnant, his parents weren't having any of it and threatened to have Althea sent to a mental hospital, claiming that she was a nymphomaniac. 1940s' justice!" She shook her head and reached down to stroke Cleo. The dog was panting heavily.

"Want me to get her some water?"

"Please. Just knock on the door."

A middle-aged woman with happy eyes answered. I explained what I wanted and she nodded. "The poor puppy! Sure, I'll get some. I'd let her in, but Mrs. Byrd would have a fit."

"I forgot about Ruby," Bernadette said once the woman had left to fetch the water. "She's a sort of companion-slash-nurse for Gran. A sweet woman. I don't know how she puts up with Althea and the rest of the clan."

Ruby came out onto the porch carrying a large plastic bowl filled with water and ice. She set it down next to Cleo, who stood up and lapped at it eagerly while Ruby reached out to pet her.

"What a dog!" she said.

"Would you turn the porch fans on when you go back inside?" Bernadette asked her.

"Of course."

With the fans creating a small breeze, Bernadette turned

back to me. "Where did I leave off?"

"Your grandmother's in-laws wanted to have her committed."

"That's right. I've got to hand it to my grandfather. He stood up to his parents and married her. The story goes that his family cut him off, thinking he'd come crawling back, but that chicken scratched his way up to being one of the top farmers in the Big Bend."

"Paula said Althea was born here?"

"Yes. Her parents had a small turpentine operation. Grandpa moved here when they got married. He volunteered for the war when he turned eighteen, but they dropped the bomb before he finished basic training. So he came back here and helped Althea's parents with their business, eventually buying them out and diversifying into tobacco and real estate. Her parents had owned around a hundred acres, but now the farm covers over a thousand and isn't used for anything other than timber and hunting."

"I can see why your grandmother would be attached to the place."

"I think she's more attached to it than to any of us. Anyway, she had two more sons, Bruce and Jack. You met Bruce. Jack was Althea's favorite by a long stretch. He was a surprise, born about twenty-five years after Bruce, when Althea was forty-five. I've seen it in other women who have that last baby after their first children are grown. That child's always their baby. Special. And often spoiled."

"Where is Jack now?"

"He died back in the '90s. Drowned. In the pond down there." Bernadette nodded in the direction of where I'd first seen her and Cleo.

"Here?" I asked, taken by surprise that there'd been another family death on the property.

"Yeah. I knew Jack pretty well. He was nine years younger than me and I'd babysit him at family gatherings. I never really thought about how odd it was that my uncle was younger than me. As he grew, he was nothing like my father or Uncle Bruce. Jack rode a motorcycle and was studying writing at school. He was also active in the student theatre. I think it was his enthusiasm for acting that got *me* interested in the theatre." I could tell that Bernadette still grieved for Jack.

"Seems odd that your grandmother would want to come back to a place where she lost one of her sons."

"You haven't met her. I think she's always blamed the rest of us for Jack's death."

"Why's that?"

"Favoring him the way she did caused most of the family to resent him. Some a little, some a lot. Bringing us back here is her way of torturing us." She paused. "Maybe that's a bit harsh. During her life, Althea's had some bitter pills to swallow."

I wanted to ask her more about her uncle's drowning, but it really wasn't relevant. I needed to get on with the interviews.

"Tell me about Tracy and Austin."

"Neither of them was very good alone, but together they were toxic."

"Paula said that Austin was possessive."

"Did she tell you that her sister wouldn't have had it any other way?"

"She said that, in some ways, Tracy was as bad as he was."

"Tracy couldn't stand a boy who wasn't obsessed with her. She'd dump a guy because he didn't call her enough. Austin and Tracy were stuck together like magnets. I gave up trying to help them ages ago 'cause I realized they liked hating each other."

"So what do you think happened today?"

"I don't know. They seemed all right when they got here on Friday. Only after they'd been here a day did things start taking a nasty turn. Might have been the drinking. Austin was hitting the beer pretty heavy. Saturday night when the rest of us called it an evening, I noticed that he stayed by the fire pit drinking with the kids."

"The kids?"

"Bridget, Rochelle and their friends."

"How did Tracy react?"

"She didn't like it. Got bent out of shape when she tried to drag him back to their cabin and he wouldn't go."

"Did it turn into a fight?"

"No more than usual. She called him a couple of names and hit his arm. He ignored her, which he knew was the cruelest thing he could do to her. Nothing they hadn't done a million times before."

"Was Paula there?"

I saw the reluctance on Bernadette's face. Finally she answered, "Yes."

"How did she react?" I asked, though I could tell Bernadette was hesitant to say anything that would appear to give Paula a motive. "You have to trust me. I'm not out to hang anything on Paula."

Bernadette sighed, causing Cleo to look up at her. She scratched the dog's head absently. "Paula called Austin an asshole and told Tracy that they should leave for a little girls' wine time."

"And did they?"

"I guess so. I headed home at that point, but I did see them walking toward Tracy's cabin."

"What about dinner last night?"

Bernadette was silent.

"Paula already told me about her outburst," I pressed.

"It got ugly pretty fast. Paula was drinking more than usual and kept bear-baiting Austin. I almost felt sorry for him and that's saying a lot." She went on to tell a story very similar to Paula's account.

"Tell me about Marty," I asked, thinking it was time to change focus.

"Not much to tell. He's... sorta withdrawn, maybe a bit immature for his age, but he's pretty much like any other kid these days. Spending most of his time staring at a phone or computer. But that's not to say a bad word about him. He likes Cleo and always comes over to pet and talk to her."

"Did you see him today?"

"Right before… everything went crazy. I was walking Cleo and he came over to see her."

"How long did he pet her?"

"Just a minute or two. Before he went off to follow his mom."

"Did he seem normal?"

"Yes. Talked mostly to Cleo, though he was polite enough to say hi and bye to me. I'm kind of used to that when I'm with her." She smiled down at the dog, who looked up with big brown eyes. "Even my best friends are more interested in Cleo when I'm out with her."

"It's the same with Mauser," I admitted.

"How is he?"

"His usual brutish self. With his black coat, he hates the summer more than most." I looked down at Cleo, who was still panting even after finishing most of the bowl of water. "Speaking of which, you better take her to the nearest air conditioning."

Bernadette nodded and stood up. "Ask Ruby where you can set up. If Dad gives you any grief, just read him the riot act. He's really just a big blowhard."

CHAPTER FOUR

After Bernadette had gone, Ruby showed me into the dining room of the old farmhouse, then left to find Owen Byrd. A massive table that could accommodate a large extended family dominated the room. On one wall was a china cabinet full of fine pieces, while across from it stood a dark wooden gun cabinet that held a beautiful collection of shotguns and rifles.

Owen Byrd liked to thump his chest. It took me half an hour to convince him to let me use the dining room as a home base for my interviews.

"Why don't I start with you?" I asked, since he was standing at the head of the table and glaring at me.

"I can't tell you anything," he blurted.

"You can tell me why you're so angry," I said, raising my eyebrows. "Look, I'm just trying to sort this out and, with some luck, leave your niece in the clear."

"What do mean by that?" he blustered.

"Sit down and I'll explain," I said, taking a seat myself.

Reluctantly, he pulled out a chair and sat facing me. I leaned forward.

"If a case like this isn't investigated properly from the start, it can linger in the minds of the public for decades. I want to be able to say definitively what happened in that cabin today. If I can do that, then your family will be able to get on with their lives. Or would you rather have some wannabe movie director make a documentary about it in a couple of years?"

Owen glared at me from across the oak table, grinding his teeth. A lock of his thin grey hair had fallen across his forehead, which was sheened with sweat even in the air-conditioned house. He swept the loose hair away before speaking.

"I see your point. Question is, do I trust you? How do I know you aren't hunting for trouble that doesn't exist?"

"You have a dead niece and a nephew-in-law in the hospital. I don't have to hunt for trouble. It's already here. I'm not asking you to trust me. I'm telling you that I have a job to do. But I'm fair. I have no axes to grind."

"You know my daughter?"

"Yes. I met her last year when I was working on a case involving one of the volunteers at her theatre."

"I remember. You were involved in that?"

"I had a lot of help, but I was the lead investigator."

Owen leaned back and looked a little more relaxed. "Dottie told me about that case, and how she ended up with that dog. The dog is okay with me, but my mother doesn't like it. Thinks big dogs are just for hunting and ought to live outside."

I saw a peculiar look cross his face and for just a moment it was as if I was looking at a young boy. Maybe a boy who had never been allowed to bring his favorite dog inside.

"You call Bernadette Dottie?" I asked, trying to make sure we were all on the same page. I'd heard him use the name on the porch earlier, but I'd never heard anyone call her that.

The question elicited a small smile. "When she was in first grade, she had a friend who couldn't seem to get Bernadette quite right. It came out as Bernadot. So we started calling her Dottie. She liked it until she got to high school and from then on, to anyone but family she was Bernadette. Guess she got too big for nicknames."

"Where were you this morning?" I asked, getting back on track. Owen's face flushed and I held up my hand. "I'm not considering you a suspect. I just need to place everyone who was on the property. I need to know who might have seen or heard something."

He nodded and looked more relaxed. "Bruce and I went out to check the feed plots and the quail fields. Sam went with us."

"Sam?" Another person I hadn't heard about.

"He's the caretaker. Sam lives in a house up front. You might have seen the dirt road to the right, just as you came in the gate. That leads to Sam's place."

"What time did you all go out?"

"We had breakfast, then took the ATV out about nine. Right after I fed and exercised the dogs."

"Dogs?"

"Damn fine hunting dogs. Young Black Mouth Curs. Florida-bred. They belong to a friend of mine. I brought them over to work with them."

"And what time did you get back?"

"We were headed back to the main house when Bruce got a call from Paula saying that something bad had happened."

My ears perked up. This was the first time I'd heard about another call. It was interesting that Paula had called her dad while Marty had called 911. That call had come in at twelve-forty-eight.

"Do you know the exact time of the call?"

"No."

I made a mental note to take a look at Bruce's phone.

"What did you see when you got to the cabin?"

"Everyone was standing around the porch and—"

"Who do you remember?"

"Myron was talking to Marty. I saw Debbie, Bruce's wife. And Dottie came over with the dog."

"What did you do then?"

"Marty told us that Tracy was dead and Austin was in bad shape, so Bruce ran into the cabin."

"You stayed outside?"

"Yep. Didn't see the point of going in. Marty said he'd already called 911."

"How long was your brother in the cabin?"

"Not long. Bruce came back out and told everyone that an ambulance was on the way and that no one else should enter the cabin."

I wondered about that. Had Bruce been trying to preserve evidence or to hide what was going on inside?

"Where was Paula?"

"Inside."

"Did you ever see her?"

"No."

"Then how do you know that she was inside?"

He looked at me with narrowed eyes. "Bruce said she was. And Marty had told Bruce his mother was inside when we got there."

"What did Bruce tell you after he came out of the cabin?"

"I don't think I should put words in his mouth." Owen was getting testy again.

"I'm just asking what you remember. I'll ask Bruce the same thing when I interview him."

"You want to have both of our statements so you can compare them. If they don't match, then you can claim one of us is lying," he challenged me.

"Not at all. I don't expect you all to have perfect recall." I didn't tell him that I'd be more suspicious if their stories *did* match. I'd consider it a sign that they had collaborated on their stories and were trying to hide something.

"He didn't say much. Just that there'd been a terrible accident and Tracy was dead."

"What did he say about Austin?"

"Only that he'd been hurt."

"He specifically said an accident?'"

"There were so many other people there. I don't think he wanted to be throwing around words like murder. My brother is a lawyer. Very careful with what he says."

"How long is this get-together supposed to last?" I asked, changing tack.

"Originally through the end of the week. Now..." He shrugged.

"You think your mother will call it off?"

Owen leaned back and laughed, though there was a rough edge to it. "You don't know my mother. She'll eat this up."

"I'm going to want everyone to stay in town at least until Friday." It was going to take time to get through all the interviews, plus I wanted to have at least a preliminary autopsy report on Tracy and a formal forensic opinion on Austin's injuries before I let everyone head home. Of course, I couldn't *make* them stay, but I wasn't going to tell him that.

"I don't think anyone will be in a hurry to leave," Owen said flatly.

"Can I speak with your mother now?"

"Be my guest. She's upstairs." He looked at his watch. "She'll be down for supper in a couple of hours. I guess you don't want to wait."

"I'd rather not."

"If you want to beard the lion in its den, it's your funeral. I'll take you up there, but I'm not going into her sitting room." As he stood up, I could hear his joints cracking.

I followed Owen up the staircase. When we reached the second-floor landing, I could tell that there had been quite a bit of work done up there. It had a more modern feel than the rest of the house.

"Mother renovated the entire upstairs to make it easier for her to get around. I told her that if she'd stay on the first floor, then it would be easier on everyone." He waved his hand dismissively. "Like talking to a wall."

"This isn't her permanent residence, is it?"

"Good heavens, no. She lords it over us from Lake City.

Dad built a white elephant there after Bruce and I were grown. He enjoyed traveling and liked the easy access to interstates going in all directions over there."

Owen pulled at the waist of his pants and smoothed his shirt before knocking on the wide oak door at the top of the stairs.

"What?" came a tart response.

"It's Owen, Mother. An investigator from the sheriff's office would like to talk to you about the… incident."

"Good! I want to talk to him too. Send him in and get out of here."

Owen opened the door and waved me in, then headed back down the stairs.

I eased through the doorway to find myself in a spacious room that took up the entire east side of the house. Through an archway leading to the front of the house, I could see a large four-poster bed, dressing table and wardrobe. The sitting room was decked out with comfortable chairs and a couch. The walls were covered with framed pictures, mostly of a rough-hewn man shaking hands with various politicians and celebrities. I recognized four Florida governors and several presidents.

Almost lost in a huge, dark leather wingback chair was a petite woman in a pant suit. Her hair was a brilliant white and her blue eyes were piercing. Looking at her, I would have guessed her to be closer to seventy than ninety.

"So what's your name?" she snapped. Her hands were moving over the arms of the chair as though she wanted to be pacing the room.

"I'm Deputy Larry Macklin with the Adams County Sheriff's Office."

"Macklin. Any relation to the sheriff?"

"I'm his son."

"Nepotism. People don't approve, but I'm all for it if the relation is competent."

I almost opened my mouth to take exception to her comment, but I figured it was best to leave it alone. "You know about what happened to your niece and her husband?" I asked instead.

"Do I look stupid? Of course I know what happened. Tracy got herself killed by that numbnut she married. Not unexpected. The only thing that surprises me is that Paula had the cojones to beat the shit out of Austin. I gotta admit, I might have underestimated that girl," Althea said with a crooked smile.

There was too much to unpack in her statement, so I decided to stick to my planned list of questions. "May I sit down?" I asked, wanting to be able to take notes.

"You goin' to be here that long?" she tossed back.

"I've got a few questions to ask you," I said in my firmest *not-going-to-take-no-for-an-answer* tone.

"Suit yourself." Althea waved me toward the more human-scaled couch.

"I understand that you called this gathering to celebrate your ninetieth birthday." I thought about offering my congratulations, but decided it wasn't appropriate under the circumstances. Besides, I didn't think she'd take kindly to anything that smacked of ass-kissing.

"That's right. I did it to watch them hop." She waved toward the window.

I wasn't sure I'd heard her right. "Hop?"

"Do you know how much I'm worth? A hell of a lot, that's how much. Everyone out there would love to get their lazy, no-good paws on it too. Only fun I have these days is teasing the crap out of them." She saw the look on my face. "Don't feel sorry for them. I've given them everything. Solid home, an education, paid for marriages and divorces. Tossed good money after bad at their kids. Not one of them worth a dime." Bitterness dripped from her tongue.

"They all can't be that bad," I said, making an ill-conceived attempt to defend her children and grandchildren.

"How would you know? You're riding on *your* daddy's coattails."

I felt my back stiffen, but took a deep breath and

reminded myself that she was ninety years old. It wouldn't serve the cause of wrapping this mess up if I got into an argument with her.

"Okay, so to torture your family you made everyone come here for your birthday," I said without too much snark.

Althea's face grew hard as she leaned toward me. "You think you're so smart. Going to come in here and figure us all out. Write up your reports and stamp 'solved' on another murder. Stand up!" she shouted.

Startled, I looked at her to see if she was serious. She was. I figured that the interview was over and did as instructed, folding my notebook. But she wasn't done.

"Go to that window and look out!" She didn't quite shout this command, but her voice was full of authority.

I didn't like being ordered around. However, my purpose in being there was to learn what these people were about. Right now, the best way to accomplish that was to go along with her. So I walked where she pointed and stood in front of the largest window in the sitting room, looking out over the land beside the house. Stretched out before me was a beautiful mix of hardwoods, pines and open fields. On this side of the house, the land sloped down to the two-acre pond Bernadette had mentioned.

"See that pond? That's where the only good thing in my life died. It's been more than twenty-five years, but do you think I've gotten any answers? They can all go to hell," she snarled.

I turned to see her slumped in her enormous chair, breathing heavily. I started toward her, but she waved me off. "Forget it. Ask your damn questions," she said, and pushed herself upright.

"I don't know what happened to your son back then. If I could help you figure it out, I would. Right now, I'm dealing with a more urgent matter. I don't care if you love them or hate them, but I'm not going to leave your granddaughter and great-grandson in limbo any longer than I have to."

"You already decided she's innocent?"

"Not necessarily. If she broke the law, I'll see that she's charged for her crimes."

"Don't let her fool you. She and her sister were always getting into trouble. She tell you that?"

I sighed inwardly. "What kind of trouble did they get into?"

"Tracy stole stuff. They caught her a couple of times. Her daddy got her off. I told him to let her sit in jail, that it might do her some good, but Bruce was soft on both of them. See where they've ended up? One of 'em dead and the other going to jail."

"What about Paula?"

"Drinking. That was her problem. She was always coming home drunk from some party or another. Drove her father crazy. Now that's what both those girls were really after. Him working all the time and both of them wanting Daddy's attention. One got drunk partying with boys while the other shoplifted and hunted down the worst men in the world."

How can anyone be so filled with hate? I wondered.

"Where were you around noon today?" I asked, trying to redirect her.

She chuckled. "Killing Tracy and clubbing that no-good Austin." I couldn't hide a look of disgust from my face. "All right. I was in this room. I don't get around as well as I used to. These days, I get up with the sun. When I'm here, I go downstairs to the dining room and have my breakfast, then I come up here for a rest. I go back down around four and spend the afternoon and evening lecturing to the deaf and stupid before retiring."

"Did you see or hear anything around the time of the murder?"

"I heard some wailing that I figure came afterward."

"Screams?" This was the first I'd heard of any noise associated with the attacks.

"No, more like a high-pitched moaning."

I looked around the room. The new windows were high quality and double-paned. I walked through the bedroom to the front window that afforded a view across the hundred-yard stretch to the cabin where Tracy had been killed. Any sound coming from there would have to have been mighty loud to be heard in this room.

"Who do you think it was?" I said quietly, without turning around.

"Paula," Althea answered, proving to me that her hearing was fine.

"Do you know what time you heard the sound?"

"About twelve-thirty."

"What did you do when you heard it?"

"I asked Ruby what the hell it was. What do you think I did?"

"Where was Ruby?"

"I don't know, but she came when I yelled for her. I told her what I'd heard, and she said she'd find out what was going on. Came back twenty minutes later and said that something horrible had happened. I could hardly get her to make sense. Took her a while to get it out that Tracy was dead and Paula had killed Austin. That's all I know about this business."

Althea stopped and got a thoughtful look on her face. "Bring me that box," she said, pointing to a small cedar box on the top of her dresser.

I retrieved the box, which was ornately carved on the lid and sides with Roman figures drinking wine and eating grapes. I noted the weight of it as I carried it over to her. Althea took a key from a chain around her neck and unlocked the box.

"A thousand dollars," she said, pulling a wrapped stack of fifty dollar bills out of the box. "All I'm asking is that I be the first person you tell when you get any information about this…" She waved toward the window. "…business."

"You're kidding me, right?" I said, appalled at the offer.

"Do I look like I'm joking?" She held the money out to

me. I had to admit that she looked dead serious.

"Why do you need to be the first to learn what I turn up?"

"Information is power. You aren't so dull that you don't understand that."

"I won't be bribed."

"Are you trying to bargain with me?" she said, reaching into the box and taking out another stack of bills.

"Put that money away," I scolded.

"Afraid to look at it?" Althea said, waving it around a little.

"How can you think that offering me a bribe is a good idea?" I said. I decided that she wasn't as smart as I'd first thought.

"You'd be surprised at the names I've got of folks who've jumped at a few thousand dollars. Doesn't matter. I learned something about you." She put the money back in the box. "And it didn't cost me anything. I'd say that's a win-win for me. Put this back on my dresser."

I did as instructed, not knowing if I'd just been complimented or insulted. "You shouldn't keep this kind of money lying around the house. Especially if you don't trust your family."

"If I thought they had the guts to come get that box, I'd have more respect for them," Althea mumbled. For all her spit and fire, I could tell that she was getting tired.

"I want everyone to stay put for a couple of days," I said, hoping she wouldn't get bent out of shape over the request. I needn't have worried.

"Ha! I'll keep them here as long as you want. I know the magic word."

"Let me guess, it isn't please."

"You're learning," she said with a wicked smile. "The magic word is 'will.' All I got to do is mention my will and they all become spellbound."

CHAPTER FIVE

I left the rattlesnake curled up in her armchair. As I went back downstairs, I wondered if I was being drawn too deeply into the family dynamics surrounding this investigation. *Investigations, plural*, I reminded myself; I still needed to contact the hospital to check on Austin's condition. If he died, I'd have two deaths on my hands.

I should have sat down and plotted out a schedule for the rest of the interviews, but instead I headed over to the cabin to check on the status of the evidence collection. When I got there, I saw Dr. Darzi and Ann carefully lifting a stretcher down the cabin steps. I caught up to them as they reached the coroner's van.

"Just in time," Darzi said cheerily.

"Anything interesting?"

"Everything seems to line up with the story being told."

"This doesn't look like much of a mystery," Ann agreed as they slid the stretcher into the back of the van.

"If the story we've been told is the truth, I won't complain."

"I'll do the autopsy…" Darzi pulled out his phone and consulted his schedule. "…on Wednesday. I'll let you know what time. Most likely in the afternoon."

"I'll try to make it. And I need to check on the victim who was clubbed. I'd like your opinion on his X-rays and any other test results."

"Of course. Billing the Adams County Sheriff's Office helps to makes ends meet."

I cringed a little, thinking of the bill. Dad had been fighting with the budget all year. "Have mercy on us."

"If you didn't need a written report, I'd do it gratis," Darzi joked. "You always provide us with such interesting cases."

"Though, so far, this one has been *meh*. Only three stars out of five," Ann said, flashing me a snarky smile as she took shotgun in the van.

I looked at my watch as they drove away. It was almost four. I went into the cabin and found that Shantel and Marcus were nearly done.

"Seal the doors and make sure all the windows are locked," I told Shantel.

"What did you think I was going to do? Leave the place wide open? You're getting mighty bossy these days. By the way, you got a week to clean out Marcus's office before I kick your stuff to the curb," she said, referring to a small office in our newly renovated evidence department that I'd taken over as a war room during an investigation in the spring.

"Some of that stuff isn't mine."

"Which is exactly what I told you would happen. I let one of you use the room and, next thing I know, it's become the community closet."

"I'll get to it next week, promise," I said, my fingers crossed behind my back. I fully intended to clean out the office, but the way my caseload was stacking up, I really shouldn't have promised.

"To the curb," she said, giving me the evil eye.

Marcus came out of the bedroom carrying a couple of evidence bags. "I didn't find anything too interesting. These are a few things that had blood on them."

I'd asked them to collect all blood evidence, just in case we ever had reason to suspect that someone else might have been in the room. Fingerprints were almost meaningless in a family compound like this, but leaving fresh blood behind would require an explanation.

"Was any of it in a place you wouldn't expect the victim's blood to be?"

"Not really. There was some in the bathroom. I took pictures and samples. Just guessing, but I'd say someone at least washed their hands."

That was interesting. Little things about this case were beginning to bother me. Paula had called her father, but Marty had called 911. Someone, presumably Paula, had washed their hands in the bathroom. But why had Paula's hand been bloody? I'd seen the two-by-four and the end she'd held didn't have any blood on it. And if she'd gotten Tracy's blood on her hands checking for life signs, why feel the need to hide it?

I left Shantel and Marcus packing up their supplies and went in search of Bruce Byrd. Off of the main house was an old summer kitchen that had been converted into a two-room cabin in a renovation worthy of *Better Homes & Gardens*. On a hunch, I knocked on the door and heard a curse from inside. The door opened and I found myself looking at Paula Reece.

"Deputy Macklin?"

"Is your father here?"

"He is… Well… He's not feeling—"

"Let him in, damn it!" came Bruce's voice from inside. Paula backed away from the door.

The inside of the cottage was as quaint as the outside. There was a large open area that served as the living room, dining room and kitchen, with a small sleeping loft upstairs and two doors in the back that I assumed led to the bedroom and a bathroom.

Bruce lay on the couch, grimacing in pain.

"Sorry, but my back is tearing me up," he said. For a

moment he struggled to sit up, but fell back against the cushions in defeat, breathing hard.

"I can come back tomorrow. I just wanted to ask you a few questions."

"No. No guarantee I'll be doing any better by then. I'd rather go ahead and tell you what you need to know."

"If you're sure."

"I was in a car accident ten years ago. The damage was too severe for a real fix. I was told that I was lucky I hadn't been paralyzed. There are days I'd rather be in a wheelchair than suffering like this."

"You don't mean that, Daddy," Paula said.

"Where's Marty?" I asked her.

"When Daddy's back seized up, he sent Marty over to be with his cousins."

"I thought it was best. Paula hasn't talked to him," Bruce said.

I saw my chance to speak with Marty being postponed. The last thing I wanted was to appear too aggressive in interviewing a juvenile.

"How are you doing?" I asked Paula.

She held out her hand, which was shaking noticeably. "I'm trying not to think about it."

"I'd like to talk to your father alone."

"I'll wait on the porch. Daddy, can I get you anything?"

"Bring me some of those pain pills."

"It's too soon to take another one," Paula told him, but she fetched a bottle of prescription pills from the dining room table and handed them to him.

"They aren't even touching the pain," Bruce groaned.

I waited until Paula had shut the front door behind her before sitting down in a chair across from him.

"I hate for anyone to see me like this," Bruce said as he squirmed on the couch. "The anxiety over all of this has caused me to tense up, which brings on the pain. Once it gets ahold of me, it's the devil to shake off."

"I'm sorry to bother you, but—"

"You have a job to do. I know. A job I want you to hurry up and finish so my daughter and grandson can get on with their lives."

"That's the goal."

"Did you talk to my mother?"

"Yes. She's an… interesting woman."

"Ha! She's a cross between Attila the Hun and a grizzly bear. I hope you don't take everything she says as gospel."

I found it interesting that the first thing Bruce wanted to do was run damage control concerning anything embarrassing that his mother might have told me.

"I understand," I said noncommittally. I wasn't there to hash over his mother's condemnations of her family. "Where were you when the attack on Tracy occurred?"

"You talked to my brother?" Again he seemed to be fishing for information about what other people had told me.

He is *a lawyer*, I reminded myself. "Yes, I did."

"I get it. You want to hear my side of events. Okay, we went out to check the feed plots and the fields. At least, that's what we told everyone. What we really did was grab a bottle of Scotch and got Sam to drive us as far as possible from the wicked witch in her castle. Which he was more than happy to do for a share of the bottle."

"When did you learn about the trouble at the cabin?"

"We were on our way back when I got a call from Paula."

"What did she say?"

"She told me that something horrible had happened at Tracy's cabin, and she needed me to come back right away."

"How did she sound?"

"Honestly, I thought she was on the verge of hysteria. Her voice was very high and it cracked a couple of times. I told her to call 911. When she started to cry, I managed to get Marty on the phone and told *him* to call 911."

"Was he upset?"

"I'd say he was in shock. I had to repeat everything several times before he understood me. When I was pretty sure he was going to make the call, I told him I'd be there in fifteen minutes, then hung up."

"Did anything else happen on your way back to the cabin?"

"No. Sam drove like the devil to get us there."

"Then what did you find?"

"Marty was pacing on the porch and Paula was inside on the couch, crying. I found Austin still alive in the bedroom, lying beside Tracy. I… didn't know what to do. I've never seen an injury like that and… and the sight of… my daughter…" His face was ashen, though I couldn't tell if it was caused by the memory of what he'd seen or from his own physical pain.

"Is there anything else you'd like to tell me?"

Bruce shook his head. "The EMTs were there minutes after I was." He grimaced from another stab of pain.

"Okay, that's all I need for now." I couldn't see the point of staying any longer.

"I should be better in a day or two. We'll bring in another lawyer to represent Paula." This wasn't a threat, but simply a statement of fact.

"What type of law do you practice?"

"Real estate law. Even if I *was* a criminal lawyer, I wouldn't represent a close relative. Too much baggage. You have to be impartial when you're advising your client."

Figuring I'd made all the progress I could for the day, I left the Byrd family farm with a dozen questions whirling around in my head. I had the feeling that something was off about the way I'd been told the events had taken place. But was I just taking a number of contradictions and misstatements and building them into a mountain? Was my natural bias taking over? Did I expect every suspicious death to be a homicide? I wanted to run the whole thing by Darlene. She had a clear, no-bullshit way of looking at things.

I stopped by the office, intending to respond to a few

emails, return some calls and go through any reports that the lieutenant had thrown on my desk. I found Darlene chatting with the desk sergeant.

"I want to talk when you have a minute," I said as I passed her on my way to my desk.

Down the hall, I saw Dad coming out of his office. Then I saw Mauser's large black head push past him and the Dane trotted over to greet me.

"What's up, goofball?" I asked, rubbing his ears as he sniffed my pants. He jumped back and did his elephantine equivalent of a puppy bow before leaping at me joyfully, again and again… and again. "Enough!" I shouted, trying to avoid another blow. Then I remembered Cleo and understood his exuberance. "Yes, I confess I saw your girlfriend."

Dad was no help. He just stood back and guffawed.

"You act like you've never had a day of training in your life," I told Mauser, who just smiled up at me with his long tongue hanging down past his chin.

"It's your own fault coming in here smelling like Cleo," Dad said.

"Way to blame the victim," I told him as I brushed drool off of my pants. Mauser, exhausted now, dropped down to the floor.

"Tell me about the Byrd case," Dad said, his demeanor switching to boss mode.

"Cases," I corrected.

"Two murders or what?"

"One murder for sure, and the other is still open. Which reminds me, I need to call the hospital." I looked at my watch and frowned. "Not that I'll get anyone now."

"Give me the short story," he ordered. For the most part, Dad kept out of investigations. However, he expected us to keep him informed so he wouldn't be blindsided when he was talking to the public or the media.

I summarized what I knew so far.

"You feel comfortable with Paula Reece on the loose?"

"I think she'll stay put for now. I'll worry more if Austin Stokes dies."

"Is there a chance he'll regain consciousness?"

I shrugged. "I won't know until I speak with a doctor. From what Dr. Darzi said, it sounds like a long shot."

"I dealt with Althea and Ryan Byrd when I was on patrol," Dad said. "He was tough. He had a lot of rental property around here, and we'd have to go evict his tenants when they didn't pay. Sometimes they were farmers who'd rented land from him. Once they were served with the eviction notice, we'd sometimes have to follow up with a no trespass warning."

"He have a lot of non-payers?"

"Byrd ran everything tight. He'd squeeze people to the limit. The only people who would rent from him were those who couldn't rent from anyone else. He ended up with farmers and tenants who were desperate. A fair amount of the time, they'd run dry and he wouldn't give them five minutes longer than the law required. I felt like a heartless bastard a couple of times. He'd evict the sick, the pregnant, didn't matter to him."

"Anyone ever strike back at him?"

Dad looked thoughtful. "Someone shot at his house in the middle of the night. There was some vandalism too. Other than the shooting, nothing serious."

"You ever catch the shooter?"

"Nah, though we had our suspicions. There was a man named... Booker... or Brock, something like that. His family got evicted. That was bad enough, but then his teenage son died in a one-car accident a few months later and the man let everyone know that he thought Byrd evicting them had led to his son's death. A stretch if you ask me, though I'm sure that getting evicted didn't help his son's drinking any. Anyway, the shooting happened about four months later. He was at the top of the list."

"I'll look it up." Having met Althea, I was interested in her family the same way people become interested in dysfunctional families on reality TV shows.

Dad looked pensive for a moment and I thought he was going to say something else, but then he just shook his head and nudged Mauser up from the floor. They were headed to a monthly neighborhood watch meeting. Dad had discovered that attendance at the meetings went up twenty-five percent if he told them that Mauser would be there.

As soon as they left, I called the hospital. There was no magic number to press for a law enforcement officer wanting information on a victim, so I had to go through several explanations of who I was and what I wanted before I got transferred to the floor nurse in the ICU.

"If you aren't family, I can't—"

"I know that. I just want to get the doctor's name and number."

"Actually, he's standing right here," she said, surprising me. Then the line went silent and I could only hope that she'd put me on hold while she talked to the doctor.

"This is Dr. Hawkins," a deep, rich voice finally said.

"I'm Deputy Macklin. I'm assigned to Austin Stokes's case."

"Are you at your desk?" he asked.

"I am."

"If I call the Adams County Sheriff's Office, they can patch me through to you?"

"Yes."

He told me he'd call me right back, then hung up. I silently applauded his caution and hoped he wouldn't take too long. My phone rang after just five minutes.

"Just wanted to be sure," Hawkins said. "I talked to a family member about an hour ago and we're just waiting on the paperwork. Mr. Stokes is being kept alive until his organs can be processed for donation."

I remembered an article I'd read on a law enforcement website warning about cases that had been lost because organs were taken before the cause of death had even been determined.

"I'm going to call Dr. Darzi's office. I'd appreciate you waiting until Darzi has a chance to examine Mr. Stokes."

"Lives are at stake," Hawkins reminded me.

"I understand that, but this is a suspicious death. I don't think you'd want to be responsible for a murderer going loose," I said, tossing the guilt back in his court.

"The paperwork is being sent back by his sister who lives in Wyoming. You probably have until tomorrow morning, at least."

"Roger that," I said, hanging up and immediately calling Dr. Darzi's office. It didn't take me too long to get Ann on the phone, and she promised she'd find out what could be done to secure forensic evidence from the body of Austin Stokes sooner rather than later.

CHAPTER SIX

Darlene was standing at my desk when I hung up with Ann.

"What did you want to talk about, cowboy?" she said in her best Western drawl.

"The two cases I picked up today."

"Two?"

I explained the situation and what I'd learned from my interviews.

"The old woman killed them with her cane," Darlene said with a grin.

"Wouldn't put it past her. I just don't think she had the opportunity or the motive. If she killed everyone she hates, there wouldn't be enough people left on the planet to make up a foursome for bridge. No, I'm leaning toward the killings going down the way they were reported, but…"

"But you're a detective and you need something to detect."

"Maybe. The phone call to her father is bugging me. Why didn't Paula tell me about it?"

"Stress, shock—hell, she might have just forgotten about it. Give her a couple of days to get her feet back under her."

"I will. I'm gonna spend tomorrow interviewing some of the other folks who are staying on the property."

"Families. I'm amazed that we don't have *more* murders at family reunions."

"No other words of wisdom?"

"In one way, it seems cut and dried. Is the sister telling the truth? If she is, then your work here is done. If not… I think you know where you have to apply the pressure."

"Her son."

"You got it." Darlene looked at her watch. "I'm gonna cut out. Got a date with Hondo tonight." Alejandro Valdez, affectionately known as Hondo, was an EMT that Darlene had been dating for almost a year.

"Where y'all headed?"

"The big city. Dinner and a movie in Tallahassee."

"Did you put in for Maxwell's job?" I blurted, wondering where I got the nerve.

Darlene looked me dead in the eye for a minute. I could almost see her trying to figure out what good it would do to withhold the information. Then she nodded.

"I'd just as soon you didn't tell anyone until it's at least gotten to the interview stage. No sense getting everyone worked up if the city is just going to toss my application in the circular file."

I sighed, not happy with the news. "Like you have to worry about that. You're a shoo-in for the job," I said morosely.

"Sugarcakes, you don't need me. And if you do, I'll be right over there at city hall. Anyway, you've jinxed me now."

"You know you'll just be doing paperwork and the city commission's bidding," I argued.

"At half again my pay and in a position that would allow me to move up to a bigger department."

"Yeah, yeah. We're just another stepping stone." I didn't rein in my petulant attitude.

"I'm touched that you care."

"Look around. Who am I going to get for a partner?"

"You could have Pete back. Or maybe Julio."

"He's doing too well as a burglary investigator."

"You're just borrowing trouble. Those pinheads on the city commission aren't going to pick me."

"We can hope," I said cheerfully.

"Screw you and the horse you rode in on."

"You're my bestie."

Darlene laughed and waved as she headed for the door. Reluctantly, I looked at the paperwork siting on my desk and dug in.

After an hour, I'd had enough and texted Cara that I was heading home. I spent most of the fifteen-minute drive considering the best way to approach an interview with Marty. If there was anything hinky in Paula's story, then I might be able to make him crack. Of course, with him being underage, everything had to be completely transparent. Acquiring Paula's consent to the interview would be the first hurdle. She hadn't put up a fuss today, but with her father almost incapacitated, would she be as cooperative tomorrow?

I decided that I was trying to see into the future, which was futile, so I turned up the radio and tried not to think about work for the rest of the trip.

At home, I found Cara making dinner. Peaceful snores from Alvin and the sight of Ivy conducting her evening ablutions was proof that she'd already fed the animals.

"I've got news," Cara said as I kissed her in greeting.

"What?" I asked with some trepidation.

"I got a two-dollar-an-hour raise!" I could tell by the huge grin on her face how excited she was.

"Excellent!"

"That's not the best part. Dr. Barnhill gave *everyone* an extra dollar an hour and said that the reason he was able do it was because of how much money I've saved him!" Cara tossed tomatoes into a salad as she talked.

"That's great. I didn't realize you'd done that much." I saw the look on her face and quickly added, "Though I know you've been working hard."

"Blame my modesty. Though I'm not being very modest

now."

"Sounds like you deserve to brag."

"When I took over as office manager, I went through all of our orders and researched suppliers. A few changes saved about thirty percent. Then there were a bunch of accounts that were in arrears. We made reminder calls to all of those folks, most of whom had simply forgotten and needed a little push. When I did my last tally, we'd gone from having almost twenty-percent delinquent accounts to less than ten percent." All of this came pouring out of her at rapid-fire speed.

"I'm impressed," I said with raised eyebrows.

"No you're not."

"Yes, I really am. All the numbers just hurt my head. I didn't think you were that much of an accountant."

"I've taken a few business classes. But it's not that. I just like making the clinic more efficient."

"I can see that."

I could sense that Cara had more to say, but she only grinned and took our salad bowls to the table.

After dinner, we watched a sci-fi show involving aliens and time travel. I had started to nod off when Cara turned to me and gave me a little poke in the chest with her finger.

"What would you think about me taking some business courses at Florida State?"

I paused the show. "Whatever you want," I said, caught off guard.

"I love working with the animals and helping Dr. Barnhill during surgeries, but I can do much more for the clinic by helping with the business side." It was obvious that she'd been thinking about this for quite some time.

"I'm a little surprised. But then I didn't realize how much you've been improving their bottom line."

"Also, if I want a better paying job in the future, I'd probably have to leave the clinic."

"What's brought all this on?" I asked.

Cara looked thoughtful. "Getting married made me start

to think about what might be down the road. I don't know." She tossed her red locks defensively.

"I'm not saying it's a bad thing. I just wasn't expecting it. I know you're happy at the clinic."

"I am. I'm just… thinking about how I can do more."

"You do plenty. It's not like we have—" I put the brakes on. We hadn't had any big discussions about kids. There'd been a few, casual, maybe-in-the-future sort of talks before the wedding, but nothing since.

"And there's the kid thing," Cara said with a shrug, as if reading my mind.

This was getting deeper into the weeds than I'd expected. I turned off the TV and faced her.

"Having children is a big decision. Do you want to talk about it?"

There was a longer pause. "If *you* want to."

I felt the ice cracking beneath me.

"I think we would make great parents. Whenever you feel you're ready, I'll be ready," I said, hoping it was the right answer. It was pushing the decision to have children onto her, but it was how I really felt.

"I didn't mean for this to be a big deal. The business school part, I mean. Having children… I'm not ready to think about that right now."

I quelled a sigh of relief.

"I'm happy with my job. Crazy as it is, and even though it's taken me a while to get there. But now I feel like a heel for not considering what you think about yours."

"I'm happy now. I guess I've gotten the hang of being the manager for the clinic and…"

"You're looking for more?"

"Possibly. I just don't know what that might be. I certainly don't want to leave the clinic any time soon."

I gave her a big smile. "I never knew you were so ambitious."

She rolled her eyes. "I wouldn't say I'm ambitious. I'm just a little restless."

"I blame your parents. All that moving around when you were growing up."

"You're probably right." Cara smiled at me playfully, signaling that the serious topics had all been covered. She leaned in for a kiss and we were soon headed for the bedroom.

CHAPTER SEVEN

I awoke at four, my mind roiling with the deaths of Tracy and Austin Stokes. After a while I gave up on sleep, dressing and sneaking quietly out of the house. My early arrival at the office was met with a stream of derision from Darlene.

"You must not have gone to bed last night," she said, "'cause there's no way you could have gotten up this early, Foghorn."

"Foghorn?" I shouldn't have taken the bait, but my mind didn't start working before nine.

"You're up with the roosters this morning. Would you prefer Leghorn?"

"How can you be so chipper?" I frowned at the piles of paper on my desk, trying to remember what I needed to get done before heading out to the Byrd farm.

"It's easy to be in a good mood this time of morning. Nothing bad has happened." Darlene took a swig from a quart-sized mug of coffee.

"Mainlining caffeine probably doesn't hurt," I grumbled.

"Honey, this is mother's milk to me. Straight black Colombian goodness."

"Didn't you have a date with Hondo last night?"

"Ha! Speaking of Columbian goodness. I sure did. Went

to a little bar where a friend of his was playing guitar and singing."

"And you still made it in before the graveyard shift went home?"

"Like the good Zevon said, I'll sleep when I'm dead."

"Enough! I need to get my act together, then head out to the Byrd farm. I've got almost a dozen more witnesses to interview."

"Let me know if you need help."

"Since I'm not even sure there will be any charges to file, I'm not going to tie both of us up."

She gave me a salute and went back to her coffee while I rushed through my morning routine of emails and reports before heading back to my car.

My plan was to sit down with Bernadette and make a schedule for interviewing the remaining members of the family. As far as I was concerned, everyone who was staying at the farm qualified as a witness. I didn't think any of them had seen what happened, but most of them would have seen Tracy, Austin and Paula interacting in the days before the deaths.

Bernadette had given me a code to get through the gate at the farm. I was ready to grind out the interviews when I drove up near the buildings and saw a little blue pickup truck that I recognized immediately. *Not possible*, I thought.

The Dodge Dakota belonged to Jessie Gilmore, a young woman who'd insinuated herself into one of my cases in the spring. She'd managed not to get herself killed, and her timely use of a broken beer bottle had saved my life. Even so, I thought she was a menace. Unfortunately, she was convinced that she wanted to be my new confidential informant. I thought longingly of Eddie Thompson. I didn't begrudge my old CI his new life of sobriety and a steady job, but I missed his connections to Adams County's slimy underbelly.

I felt my blood pressure rise just looking at Jessie's truck. *How did she hear about this and how did she manage to get out here?* I took a couple of deep breaths and reminded myself that she'd been keeping a low profile since April. Her close encounter with real violence had left her a little shaken.

I parked and went hunting for Bernadette, keeping an eye out for Jessie. I found both of them sitting with Cleo on the front porch of a small hunting cabin a few hundred yards behind the main house and on the other side of the pond where Jack Byrd had drowned. Cleo stood up as I approached, while Jessie looked nervous and Bernadette gave me a sad smile.

"They really did put you and Cleo outside the circle," I said.

"You heard Dad. Althea doesn't like Cleo in any of the houses." She reached out to pet the dog. "Doesn't hurt our feelings. Quieter out here."

"Jessie," I said evenly.

"I only came out here 'cause Bernadette asked me to," Jessie said with a defiant tilt of her chin. I noticed that she'd changed the streaks of color in her dark hair from acid green to a startling blue.

"I know all about the excitement y'all got into this spring," Bernadette said. "I really did ask her to come out and stay with Cleo and me. I wanted to have one friendly face around."

"I didn't know you knew each other."

"Bernadette brings Cleo into the library to read with the kids," Jessie informed me. "One of my jobs is to get the kids signed up for times with them."

"Jessie's a very smart young lady. Not a bad actor, either. I talked her into taking a small part in a play at the theatre last month." Bernadette smiled at Jessie who, surprisingly, blushed.

"She *is* a good actor," I said with a level dose of sarcasm. Jessie had played me a couple of times.

"Have you made a decision about Paula?" Bernadette asked.

"Not yet. I want to talk to everyone else who's been here

since Austin, Tracy and Paula arrived."

"Dad told me that Austin isn't going to live."

"He's still on machines at the moment," I said, causing her to shake her head sadly.

"I just hope Paula doesn't have any legal problems."

"I can't promise that."

"I thought you might need a cheat sheet, so Jessie and I worked one up for you. Come on in."

I followed her into the cabin, with Cleo nudging my hand for attention. Jessie was right behind us.

"I came to help Bernadette, but if I can help *you* with the investigation…" she said slyly, and I saw some of the mischievous Jessie that drove me crazy.

"Right now I just need to get everyone's story. I guess you had something to do with the cheat sheet?"

"I might have suggested it," Jessie said with a coy glance toward the floor. I sighed.

The inside of the cabin was rustic and workman-like. The walls were plywood and the floor made from rough pine boards. There were two sets of bunk beds against one wall, while the other held a basic kitchen area. The only concession to comfort was a double bed in one corner with a nightstand and a colorful braided rug on the floor. A lumpy couch provided the only seating.

"I wrote down all the names I could think of," Bernadette said, handing me two pieces of paper ripped from a yellow legal pad.

"What I want to do first is interview Marty," I said.

Bernadette gave me a guilty look. "He's not here. Dad took him into Tallahassee to pick up some feed for the dogs. He was feeling bad for the kid and thought it would help take his mind off things. I know you want us all to stay here for a while, but we didn't think a trip into town would be a problem."

I sighed. In truth, I hadn't told them they couldn't go *anywhere*, and I hadn't expressed any particular concern about Marty.

"Okay," I muttered, looking at the list. "If I can't start with the youngest, let's do the oldest. I've already talked to Althea, Bruce and your dad. Which means that your mom or Bruce's wife, Debbie, can be next."

"Mom won't be here before noon."

"Fine. I'll start with Bruce's wife."

"Have you seen my aunt?" she asked, her hands making air quotes.

"I don't think so."

"Ha! You'd remember. I'll take you over there. She'd never walk this far across country." Bernadette chuckled. "Besides, she's afraid of Cleo."

We headed back out the door and I turned to Jessie. "You can stay here with Cleo."

She gave me a wounded expression as the dog leaned against her for an ear rub.

"I take it that you don't approve of your aunt?" I asked Bernadette as we walked across the meadow on our way to the other houses.

"She's my uncle's second wife. The whole affair is so cliché. Debbie turned thirty-two last year. Blonde, gold earrings hanging down to her shoulders, bracelets jangling on her wrists and a very prominent diamond ring on her finger. Uncle Bruce went full midlife crisis with this one."

"I saw Bruce yesterday. He was having some serious back pain, but there wasn't any sign of his wife."

"I saw her in front of Austin and Tracy's cabin yesterday when Marty told them what had happened. Predictably, Debbie looked freaked out and went running back to her place. I never saw her after that. Paula and Debbie don't get along. Since Bruce has a soft spot for his daughter, Debbie's learned to just disappear when Paula's around."

Bernadette knocked on the door of the cute cottage I'd been in yesterday. I would have told her that I'd take if from there, but I wanted to see how the family interacted. Bruce, Debbie and Paula would react differently around each other and Bernadette than they would with me on a one-to-one basis. I'd gotten some good leads in the past from sideways glances exchanged across a room.

Paula opened the door and let us in. Bruce was still lying on the couch, looking the worse for wear, though he'd obviously been up at some point as he'd managed to change clothes.

"Sorry that I still can't get up to greet you," he said with obvious frustration.

"No worries. I actually came to talk to your wife."

He frowned.

"As a lawyer, my first inclination is to tell anyone who needs to hear it not to talk to the police voluntarily, though I've already stretched that rule." He sighed. "However, I don't think anyone could possibly think that Debbie has anything to do with this business. Debbie!" He yelled her name at the top of his lungs, then grimaced from the pain of the effort.

I looked over at Paula, who was already making her way to the back bedroom while Debbie appeared at the top of the stairs leading to the loft.

"I'm coming, honey!" Debbie said lightly. Then she looked down from the landing, saw me and stopped. The hesitation only lasted a moment, then she gingerly made her way down the steep stairs while wearing ludicrously high heels.

Bernadette rolled her eyes. "I'm heading back to my cabin," she said and made a quick exit.

"Debbie, this is the investigator who's handling the deaths of—" Bruce choked up for a moment. "Of Tracy and that *monster*." His pain was clearly affecting his diplomacy.

"I'm pleased to meet you," Debbie said with honey-sweet vowels. "Of course, the circumstances are just horrible."

"I'd like to ask you a few questions."

"Ask away." She fluttered her hands in the air.

"In private?" I looked at her husband to see if he would object, but Bruce had already closed his eyes.

I noticed that Debbie had also turned toward him. A

frown crossed her face when she realized he wasn't going to argue.

"I guess so… sure." She glanced around. Her eyes lit on the door to the back room and a look of frustration mixed with anger spread across her face. "Let's go out on the porch. It's still early. How hot can it be?"

Once we'd settled into the white wicker chairs on the narrow porch, she wiped away a few drops of sweat from her forehead in a dramatic gesture.

"I spoke too soon. The air is literally dripping out here."

"I won't keep you long. Start by telling me where you were from eleven o'clock yesterday until you learned that something had happened at the Stokeses's cabin."

Debbie gave me a hard look. There was some steel in this magnolia.

"I was going through my feeds," she said, holding up the phone that she'd had in her hand the whole time. "I'm close to being a full-fledged influencer. I've got three thousand followers."

"Where were you when you were looking at your… feeds?"

"Here, of course," she said, flipping up one of her hands to indicate the cabin.

"Were you alone?" I asked, and for just a split second I saw hesitation. Did her relationship with Bruce meet *all* the criteria of a May-December marriage?

"Bruce was out doing something with his brother. Feeding the deer or something. Silly, since they're just going to shoot them come fall," she said, blatantly sidestepping my question.

"Who was with you?" I responded, showing her that I wasn't a complete idiot.

"Nobody really. I mean, Myron came by for a minute. Just a minute, mind you."

"Myron?"

"He's Bruce's second cousin or something," she said indifferently, no doubt hoping that I would move on.

"And he'll corroborate your account?"

This time the hesitation was paired with a frown and furrowed eyebrows.

"Am I… like… under oath or something?"

"What do you think?" I could avoid a question as easily as she could.

She sighed dramatically. I was beginning to realize that she did *everything* dramatically.

"He *should*," she pouted. As if a light bulb went on over her head, her body language shifted from *you're-pressuring-me* to *aren't-I-pretty?* She sat back in her chair, pushing out her chest and giving me a sad little smile. "I guess I might need a little… discretion."

"Just the facts, ma'am," I said in my best Joe Friday voice. While the reference was lost on her, my tone wasn't.

The pouty look came back. "Jeez, we were just flirting. That's all. A little harmless flirting with the only guy around here who isn't enslaved to that bitch in the tower." As soon as she said it, she looked nervously over her shoulder at the doors and windows of the cottage, then lowered her voice. "I swear it was nothing."

"All I'm interested in are the two deaths."

"Is Austin really and truly dead?" Her eyes took on the look of a frightened child. I couldn't tell if it was simply another act.

"Last I heard, he was on life support."

"But…"

"The doctors say he's brain dead. They're keeping him alive because he was a registered organ donor."

"Oh…"

"Does your husband know you were with Myron?"

"I know what you think. Like everyone else, you think I married Bruce for his money. This whole rotten family thinks that. They took one look at me and made up their minds. I never had a chance." I could see her teeth clench as she spoke, a look of disgust on her face. "It's never been about the money. Bruce and I have a good life. We make each other happy. Except when we're around his family. I can't stand them." She stomped her foot for emphasis.

"Except for Myron?"

"He's an outsider like me. We get together at these family torture sessions and have a few laughs. I'd go crazy here if it wasn't for him." She was talking from the heart now.

"And his wife?"

"She's all right. Not that she'd understand about us. Ellie is… a little odd. That's why I'm not sure Myron will say he was with me. He wouldn't want to hurt her."

"I can't promise to keep y'all's little rendezvous secret, but I'll do what I can," I said honestly. "Let's move on. You were with Myron… flirting. Then what happened?"

"We were… We heard loud voices coming from Austin's cabin, so Myron left by the back door while I went out the front to see what was going on."

"You were afraid that your husband might come back?" I assumed.

"Or that one of the busybodies might see us and say something to Bruce or Ellie. The whole crew just loves to stir up crap. And you want to know why?" Her eyes were suddenly on fire.

"Why?"

"The money." More hand-waving. "That's what this is all about. The queen bee's money. That old witch is going to live to be a hundred just so she can keep watching her children fight over the money."

"How much money are we talking about?"

"Ho, ho! Millions. Mostly in property. Some in stocks and such. She lets Bruce manage some of it. For free, of course. If he was investing that kind of money for someone else, he'd be making a good living off of the commissions alone. You know what she gave him for Christmas last year?"

A subscription to the jelly of the month club? I thought. But I let her answer her own question.

"A five-hundred-dollar gift certificate to JoS. A. Bank.

What a joke! Her investments made over a hundred-thousand dollars last year alone. What's he get for his trouble? A gift certificate to a clothing store 'cause she says he looks like a bum."

"Who inherits the money?"

"No one knows. At least, that's what Bruce says. He claims she didn't let him draw up the will. She keeps it with some lawyer in Lake City."

The money had me curious. Could that have been a motive for killing Tracy and Austin? It seemed unlikely. If Althea had been the victim, then it would have made some sense. But why kill off two people if it wasn't even clear that they were included in the will? I was definitely heading off on a side rail that didn't seem to be going anywhere. It was time to get back on the mainline.

"How well did you know Austin and Tracy?"

"Tracy listened to everything that Paula told her about me. Tracy told me once that she'd hated me before she even met me."

"And Austin?"

"I didn't think he was that bad, though there was a lot of hate directed at him. But he was always nice to me." There was no hint of the flirtatiousness she'd shown when talking about Myron.

"What did you think of their relationship?"

There was a long pause while she pursed her lips in thought. "You've got to remember how bad Tracy and Paula have been to me. Any time one of them was getting slapped down, I was, like, all for it."

"Slapped?"

"Not literally. I never saw Austin lay a hand on either one of them. Still, he didn't take any of their mouth either. If they got in his face, he'd put them right back in their place. I was like 'Rah! Rah!', cheering that shit on."

"How had Tracy and Austin been getting along since they got here?"

"I saw them every evening. It was just like always. They'd

put on a show for a while, trying to convince the witch that they were all lovey-dovey, but they couldn't keep it up. I didn't see as much yelling this time. Just lots of cold-as-Christmas stares."

"More or less than usual?"

"Maybe there was more of it from Austin. Like I said, less heat and more ice."

"What about Paula? Did she interact with them differently?"

"Interact? That's a funny word for those three. Paula is a real piece of work. She played the same role with them that she does with Bruce and me. She picked a side and stuck with it. Stuck like glue to Tracy and shot back glare-for-glare at Austin. I'm not really surprised about what happened yesterday. Just sayin'."

"You aren't surprised that Austin killed Tracy?"

"No, that *did* surprise me. I've seen lots of couples like them. Those two just loved to hate each other. I never thought either of them was unhappy with the arrangement. That was just their thing. As long as neither one crossed the line, they were happy to keep it up. No, what I wasn't surprised about was that Paula killed Austin."

"You think she wanted to kill him?"

Debbie laughed. "Austin and Paula have wanted to kill each other since day one."

"Why?"

"Because Paula is a jealous bitch and can't stand for anyone new to come into her family," she said with a double helping of bitterness, then leaned toward me. "And the night before, Paula crossed a line. She started picking at Austin and even Tracy couldn't get her to stop. That's what four gin and tonics can do to you. I thought Austin was going to punch Paula right in the snout."

"Tell me about the fight."

"Everyone knew that Austin had lost his job… again. But we weren't supposed to talk about it. Well, Paula comes to dinner and I'm pretty sure she'd already hit the bottle, talking real loud and asking Austin how his job was going, knowing full well he didn't have one. On and on she went. Tracy tried to cut her off and Paula just kept sidestepping her. I wish I could have videoed Paula ranting at Austin. That would have gone viral for sure."

"How did it end?"

"Tracy dragged Austin away before he hit Paula."

"What did Paula do?"

"She laughed, but when she saw no one else was laughing, she got another drink and went into the family room. When Bruce and I left, she was snoring away on the couch."

"Was Marty there?"

Her eyes softened and the vindictiveness in her face eased a little. "That poor kid. Anyone could have seen he was mortified. I've got nothing against Marty. He's always tried to be nice to me."

"Tried?"

"His mother has poured poison in his ears, same as everyone else. I could see her doing it. He'd look my way and she'd lean over and whisper to him."

"How did Marty get along with Austin and Tracy?"

"Okay, I guess. Whenever Tracy and Paula got together, there wasn't room for anyone else. As for him getting along with Austin, his mother wouldn't let that happen. No way."

"Who else didn't like Austin?"

"I keep trying to tell you. This family doesn't like anyone who comes in from the outside. I'll admit that Austin was rough around the edges, but he didn't deserve the type of hate these people felt for him. The only time they treated me like part of the family was when they were trying to talk me onto the hate-Austin bandwagon. It was just another strike against me that I didn't go along with it. You think I'm a gold digger? Let me tell you, if I was then I would have been loud and proud hating on Austin, 'cause that would have earned me brownie points with the powers that be."

"Let's go to the moment yesterday after you and Myron

left this cottage. What did you do and see?"

"Let me think." The shift in topic caused her to pause and regroup. "There was a lot of stuff going on around their cabin, so I walked over there. Marty came out crying. Ellie was there. I saw Myron come around from behind my place."

"Ellie was where exactly?"

"She was walking toward the cabin. Myron saw her and went over to her."

"You said you and Myron had heard a commotion when you were still inside. Could you tell who was causing it?"

"I'm pretty sure it was Paula. Yeah, I saw Paula go back in the house as Marty was coming out."

"Had she been talking to someone?"

"I think she was yelling or crying or something. I knew right off that whatever had happened was bad. Once she went back in the cottage, it was hard to hear 'cause the windows were closed and the air was on." She looked down at the floor.

"Was there anyone else around?"

"Ellie had the kids with her! That's right."

"Kids?"

"Myron's boy Elijah, and Ellie's girl Jeanette. They were both married before."

"How old are Elijah and Jeanette?"

"Sevenish... maybe a little younger. I'm not a kid person, if you know what I mean." She made a face.

"Go on."

"Well, I just watched. Myron and Ellie went over to talk to Marty. Thing was, Marty just kept crying and hitting himself. At one point, Myron stepped around him and went into the house. When Myron came out of the house, he was freaked out. He was shaking his head and looking confused. He said something to Ellie, who took the kids and headed back to their camper."

"What did you do?"

"I just kind of froze. I'd heard Marty say that Tracy was

dead, but I didn't understand what was going on. Myron talked to Marty and hugged him and stuff. I saw Dottie and Cleo too. Then Bruce and Owen came driving up. Myron kind of let Bruce take over. I went back into the cottage then."

"You didn't talk to your husband?"

She shook her head. "He didn't look right. Something about the expression on his face scared me."

"When did you find out the full story?"

"I watched out the window and saw the police and ambulance arrive. Later, when Bruce and Paula came to the cottage, I heard them talking and figured it out." Debbie seemed shaken by the memory of the events.

"What did Bruce tell you had happened?" I asked.

She frowned. "Now, I know Bruce wouldn't want me telling you things he told me. If you want to know that, you'll just have to ask him." She stood up. "I think I'd better be done talking."

"I may need to speak with you again."

"We'll see." She turned and headed back inside without another word.

Her abrupt end to the conversation was a little odd. But considering her precarious situation with the family, I guess I shouldn't have been surprised.

CHAPTER EIGHT

Walking off the porch, I saw four people headed toward me. They were all young, in their late teens or early twenties. A tall, dark-haired man appeared to be the oldest, and he was holding hands with a younger brunette who was a foot shorter than he was. They were clearly a couple. He made eye contact with me and the group turned in my direction.

"Are you the detective?" the older man asked as they caught up with me.

"I'm Deputy Macklin with the Adams County Sheriff's Office."

"You're looking into… the deaths?"

"That's right. And you are?"

"I'm Andy Hagan. This is Roch," he said, pronouncing it "Rock" and putting his arm over the shoulder of the young woman. "That's Cory and Bridget."

A blond-haired man and the other girl with him both looked uncomfortable, shifting their weight from foot to foot and not letting their eyes meet mine for more than a second.

"Are you part of the family?"

"I'm just Roch's boyfriend. Roch and Bridget are sisters. They're like great-nieces to Mrs. Byrd. Cory's their cousin, something like that," Andy explained.

"And you all were here yesterday?"

"You mean when… things happened?" Andy seemed very open, but looked at the others for support.

"I meant are you staying here on the farm? But, yes, were you present when the deaths occurred?"

"Yeah, but we were out on a hike when things happened." He looked a little uncomfortable.

"All of you were together?"

"Yes," said Roch.

"When did you go on the hike, where did you go and how long were you gone?"

"Wow, I…" Andy pursed his lips and scrunched up his eyebrows in concentration. "Around noon?"

"You sent a text," Roch reminded him.

He took out his phone. "That's right. We took a selfie and I sent it to a friend of mine." He pulled up the text and showed it to me. "I sent it just after noon."

I looked hard at the picture. "Where was this taken?"

"Right over there." He pointed to a spot about fifty feet from where we were standing. In the background, I could just make out Tracy and Austin's cabin.

"May I?" I asked, holding out my hand for the phone.

He passed it to me. I looked more closely and thought I could make out two people in the background of the photo.

"I can text it to you," Andy offered.

The photo was taken about thirty minutes before the killings. Was there anything I could learn from it?

"That'd be great," I said, handing the phone back to him along with my card.

He poked at his screen until my phone vibrated with a text alert. I opened it and tapped on the picture, expanding it. Sure enough, I could make out Austin and Tracy standing near the cabin. Later, I'd download the photo to my computer where I could enlarge it further.

"You think that could help?" Andy asked.

"I don't know."

"Paula didn't do anything wrong," Bridget spoke up, a frown on her face.

"We're still in the early days of the investigation," I said neutrally.

"She *did* kill Austin," Cory pointed out.

"He probably deserved it," Bridget shot back.

"Whatever," Cory said, backing down.

"How old are you all?" I asked. A month earlier I'd arrested a young man who I'd assumed was at least twenty. When he finally gave me his date of birth, I found out that he was barely seventeen. I'd stopped guessing at ages.

"I'm twenty-five," Andy piped up.

"Twenty-one," Roch said.

"I'm not sure what business it is of yours," Bridget said, trying to sound tough.

"I'm just trying to get all the facts." I wasn't going to argue with her.

"I'm twenty," Cory said.

"Fine, I'm nineteen," Bridget pouted.

I turned to Roch. "Is Roch a nickname?"

"What? Are you going to look us up or something?" Bridget grumbled.

"Ignore her. She's just in a pissy mood," Roch said. "My full name is Rochelle and I hate it."

"I appreciate y'all coming over and talking to me," I said, ignoring all the young adult attitude. "I may need to ask you more questions later."

"Why? We weren't here when the murders took place," Bridget groused. She fiddled with a necklace made up of dozens of animal figures carved out of wood.

"Give it up, Bridget," Cory told her, then they all headed down the hill toward the pond.

"You can call me any time. You have my number," Andy said over his shoulder.

I decided that Myron would be next on my list. I wanted to explore his relationship with Debbie. A voice in my head kept asking what this had to do with the killings, but I didn't have an answer. Something just felt odd, and I remembered some words of wisdom that Dad had shared with me when I joined the department: Everyone's a suspect until they aren't.

Two large RVs were parked near the main house. I figured one of them had to belong to Myron and Ellie. When I got there, it wasn't hard to identify. Under an awning attached to the largest RV, a woman was sitting with two small children.

The woman looked up as I walked toward them. Even from forty feet away, I could tell that she'd been crying. The children were dressed in matching overalls as they played with plastic cars. The olive-skinned boy was showing admirable tolerance as the blonde girl snatched away his toy.

"Ellie Morgan?"

"Yes," she said, making it sound like uttering the word was a huge burden.

I introduced myself. She nodded and looked at the children.

"I don't want to talk about… any of that stuff in front of the kids," she said flatly.

The RV door opened and a burly, deeply tanned man looked out.

"I'll watch the kids," he said.

"Are you Myron?"

"I am." He looked at me the way a boxer looks at his opponent during the weigh-in.

"You're actually who I want to talk to."

This got me a frown from both of them. The kids were also looking at me by this point, but at least *they* were smiling.

"You go on," Ellie said to Myron.

"You can come inside," he said to me, stepping back from the door.

The inside of the RV was bigger than I would have imagined from the outside. Not magical-Tardis bigger, but certainly comfortable.

He waved me to the built-in dining table. I sat down on

the bench closest to the door while he squeezed in across from me.

I debated whether I should set him up to hang himself, or be open and let him know that I had already talked to Debbie. I decided to play hardball.

"Can you tell me where you were yesterday between ten and noon?"

"Man, you know who did what to who. Why are you coming at me like that?"

"I'm trying to establish where everyone was when the incident occurred."

"You're telling me that you aren't treating me any differently than the rest of the family?"

"That's right."

"Sure," he said, making it sound like a curse. "I was just walking around until I heard Marty all upset. Then I went over to the house and tried to get him to make some sense. He was out of his mind. When I went in to see about his momma, I knew why. Crazy. Just crazy."

"Before you heard Marty, you weren't with anyone?" I asked, all innocence.

He tried to incinerate me with his eyes.

"What is this, man?" He pulled out his phone and showed me a text he'd received from Debbie. All it said was: *The cop knows*, followed by a sad face emoji. "This is bullshit. Why did you come in here trying to play me?"

"So tell me the truth."

"Fine, I was talking with Debbie. We heard yelling outside and I went to find out what it was. Then Marty is crying and I find Austin and Tracy dead. Okay, Austin wasn't dead, but he sure looked like it."

"Talking with Debbie?"

"Man, please. Yes, I was talking. Nothing else." He leaned toward me and lowered his voice. "Not that she isn't hot. If I was single, sure, I'd tap that, but I'm married, got kids. Besides, there's people all over this damn place." All of this had the ring of truth, though not necessarily the whole truth. I decided to let it drop for now.

"Tell me exactly what happened after you left Debbie."

"We heard some noise, so I went out the back. I wanted to make sure it wasn't Ellie or the kids, you know. Didn't take me long to figure out where all the commotion was coming from. That boy Marty was standing on the porch, all torn up. Crying and such. Not knowing what happened. I just tried to help him."

"What do you do for a living?" I asked, both because I wanted to know and also to break up his narrative. It was possible to trip up a liar by asking questions they weren't expecting.

"I sell motorcycles at South Alabama Motorsports in Dothan and teach motorcycle safety classes on the weekends. Funny you ask, 'cause seeing Marty and going toward that house felt like going up to someone who's had a bad crash. That's how he was. All rubber-legged."

"What did he tell you?"

"Not much. He couldn't hardly talk. His voice was all shaky. He choked up when he tried to put words together."

"Did he have any blood on him?"

"Some on his hands. He got some on me."

I leaned forward. "Do you have the clothes you were wearing?"

"What? You think I threw them away?"

"Can I see them?"

He got up and walked to the back of the RV, surprisingly light on his feet for such a large man. I didn't feel more than a little vibration as he went to retrieve the clothes.

"I figured you didn't need to see my underwear," he said, showing several smears of blood on his shirt. His pants looked clean.

"I'd like to take these in case we need to have them tested," I said and saw him grow tense.

"What, you think I had—"

I waved my hands. "No, I don't think you had anything to do with this. But I'll be candid with you. I'm not sure what happened inside that cabin. My focus is on Marty and Paula. All I'm doing right now is collecting information."

He handed me the clothes. "Marty said that he touched Austin. He thought he was dead."

"I need to clear this up to everyone's satisfaction now so that Marty and Paula won't have to worry about it ten years from now. Does that make sense?"

"I can see that," he said begrudgingly.

"Did Marty say anything intelligible when you got to him?"

"I think he said something about calling 911 and that they were dead."

"Had he called 911 already?"

"I don't know. I just heard that and the word dead. I knew something bad had happened. I figured it was an accident. I've got my CPR certification, so I thought I might be able to help."

"And…"

"I went inside." Myron's face glazed over and I knew he was replaying the events in his head.

"Tell me what you saw."

"It was bad. Tracy, man, she was lying there… ugh. I just… She was obviously dead, her tongue… For some reason, that was worse than Austin, though he had blood all over him. I just reached down and felt his wrist. I was pretty sure I felt a pulse."

"Where was Paula?"

"When I went inside, she was sitting on the couch all kind of curled up and whimpering. When I leaned over Austin to see if he was alive, I saw her standing in the doorway of the bedroom watching me."

"Did she talk to you?"

"I asked her what happened. I think she was in shock. She just stood there hugging herself and making little sad sounds. I told her I thought Austin was still alive, which kind of woke her up. She took her phone out and said she had to call her dad. That seemed odd to me. But freaked out people do weird shit. All I knew was that someone needed to call 911 and it wasn't going to be me."

"Why didn't you want to make the call?"

He gave me a look like I was a fool. "I didn't have nothin' to do with any of that and didn't want my name comin' up. Yet here you sit anyway. No, man, Marty was better when I got back out on the porch. I told him that he had to call 911. He said he already had and that's when I saw Bruce and them drive up."

"Who else did you see while all of this was going on?"

"I saw most of the family. People kind of came and went."

"What about the younger family members?"

"Ellie had our kids there."

"I meant Andy and Rochelle, that group."

"Noooo. Didn't see them. Sam was driving the ATV for Bruce and Owen."

"Did anyone besides Bruce interact with Marty or Paula?"

"Dottie came over with that horse of hers and talked to Marty."

"Did you hear what they talked about?"

"She was just trying to calm him down. He likes that dog of hers."

"What did you think of Austin and Tracy?"

"As a couple? One word: trouble. I called them the family entertainment. Every time we got together, those two would find a way to get into a pissing match. Half the time I think they were just doing it so everyone would make a big deal over them. Like all that viral stuff on the Internet. People act crazy for attention."

"Are you surprised that Austin killed Tracy?"

"Hell yeah! Who does that shit?" He looked down at the table. "It was awful. I'm going to be seeing her face in my nightmares for a long time."

"What about Paula?"

"What about her?"

"Are you surprised that she killed Austin?"

"To protect Tracy? Nope. They were thick as thieves. The only thing they ever argued about was Austin. Paula hated him. If she saw him choking Tracy, I expect she'd do anything to stop him."

"Did any of them act different this week?"

"Nope," he said way too fast.

"Take your time. Think about the last couple of days. Did anything seem odd?"

"Austin was his usual obnoxious self. Tracy would do things to provoke him and then go batshit on him when he got upset. All normal. Paula and Tracy would get into a huddle and talk. I figured it was about Austin most of the time. No different than all the rest of these family encounters."

I felt my phone vibrate for the third time in the last four minutes. Excusing myself, I pulled it out to find two missed calls and a text from dispatch, telling me to get on the radio. In case I missed it, there was a second text simply reading: *Urgent.*

Wondering what the hell was going on, I thanked Myron for his time and ran for my car.

CHAPTER NINE

I called dispatch before I got to the car. I could hear the tension in Marti's voice as soon as he answered.

"Armed robbery at the Supersave with a shooting in the parking lot. Johnson is in charge of the perimeter. He's been burning up the radio. All hands on deck."

I heard the calls going out as I got into the car. They called my name and there was a little back and forth as I was instructed to park at an intersection about a mile from the Byrd farm.

I took a quick look back at the houses before I sped out to the main road. I didn't really want to abandon the investigation to go play roadblock, but my more sensible side argued that an armed suspect on the run was more important than a couple of killings that were probably better sorted by the State Attorney, who'd ultimately have to decide whether to prosecute Paula or not.

I drove to my assigned position and parked my car where I could easily drive it onto the road as a barricade if I needed to. That would be a measure of last resort. It would have been handy if I'd had one of the department's spike strips, but the portable tire shredders were expensive and the six that we had were all in the hands of our SWAT team.

I listened closely to the radio. No one had spotted the suspect since he'd fled into a low-income neighborhood about a mile from the courthouse square. There were a dozen deputies like me, just sitting and watching, while others were driving up and down Calhoun's streets, looking for the suspect's white Toyota Camry. Five such vehicles had already been spotted and checked out.

I found a granola bar in the glove box and was concentrating on what might well have been my lunch when the radio exploded. Shots had been fired. A Florida highway patrolman had flushed the suspect, who was tearing up the tarmac trying to get out of town. Like a ball on a roulette wheel, he seemed about to commit to one escape route after another until he finally picked my direction. My body did a full adrenaline dump as I moved my car into the road. Three of our cruisers were in hot pursuit.

The calls were coming in fast when, with the suddenness of a bolt of lightning, it was over. The Camry had hit a curb and flipped, ending the chase. Breathing deeply, I moved my car back off the road, then waited for a lull in the radio traffic to tell them I was leaving my position.

"Negative. Hold in place."

"Is there a second suspect?"

"Negative."

I wanted to ask why I had to stay parked at the intersection, but then a bunch more chatter from the deputies and EMTs blew up concerning the health of the suspect, who'd apparently suffered serious trauma from the accident. I found out later that he'd sold the air bags out of the car a week earlier to buy drugs. Talk about karma hitting you upside the head.

I was impatiently cooling my heels, wondering how long I should wait before calling in again, when I saw Dad's official sheriff's SUV pulling off the road across from me. *What have I done now?* I thought.

I got out of my car as he was stepping down out of the SUV.

"My side or yours?" I asked.

"You're parked in the shade," he said and jogged across the two-lane highway.

"What's up?"

"I just wanted to have a chat with you," he said in an uncharacteristically passive tone.

"Okay."

"What have you learned out at the Byrd farm?"

Why does he want to talk about this here? I wondered. *He could have called me into his office where it's air-conditioned.*

"I'm not much further along than I was yesterday. I know that there was a lot of animosity between Paula, Austin and Tracy, the female victim. Paula resented the way her brother-in-law treated her sister. There may have been some jealousy on Paula's part. She and Tracy were very close. But there'd been an ugly scene the night before. Complicated family dynamics."

"Nothing you can hang your hat on?"

"Not unless something jumps out in the autopsies."

"Do you think there's a chance of discovering physical evidence to support a murder charge?"

"Unlikely. I don't think Paula has told me everything, but I haven't done a full interview with her. I was giving it a day or two. Any evidence to convict would have to come from witness testimony. And I still need to talk to her son Marty."

"Johnson's grumbling about you taking two days to work on a case that seems pretty cut and dried."

Is this why he tracked me down out here? Because Lt. Johnson is irritated with the way I'm allocating my time? Aloud, I said, "The situation is unique. We've got a bunch of witnesses who live out of the area. If I don't interview them now, it'll be a lot harder to do in the future."

"Makes sense to me. I just thought you ought to know so you can discuss it with him before it becomes a problem," Dad said, then glanced down at the ground, almost as though he were nervous about something.

I waited while he seemed to be gathering his thoughts.

When he still didn't say anything, I asked, "Is there something else you want to talk about?"

A few beads of sweat trickled down his forehead. "It's hot out here," he said, taking his hat off and wiping away the sweat. "We can talk later."

"We can sit in the car," I offered, wanting to know what the hell was up.

"That's okay." He had already turned and was crossing the road.

I shook my head and got back in my car. Dispatch said I was free to go, making it clear that Dad had been the one to ask that I be held at my post.

I made it back to the Byrd farm by two-thirty. I had time for another interview and a talk with Jessie. I wanted to make sure she understood that she was to steer clear of this investigation.

As fate would have it, I saw her as soon as I parked my car. She was leaning through the passenger door of her truck, rooting around for something.

"I want to talk with you."

"I thought you might," she said, backing out and holding up a white cord. "I had to get my phone charger."

"How have you been?"

"Good. I'm still a little wigged out about the fact that I stabbed a guy."

"If you hadn't, then he might have killed me or hurt someone else." Both of us had our heads down as we walked toward Bernadette's cabin.

"Yeah. It helps to think that."

"You still want to be in law enforcement?"

"Yep."

"You know you can't interfere in this case?"

"I really did just come out here to support Bernadette," she said. "And to help with Cleo." She seemed sincere.

"No snooping," I said forcefully.

"I hear you," she answered, only slightly petulant.

"Why were you so determined to get involved back in the spring? What's driving your interest in law enforcement?"

Jessie had been adamant when I'd first met her that, even though she'd had a brush with the law when she was younger, she was resolute in her desire to become a cop. Now she walked a dozen steps without answering.

"Do you remember the girl who went missing?" she finally asked.

My mind started to review a hundred different flyers from just the last few years. "I'm not sure I know who you're talking about," I said diplomatically.

"Terri Miller. She disappeared in May five years ago."

"I remember. I was still on patrol and went door to door talking to people. In fact, when we first started working the Four Seasons case, we thought there might have been a connection between the Miller disappearance and the body found at the nursery, since Terri had worked nearby."

"I help her mother keep the missing posters fresh. I went by to replace the one at the nursery on the day the body was found. That's why I was so keen to work with you."

"Did you know Terri?"

"Kind of. She worked at the Dollar Saver, and I spoke to her a few times. I saw her the day before she disappeared and she was so happy." Jessie got a faraway look in her eyes. "Terri was stocking soup or corn or some kind of canned goods and I was looking for ramen noodles. We got to talking. She said she'd just gotten a fifty-cent raise and had been accepted at FAMU for the fall. I was thinking about going back to school, so I asked her about FAMU and why she wanted to go there. Terri told me she planned to study agriculture, which I thought was really cool. When I heard the next day that people were looking for her, I kind of freaked out... even joined some of the search parties."

"So now you want to be a cop?"

"Exactly. I want to find out what happened to Terri. Her mom has run into a lot of road blocks. Your office won't share information with her," Jessie said accusingly.

"When you're investigating a case, sometimes you have to withhold information. You can't go around giving out everything you know. That just muddies the water when it's time to prosecute someone."

"But no one *is* investigating Terri's case!" She stopped walking and faced me.

"That's not true. Pete Henley is still working on it. He keeps the files on his desk and goes through them regularly. And, knowing Pete, I'm sure that he calls Terri's mother from time to time and checks in with her." I was confident in defending Pete. I knew for a fact that the Miller disappearance ate at him.

"Yeah, maybe. But I want to read the file and know what's being done."

"If you become a cop, then you'll be bound by the same rules as we are. Which means you couldn't share everything with Terri's mom and you'd have tons of other work to do. You wouldn't be able to focus all of your energy just on finding Terri."

"I know. I'm not stupid. It's not just about Terri. She just… I realized that people disappear all the time. It's scary."

"It would also take years before you'd be able to become an investigator."

"What part of 'I'm not stupid' don't you understand? I get it. But I have to start somewhere. I just need to get into the academy." Her expression had gone from anger to frustration.

"You stay clear of this mess and I'll see what I can do to help."

"You said that before."

"It hasn't been *that* long. Plus, you were pretty wigged out after that stabbing. And there was the little distraction of my wedding and everything. Hey! Do you want to get in or not?" I asked with a smile.

"Yes."

"I'll talk to Dad. He's got friends."

Her pace quickened and we were soon at the hunting cabin. We found Bernadette out back with Cleo. She'd found an old kiddie pool and filled it with water for Cleo to play in.

"Have you found out anything?" Bernadette asked as we walked up.

"There's still a ways to go," I said and Bernadette frowned.

"It's just so hard on everyone. I know it's tearing up Uncle Bruce and Paula."

"I'd like to talk to your mother. You said she's staying at your house?"

"That's right. She wasn't here yesterday during the… deaths. She called me later and said she was too upset to come out."

"I'd still like to have a word with her. Would you mind giving her a call and making sure she knows I'll be coming by?"

Normally I wouldn't have warned someone before coming to interview them but, from all accounts, the woman hadn't been on the property at the time of the attacks. Plus, it would save me time if I knew for sure that she'd been home when I got there, and I'd spend a lot less time on explanations.

"Sure," Bernadette said. "The hard part isn't getting to talk to her; it's getting away from her." She picked up her phone and tapped the screen. "Hey, Mom. Yes, I know…"

I listened to Bernadette's side of the conversation for a while, but after ten minutes there was no sign of it ending and she waved for me to head on into town.

Bernadette's mother answered the door while still talking on the phone with her daughter. I felt sorry for Bernadette.

"He's here, I got to go," she finally said and disconnected the call.

Karen Byrd looked like she'd stepped out of a *Southern*

Living magazine circa 1980. Her grey hair was done, her clothes were perfect and she was wearing a tad too much perfume.

"Don't stand out there in the heat, come on in." She turned her back and walked down the hall, leaving the door open for me to follow. "What do you want to drink? Dottie has a very well stocked bar. But, of course, you're on duty so no drink for you, I suppose."

I followed her into Bernadette's living room. The house was a beautiful Victorian that Bernadette had furnished with classic period pieces. Karen waved me toward a couch while she fixed a drink at a small wet bar, then carefully sat down across from me, trying not to spill her full cocktail glass.

"Don't you dare judge me," she laughed. "I have to drink when we come down to these dreadful reunions. Althea's cattle calls, that's what they are! How I managed to get the most hateful mother-in-law east of the Mississippi, I don't know. All I do know is that I can't spend more than half an hour in her presence. If I did, I'd surely throw a glass of whatever was in my hand straight into that viper's face."

"I met her yesterday. She *did* seem a little intense."

Karen laughed. "Intense. My, you do have a way of putting things. Now, you go ahead and ask me anything. I may detest Althea, but I've always liked Tracy and Paula. If I can help, I most certainly want to do all that I can."

"What did you think of Austin?"

"A rogue. He could be a real bastard, yet… I understood Tracy's attraction to him. He was the kind of bad man that some women love to hate. Not me! I like my men tame. At least the one I'm married to." She followed this with a wink that made me feel very uncomfortable.

"Did you see any of them this trip?"

"I saw all of them. Only once all together, Sunday night. We had dinner at the big house with the queen herself in attendance. Hold on. If your next question is whether I saw any tension between the three of them, then you can forget it. Everyone there was tense. That's what the old bat does to all of us. And truth be told, I was too busy watching my own P's and Q's to notice what anyone else was doing. Owen had put me on notice that if I said anything to cause a scene, then I would be spending my birthday at home rather than on the cruise we've planned. Owen wasn't kidding, which made for quite the dilemma for me. You might have noticed that I'm a wee bit of a chatterbox. I just knew that, in that crowd, if I opened my mouth I would say things that would have me stuck on dry land next month. I had to concentrate like a tightrope walker to keep my mouth shut."

"And you weren't out at the farm yesterday?" I asked, trying hard to hide my amusement.

"That's right. My routine when we're forced into one of these nightmares is to wake up here at Dottie's around ten. I make myself some breakfast, read whatever book I'm working my way through, then I start to lubricate myself at Dottie's expense until around four when Owen picks me up and forces me to join the festivities. I last about two hours before Owen sees that I'm losing my cool. He hustles me out to the car and back here, where I go to bed. Soap, rinse, repeat."

"How did you hear about the deaths?"

"Owen called me… I guess it was about one o'clock." She picked up her cell phone and looked. "Five after, to be exact. He told me that Tracy was dead and Austin had been rushed to the hospital."

"What else did he say?"

"Not much."

"Did he mention Paula?"

"Let me think…" She looked off into the distance and tapped her forehead with her finger. "No. I don't think he did. Really, the call…" She looked at her phone again. "… only lasted for a minute-and-a-half. He did tell me that he wouldn't be picking me up. Said that he would have to look after some things and help take care of his mother, which is ridiculous. That woman could handle Mongol hordes with one hand tied behind her back. Of course, I was delighted.

Not about the deaths. Just about having an evening off from the ritual abuse of dinner at the farm."

"He didn't mention what he was having to look after?"

"Just things. I assumed who he really had to look after was Bruce. That man loves his daughters." She paused. "I should pay a call on him. The poor man. He struggles with his back too. And that wife of his." Karen rolled her eyes. "She would be right at home in *The Best Little Whorehouse in Texas*."

I had to bite my tongue to keep from suggesting that Karen would be perfectly cast as the madam. Instead, I said, "I just want to be clear. You never went near the farm yesterday?"

"That's right. Like I said, I was—"

"And you didn't talk to anyone but Owen?"

"Right again, and he didn't tell me anything."

I stood up before she could go off on another tangent. "I've got to get back to the office. If you think of anything else, will you give me a call?" I gave her my card with a little hesitation. I didn't want to get stuck on the phone with her.

"I sure will," Karen said, taking the card and talking my ear off all the way to the car.

CHAPTER TEN

It was after five when I got back to the office and I was glad to see that Lt. Johnson wasn't around. If Dad was right and Johnson was in a snit about how much time I was devoting to the Byrd case, then I didn't want to run into him. Mainly because I knew I couldn't defend my focus on the case. It wasn't like we were hunting a suspect or trying to find a body or a murder scene. We had everything and were just waiting for test results. If they didn't show anything to contradict the witness statements, then there wouldn't be much I could do. And my excuse that most of the witnesses would soon be leaving the county didn't cut much ice in this age of email and FaceTime.

I checked in at my desk to tackle a few emails and sort the growing pile of reports. I was heading out the door when I saw Dad coming down the hall. He had a piece of paper in his hand.

"Wait up!" he shouted. I stopped and wondered if he was going to bring up whatever he'd been hinting at earlier.

"I've got time to talk," I told him, hoping to nudge him into revealing the mystery topic.

"No, I just wanted to ask you to touch base with Dr. Horvath." Dad handed me the piece of paper in his hand. It was a report of a robbery.

"Who stole from Dr. Horvath?"

"That's what we're supposed to find out," he said with a heavy dose of sarcasm.

"Dumb question," I admitted, and gave up asking questions to scan the report. Someone had stolen several packages that had been left at the large animal vet's house. "You want *me* to look into this?" I said, not meaning to softball another opportunity for sarcasm his way. I quickly added, "Julio is handling robberies."

"And he's going to be busy helping to sort out the mess from this afternoon."

"And Dr. Horvath is a friend. Say no more."

Betty Horvath took care of Dad's horses and most of the other livestock in the county. She was a great person and I understood why Dad wanted to give this a little extra attention. I was just feeling overwhelmed, thinking of the stack of reports I'd just left on my desk that was only getting higher with every minute I spent on the Byrd case.

"Is there a problem?" Dad asked.

"Not with this," I said, holding up the report. "But didn't you have something else you wanted to talk about?" I saw his cheeks flush.

"I told you we'd deal… talk about that later." He brushed past me and headed straight for the door.

I followed him out of the building. I was almost to my car when, feeling the luck of an unlucky Irishman, I saw Lt. Johnson pulling into a parking spot near me.

He signaled for me to wait for him. For a second it crossed my mind to make a mad dash for my car and home. Instead, I decided to be proactive.

"I know I'm getting behind," I said as he got out of his car, before he had a chance to berate me.

Johnson's dark face was thunderous. "Everyone needs to stay in step. I cannot authorize you to work on your own time and I know you're aware of the situation in regard to overtime. Point being, the work has to be done, and done in a timely manner. You need to look at your cases and prioritize them. If they're not going to lead to an arrest, then you can't spend time satisfying your curiosity."

Johnson had been an officer in the Army for twenty years. He did things by the book and he obeyed orders. I understood what he was telling me. However, the suggestion that I was investigating the Byrd cases just to satisfy my own curiosity ruffled a few of my feathers.

"Would you prefer that I take the word of a person who's just killed someone at face value, or do you think it's prudent to interview witnesses and establish whether she's telling the truth or not?" My voice was flat without any nuance whatsoever, but I still saw the pilot light flicker in his eyes.

"I'm not telling you how to do your job. I'm just reminding you that you can't devote all of your time to the cases that interest you and neglect the rest of your workload."

"Understood," I said tersely, reminding myself that Johnson's position as supervisor of the criminal investigations division required him to look at the big picture.

"I don't want to see your backlog get any higher." Johnson gave me a hard look, then turned his back on me and headed for the office.

I counted to ten, knowing that he had probably spent all afternoon at the robbery suspect's crash site, overseeing Julio's handling of what was, at least temporarily, a high-profile case. Julio Ortiz was a very good investigator, but he was a little green to be dealing with a case that would have had all the local news channels on the scene.

I chewed my lip and walked to my car, considering how I was going to thoroughly investigate the Byrd deaths, keep up with my ever-growing caseload *and* still deal with the unexpected, like the robbery report Dad had tossed to me.

I drove home with the radio playing classic rock, trying to clear my head and relax. I remembered how Reverend Pritchard, the minister who had performed our marriage ceremony, had told us that we would need to make our home a sanctuary… or something like that. A place where Cara and I could take refuge from the world and be with each other. I was looking forward to that tonight.

Cara was still dressed in her vet scrubs when I came in the door. She was standing in the kitchen, just staring at the refrigerator.

"What's up?"

"The refrigerator was making a funny noise and now it's not making any sounds at all. On top of that, the freezer doesn't seem to be very cold." Her voice was weary.

"Seriously?" I felt all my hopes for a trouble-free evening melting away like our ice. "Open the freezer."

The ice was wet and there was water dripping down the sides. I clicked the on-and-off switch a few times, and moved the dial that regulated the thermostat back and forth. The compressor didn't kick on. "Let's push it away from the wall," I said, not even trying to keep the irritation out of my voice.

"Let's just call a repairman."

"It's six-thirty. I don't think there are twenty-four-hour refrigerator repairmen. If there are, they're in Tallahassee and I don't want to pay for an after-hours emergency service call all the way out here. I just want to look at the back and see if there's anything obviously wrong."

"Do you know anything about refrigerators?" Cara asked.

"No. But… I don't know. I just want to look and see if I can tell if something is… out of whack. I would recognize a wire pulled out or a… I don't know, a tube loose or something."

She frowned uncertainly.

"Just help me move it."

We moved the appliance away from the wall, with Alvin giving us occasional barked instructions. Of course I couldn't see anything wrong. I shot out a couple of curse words in exasperation and gave the back of the refrigerator a good whack with my fist. This calmed me down a little but did nothing to fix the refrigerator. I took a deep breath and looked at Cara, who seemed on the verge of tears. I knew she was more upset by my behavior than the broken refrigerator.

"I'm sorry," I told her. "It's been a rough day. Dad's acting weird and the deaths at the Byrd farm are eating up time I don't have. Johnson's pissed because my caseload is getting out of hand, which doesn't make me any happier than it does him."

I paused and looked at the refrigerator. "We need to throw out the frozen food. This is the original refrigerator that came with the house. It's at least twenty years old. We'd probably save energy and money with a new one. I'll see if Dad or Pete wants this one for their garage. If one of them wants it, then they can see about getting it fixed. We'll just buy a new one."

We got down to the business of cleaning out the refrigerator.

"Austin killed Tracy, right?" Cara asked as we worked.

"I can't see any other scenario that makes sense. If he didn't, then it would have to have been Paula or Marty. I guess if Paula came in and found that Marty had killed Tracy, then she might kill Austin to cover it up. But that's wild speculation. Marty seems pretty mild-mannered. Anyway, if that's the case, then it would be hard to prove. It's not like DNA is going to be helpful. Practically everyone in the family has been in and out of that cabin, both before and after the murders.

"There were no signs of a sexual assault. The positions of the bodies and the blood evidence looked consistent with Paula's story. There are a few inconsistencies, but nothing that can't be explained." I paused and thought about what I'd just said. "You know, Johnson's right. I should just do the formal interviews with Paula and Marty and, if Darzi's autopsies support her story, I should pass it on to the State Attorney and let him decide if he wants to prosecute her for manslaughter."

"You don't need to beat your head against the wall," Cara agreed, filling up a garbage bag.

"I feel better just saying it out loud. Maybe I was trying to find a conspiracy where there isn't one. Besides, I have plenty to do. And Dad's acting so weird."

"What do you mean?"

"Like he's got bad news and just can't bring himself to tell me."

"He's not going to fire you," she said with a laugh.

"I'm fairly sure of that. I don't even think he's going to demote me to patrol."

"Has he been to the doctor recently?" Cara asked slowly. This was a thought that hadn't occurred to me. Cara saw the look on my face. "I didn't mean... I'm sorry I brought it up."

"I don't know. But I doubt it could be anything like that. I thought he was going to tell me whatever it is when I was leaving this afternoon, but instead he just threw another report on my desk. Dr. Horvath had some packages stolen, and Dad told her he'd look into it. Which means *I'll* look into it."

"What kind of packages?"

"UPS delivered them to her house. Someone swiped them before she got home."

"I think she runs her business out of her house. Being a large animal vet, she doesn't have a regular office since almost all of her business is barn calls."

"I'll touch base with her tomorrow. Maybe I can give her some ideas about how to make sure her package deliveries don't get pilfered."

"What's for dinner?" Cara said, holding up a frozen pizza.

"Sounds good to me."

On Wednesday morning, I woke up determined to stick to my plan. I would work on my backlog, check in with Dr. Darzi and follow up with Dr. Horvath. Another point on my agenda was to find out what Dad was hiding from me. But my plans were derailed before I even got out of bed.

I rolled over to pick up the ringing phone, hoping it was a call that I could let go to voicemail. When I saw that it was dispatch, I knew it wasn't going to be good news.

"We just got a call from Paula Byrd. Her father is dead."

CHAPTER ELEVEN

We have just jumped the coincidence shark, I thought on my way out to the Byrd farm. Three deaths in three days. One was clearly murder, the other was probably justifiable homicide, but what the hell had happened now? According to dispatch, Paula had found her father this morning, lying on the couch and unresponsive.

Dispatch had called for both me and Sergeant Will Toomey. Both Toomey and the ambulance had beaten me to the property. Dispatch had gotten the key code to the gate and given it to both of them. At this rate, I thought they should just distribute the code to every first responder in the county.

As I parked, I could see members of the family watching from the various campers, houses and cabins. Jessie and Bernadette were walking Cleo down by the pond. Jessie looked up and gave me a brief nod as I walked toward Bruce's cottage. I saw Owen on the front porch of the main house, his head in his hands and his shoulders hunched.

Hondo had pulled his ambulance right up to the converted summer kitchen. He was coming out of the cottage as I walked up the steps. He shook his head and I turned to walk with him back to the ambulance.

"Thoughts?" I asked him.

"Overdose. There's a bottle of Percocets next to the couch. Not many pills left in the bottle. The kicker is that I could also smell whiskey on his breath. Not a good combination. Of course, it's all guesswork until the toxicology comes back. Toomey says he already called Darzi."

I nodded. "Any signs of trauma?"

"No. Like I said, it looks like a classic overdose. I could see that he was dead as soon as I walked in. The woman was all over me. Telling me I had to revive him. Wanted me to use the paddles on him. Crazy! He'd been dead for hours. I told her I needed to leave him the way he was for forensics and Toomey backed me up. Everything is exactly how I found it when I got here."

"Appreciate it, Hondo."

"I got your six, man," he said, closing up the back of the ambulance.

I went into the cottage where I found Toomey watching over the body. I could hear weeping from the back room and assumed it was Paula.

The body of Bruce Byrd lay half off the couch, his head hanging almost to the floor. The Percocet bottle was sitting on the side table. I looked closer, trying to recall how full the bottle had been the day before. Maybe three-quarters? Now there were only five or six pills lying on the bottom of the bottle. The label said that the prescription was for sixty pills, which seemed like a lot for a powerful and addictive painkiller. I knew that there were addicts who downed forty pills in a day, but they'd built up a tolerance over time. Had Bruce been an addict? He was a lawyer, and money and power could buy almost anything. With such severe back pain as Bruce had claimed to have, it wasn't surprising that he'd have needed some powerful juju to deal with it.

I remembered how Bruce had complained that the pills weren't cutting the pain. One of the downsides to Oxy was that a patient could build up such a tolerance that they needed more of the pills to do the same job. Had Bruce just misjudged what his body could take?

There was a glass on the table beside the couch, with a small trace of amber liquid in the bottom and the recognizable smell of whiskey.

"Sarge, did you call out the crime scene unit?"

"I thought I'd leave that decision to you. We've already had visits from Major Parks at two of our supervisor meetings about unnecessary call-outs."

I nodded and called Shantel.

"I can understand why you want me," she said. "You're closing in on a new world record for coincidences out there. Three bodies, three days."

"Thanks for the count. I keep losing track," I said, rolling my eyes. I expected nothing less from her.

"We'll be on our way shortly," she said.

"Mrs. Reece?" I called out as I walked toward the bedroom. I could still hear her sobbing.

Paula was on the bed, dressed in a T-shirt and jeans, with her face buried in the pillows.

"I need to talk to you," I said quietly.

She kept her face buried, but the sobbing became more intermittent as she tried to catch her breath.

I walked over beside the bed. "I know you're grieving, but we have to sort this out."

Paula rolled her head so that she could look at me. Her eyes were swollen and her entire face was red and damp from her tears.

"I don't understand any of this," she muttered, looking at me with wide brown eyes.

"I think you need to call your doctor too."

"Maybe."

"Where's Marty?"

"He's staying in our camper. Dad insisted that I stay here with him. I wanted to. He was in so much pain from his back. All of this is my fault." Paula let out an agonizing wail and curled back up in a fetal position.

I pulled a chair over and sat down next to the bed. "I can only imagine how much grief and shock you must be experiencing."

"My sister *and* my father," she said with her eyes clamped shut. I noticed that she didn't mention Austin.

"Right now, the best way you can honor them is to explain to me exactly what happened so that the legal aspects of your father's and sister's deaths can be dealt with. Then you and your family can mourn for them in peace." I tried to be gentle. "Would you like a glass of water?"

Paula wiped at the tears and opened her eyes again. "Please," she said with a voice like a child.

I found my way to the kitchen, and when I came back she was sitting on the side of the bed.

"I can't go out there," Paula said as she took the glass. "Not until they've taken his body away. Do you believe in God?"

"I have to," I said honestly.

"I used to. Now..." She drank deeply from the glass.

"Anyone who has been through what you have in the last few days would feel blindsided and angry." A pesky voice in my head added, *Unless they did it.* "Tell me about this morning."

"I... uh... I woke up. I've been sleeping in this room so that I'd be close if Daddy needed anything."

"What time did you wake up?"

"I didn't sleep very well last night, thinking about... everything. I was up around six-thirty, give or take a few minutes. I went straight to the kitchen so I didn't see... Daddy at first. I turned the coffee pot on and got out some bread. He likes toast in the morning. That's when I thought I ought to see if he was awake. I... saw him lying half off the couch and knew that something was wrong."

"Did you check to see if he was alive?"

"I... He was cold, but I've heard stories of people being revived. I tried to get him back up on the couch. Every time I tried he... slipped back off. I called 911. Then when they showed up, they didn't even try and revive him."

"Did you hear anything during the night?"

"Like I said, I couldn't really sleep. Yes, I heard Daddy moving around several times. With the pain, he has to brace himself and… well… he makes a bit of noise trying to get off the couch. I thought I heard him get water the last time."

"You heard him get up, but didn't go to see if he was all right?"

"Oh no. Daddy had already gotten mad at me a couple of times for hovering. I made him promise me that if he needed my help, he'd call for me."

"Where's Debbie, your stepmother?"

"She went to stay at Dottie's house with Karen."

I wondered how those two would get along.

"When did she leave?"

"We got in a fight yesterday afternoon. She told Daddy that he had to choose between her or me. He said he wasn't going to kick me out. Ten minutes later, she stormed out the door with her luggage."

"Only you and your dad were in the house last night?"

"Yes. He was okay when I went to bed."

"How many pain pills did he take?"

"I don't know. I got mad at him yesterday morning for taking so many. He was pissed off at me, but I took the bottle into the kitchen. Is that what killed him? I should have thrown them away!"

"We don't know anything yet." I heard someone come into the house, then Shantel's voice. Toomey would let them know what was going on. "What did you and your stepmother argue about?"

"Dinner. I wanted to make something here while she wanted Daddy to take her out for dinner. There wasn't any way that he could have driven a car. Debbie just wanted to go out and didn't care how much pain he was in."

"Can you remember exactly what she said to your dad?"

"Not really. She was pacing up and down the room, saying that she needed to get away from Gran. And how all she wanted to do was go out for a nice dinner. Somewhere that the witch can't lord it over her. Stuff like that."

"What did your dad say?"

"He was going to take her out. Until he tried to get up and collapsed from the pain."

"Then she walked out?"

"No. That's when I told her to leave Daddy alone. At that point, she turned to him and said it was her or me."

"After he told her he wasn't kicking you out, she left?"

"She grabbed the keys and told him she wasn't staying here another night. When he asked her where she was going, she called Dottie and worked it out. Debbie is such a bitch. She hurt him so bad." This devolved into a crying, cursing jag aimed at Debbie.

"Has anyone called her?"

Paula gave me a rather odd look, a cross between anger and shame, then glanced over at the clock beside the bed. "They probably aren't up yet. Of course, someone else might have called."

"Who else came to see your dad yesterday?"

"Just about everybody came by at one time or another. Everybody but Gran. She sent Ruby over to see how he was doing."

I got her to tell me about the rest of the family's comings and goings. Most of them had talked with Bruce for just a few minutes, then left.

"I could tell that being around me made them nervous. They think I'm a murderer." There was a brief pause before she added, "I guess I am."

I wanted to contradict her, but she *had* killed Austin. It might have been in the defense of her sister and justified, but she had still killed another human being. It changes you and changes how people perceive you.

"Time can heal many wounds," I said, knowing that I was just tossing out a cliché because I couldn't come up with anything else that would offer hope.

"The worst part is that I don't know what I'm mourning

the most. I've lost a father and a sister, and I've killed my brother-in-law. Still, there's a part of me that sees all of it through the eyes of a selfish child who feels cheated and unfairly treated."

"Most of us have selfish thoughts. And when someone in our family dies, it's natural to feel cheated. It speaks to how much you valued having them in your life."

Paula reached out and touched my hand. "Thank you."

I gave her a small smile and thought how odd it was for me to be comforting a suspect. I always tried to be respectful of the people I interviewed, but I felt a special empathy for Paula. Maybe it was the degree of loss that she had suffered—father, sister and her own innocence in a matter of days. What else would she lose? She'd be lucky if many of her relatives didn't shun her. How would this affect her son and their relationship?

"I want to see Marty," she said, leaving me with the sensation that she had read my mind.

"I just have a few more questions." In truth, I had a lot more questions, including many concerning the death of her sister and brother-in-law. I'd put them off to give her time to recover from the trauma, but I couldn't give her the same luxury this time.

"I'm going to treat your father's death as suspicious," I told her.

Her eyes got wide. "What do you mean?"

"I just feel like three deaths in three days is... troublesome. Let me ask you this: is there any chance that your father committed suicide?"

"No way! Never, and especially not now. Not when I needed him. He promised that he would get me a great lawyer, and stand by me if charges were brought against me for Austin's death." Paula was adamant.

What if he had found out she was guilty of the premeditated murder of Austin Stokes? Or worse, the murder of both Austin *and* Tracy? Could he have lived with the knowledge that one of his daughters had killed the other?

Maybe he had confronted Paula, so Paula had killed him too. *Wild speculation*, I reminded myself.

"Like with the deaths of Tracy and Austin, I need to give your father's death the highest level of scrutiny to avoid losing valuable evidence in the event that he… his death was something other than an accident." I was trying to avoid the M-word.

"You mean murder?" She wasn't having any of my discretion.

"Or suicide. I know that you don't believe your father would have killed himself, but it's very common for relatives to be unaware of someone's intentions."

"Murder and suicide both seem impossible. An accident, maybe." She shook her head.

"I'm asking for your cooperation," I said bluntly.

Before she could reply, there was shouting from the front room. We ran to the sound of the argument and found Owen standing at the front door, enraged. Toomey was standing in front of him, and Bernadette was holding onto her father's arm.

"Dad, you can't go to him yet."

"He's my brother!" he shouted and shook her off his arm. He tried to push past Toomey, who wouldn't budge.

"Sir, I respect your grief and understand your desire to go to your brother, but this is being treated as a crime scene."

"A crime scene! You people are mad! Has a doctor been to see him?"

"Dad, Uncle Bruce is dead."

"I can see that! Let me go." His eyes were wild and unfocused.

I walked over to them. "I'll take him in to see his brother," I said to Toomey.

"Mr. Byrd, you will need to follow my instructions." I stood blocking his way. I wasn't going to take him over to Bruce's body unless I was sure that he wouldn't try to touch it or disturb anything. "Do you understand?" I said, loud and firm.

He shook his head and looked at me. His face relaxed a bit and slowly he nodded. "I… I… understand. Yes. Of course. I just need to… see him."

"You cannot touch him." I stared hard into his eyes.

"Yes. Okay."

Slowly, I took him to where his brother lay slumped off the couch. Off to the side I saw Shantel, camera in hand, staying clear.

"I can't understand any of this," Owen said in a weak voice that cracked with emotion. Tears were streaming down his face. "This was a summer kitchen when we were growing up. I remember us sitting, I guess about here. There was a long pine table where Aunt Ruth would roll bread. She'd toss us pieces of dough rolled in cinnamon." He stopped talking and looked down at his brother. "He can't be gone."

His legs started to buckle, and Toomey and I caught him before he hit the floor. We half carried him to a chair by the front window as he tried to catch his breath. Owen was sweating heavily.

"I'm going to loosen your shirt," I said, and unbuttoned the top buttons as he tried ineffectually to brush my hands away.

I called for Bernadette and she came in and took his hands in hers. "Take long, slow breaths," she told him.

"I'll get him some water," I heard Shantel say.

When Shantel came back with the water, I turned to her and asked, "Are Darzi's people here?"

"Linda's here with someone new. I asked them to wait outside 'til I was done recording the scene."

"Explain the situation to her and ask Linda to come take a look at him." She was an assistant pathologist and had more medical training than any of the rest of us.

Linda gave him a solid going-over. "He should be fine. I think he just needs to lie down for a while. Drink plenty of fluids and stay in the air-conditioning. It's likely he just got overheated and had a panic attack. Might have even started to drift into shock. How are you feeling now, Mr. Byrd?"

"Better. Lying down sounds good."

"I'll help you back to the main house," Bernadette said.

"What about Bruce? What are they going to do with him?" Owen asked her.

"They'll take him to the hospital," she said honestly, leaving unsaid the hard truth that his destination was the morgue.

CHAPTER TWELVE

After Bernadette had escorted Owen out of the cottage, Linda turned to me. "You have quite the little corpse farm going on out here. We had your last two victims scheduled for this afternoon. Maybe we can make it a trifecta." She didn't put much heart into the joke and, to be honest, I couldn't appreciate the usual graveyard humor.

"The sooner the better. I'm having a hard time getting a grip on this one."

"The first two seem pretty clear. Couldn't this one just be a coincidence? Or is it possible that he overdosed accidentally or on purpose because of the deaths of the other two?" Linda's voice was sympathetic.

"I've considered that. Anything is possible at this point. What I need is more evidence."

"I'll assist Dr. Darzi so we can get all three autopsies done today."

"I appreciate it. These people will be going home soon, and I've got pressure on me from the lieutenant to wrap this up. Of course, that was *before* this death."

"I don't see much that's unusual. Though most of the overdoses we see are addicts who've tried to quit and, when they relapse, they overestimate their tolerance for the drug.

Or they're using a drug that doesn't tolerate miscalculations, either in the making or the using."

"It looks like he might have been drinking."

"Alcohol and Percocets are bad news, especially in a man his age. Could be a case where he just stopped breathing."

"I'll try and make it to the autopsies."

"The first two are scheduled for three and four this afternoon. Add this one and we'll be running close to six, even with both me and Dr. Darzi working on them."

"Thanks." I got out of the way to let her work.

"This is Duke," Linda said, indicating her young new assistant as they started to poke and prod the late Mr. Byrd. Duke gave me a boyish smile before he knelt beside the body.

I went back and told Paula to stay in her room until they had removed her father's body. No one should see their loved one being examined by a coroner.

"What do you want us to collect?" Shantel asked.

"The glass, the prescription bottle, then do a search in a ten-foot circumference of the couch. My main interests right now are the contents of the glass and bottle, and any fingerprints that might be on them. I'm going to look around and see if I can find the bottle that the liquor came from."

There were half a dozen bottles of liquor in a cabinet next to the refrigerator. In the front was a half-full bottle of Scotch that looked high-end to my untrained eye. At least, the label looked fancy.

I asked Shantel to fingerprint and collect the bottle, then I went to get Karen's number from Paula. I'd decided that talking to Karen would be better than calling Debbie directly.

The phone went on ringing long enough that I expected to talk to her voicemail. Finally, I heard a very groggy Karen ask me who was calling. I looked at my watch. It was almost ten o'clock.

"This is Deputy Macklin." I let that sink in.

"Oh. You should warn a lady when calling before noon,"

she said in honeyed tones.

"Is Debbie there?"

"Oh my lord, yes," Karen groaned. "That woman is crazier than I am. Though I do have to admire her ability to hold her vodka."

"Do you know if she's awake?"

"I doubt it. What do you need with that little bit of nothin' when you can chat with me?"

"I need your help. Something has happened to her husband."

"Bruce?" There was a pause. "I guess that explains all of the calls from Owen. I was ignoring him. What's happened?" She was awake and concerned now.

"I'm afraid that Mr. Byrd has died."

There was a longer pause before she said, "Oh no. Poor Owen. I need to call him."

"He was pretty upset. Bernadette is looking after him."

"Owen has his issues, but he loved his brother. With their battle-axe of a mother, they had to rely on each other."

"Debbie doesn't know yet."

"That poor, silly woman. She'll go crazy. I see why you called me."

"I'll tell her, but I just wanted you to know what was going on so you can help her through this."

"What happened to Bruce?"

"Looks like a drug overdose."

"I don't understand."

"We think he may have taken too many Percocets."

"Drugs are too dangerous. That's why I stick to alcohol. Don't worry, I'll tell Debbie. But I should warn you, she'll want to come straight out there."

"That's fine. I need to talk to her anyway. His body will be taken to the morgue in Tallahassee for an autopsy."

"I guess that's necessary. So much tragedy in just a couple of days."

I told her to have Debbie call me if she had any questions, but it was unnecessary. As Karen had predicted,

Debbie arrived as they were placing Bruce's body into the coroner's van. There was much wailing and gnashing of teeth as we struggled to keep her from disturbing the body. I'd already sent Toomey on his way, so it took the combined strength of me, Linda and Duke to rein Debbie in.

"That bitch of a daughter killed him!" she screamed.

How long would it be before Paula came out of the house and started screaming at Debbie? I was regretting letting Toomey leave.

"You need to calm down," I said, holding firmly onto Debbie's arm. "You are justified in your grief, but we need to get on with our investigation." As soon as I said that, she stopped fighting us.

"You sure the *hell* need to investigate his death. She murdered him!"

"We don't know that. But I promise you, we're going to find out what caused his death." I nodded to Linda and Duke and they closed the van doors.

Debbie turned and looked at the back of the van as Linda and Duke made their hasty escape.

"Where are they taking him?" she asked softly.

"They're going to perform an autopsy on him this afternoon."

She looked at me and, for a moment, I thought she was going to protest. Then she nodded. "I need to know what killed him."

"Come with me," I told her.

"Where are we going?"

"Let's walk down to Bernadette's cabin."

Debbie looked down at the high heels she was wearing. "I should have dressed more sensibly for walking around in the sticks," she said. "I wasn't thinking."

"Did Karen come with you?"

"She went straight to the big house, looking for Owen."

"Good. Now come on. It's not that far of a walk down to the cabin. You need to be with someone."

"I know what you're thinking and you're right. Dottie's

the only one other than Karen who can put up with me. I don't think Karen could if she wasn't half lit most of the time." Most of Debbie's spit and fire was gone.

"Where were you last night?"

"I guess you heard that I had a fight with Bruce. Oh, how am I going to live with that? The last thing I said to him was that I didn't care if he got better or not. Damn it!

"Anyway, I called Karen and went over there, and immediately we were three sheets to the wind. Reviewed every boyfriend, husband and casual affair we'd ever had. God's honest truth, I don't remember much after midnight."

"Was there anything different about Bruce yesterday?"

"Different?"

"More depressed, happier, angrier, more tired, more energetic? Anything that struck you as different."

"Not really. He's been in pain since Monday. I know I wasn't very… nurturing. It's just not my nature. That doesn't mean I didn't love him. Our fight yesterday was more of… Okay, the truth is… I can be sort of petulant when I don't get my way. But gawd! Look at this place." She swung her arms around before pointing them straight at the big house. "And that witch up there. What wife wouldn't have a problem with her?"

"So the argument wasn't anything new? Did you all argue a lot?"

"About his family, yes. When we could forget about them, we had a great time. He worked a lot, which was a bummer. But he took me places. Two cruises last year. Mamma Rattlesnake hated that. Bruce wouldn't use his phone when we were on the ship. He thought it would be too easy to hack it or something. So he'd go a week without talking to her. You should have seen him. He was… fun. I've been waiting for ages for her to get stuffed in a hole and covered up. But now Bruce is dead."

"Tell me about the Percocets he was taking for the pain."

"They weren't helping much. That was something else that was driving me crazy."

"What?"

"Him complaining 'cause he couldn't get any relief from the pain."

"How many was he taking?"

"I don't know. He knew I don't like pills, so he didn't talk about it much. Except to complain. I told him that he should try acupuncture, or maybe a different chiropractor."

"How long had he been taking them?"

"He didn't take them much. Just had them for, like, an emergency. His doctor prescribed them. I think he got the prescription filled before we came down here. Bruce knew how stressful this trip was going to be. His mother was already badgering him before we'd even packed."

"Badgered him about what?"

"The usual. About me. About Tracy and Austin. He advised her on her legal stuff. She has a business lawyer who does all her actual work, but ol' Althea doesn't trust anyone. She was always making Bruce go over paperwork that the other lawyer had prepared."

"Was there anything in particular this time?"

"You have to understand, there was *always* an urgent document he had to review. I swear, I stopped listening to it years ago."

"Did your husband seem more… anxious or worried this time?"

"No. He was at the same level of crazy that he always was when his mother tightened the screws."

We were passing the pond. Jessie and Cleo came out of the cabin when we approached.

"Oh no, not that dog. When did they start making dogs that big?" Debbie said, and I had to look at her to see if she was serious. I couldn't tell.

"She's a very sweet dog. And well disciplined," I said, thinking about the huge contrast between Cleo and Mauser. Debbie didn't have a clue what a *real* monster dog was like.

"Jessie!" I called. She raised her hand in greeting and brought Cleo over to us. The dog approached Debbie slowly, and she nervously reached out a hand for Cleo to sniff.

"Isn't this what you're supposed to do?" she asked.

"That's right, just let her smell your hand," Jessie told her. Cleo moved in closer and leaned gently into Debbie, as though feeling her grief and anxiety.

"Wow. You're a real horse," Debbie said lightly, patting Cleo as the dog stood motionless, seeming to know that a sudden movement would frighten the woman.

"Is Bernadette still up at the main house?" I asked Jessie.

"Yep."

"Would you mind staying with Mrs. Byrd?"

Debbie turned to me. "Don't call me that. This family never wanted me and now that Bruce is dead, I don't want anything to do with these… people. I'm not talking about Dottie and Karen. They've both been all right."

"We can go inside. Cleo's about had enough of the heat," Jessie said.

After they went inside the cabin, I walked up toward the main house. On the porch, I found the group of young folks I'd met the day before. They were playing some game that involved one of them putting their phone on their forehead while the others shouted out clues to the word that appeared on the screen. They stopped playing when they saw me.

"We didn't mean any disrespect," Andy said.

"I didn't think you did," I told him.

I noticed that Marty was sitting in a rocker, a little way down the porch from the others. Technically he was part of the group, yet he was clearly emotionally separate. It had to be hard for him, being younger than the rest and so much more a part of the horrific events that had transpired over the last couple of days.

"Did Bruce have a heart attack?" Cory asked.

"We don't know the cause of death yet. There will be an autopsy. After that, we'll know more."

Marty was following every word. His gaze went from person to person as I spoke.

"Did any of you visit Mr. Byrd yesterday?"

"Bridget and I did," Roch said. "Actually, we went to visit Paula."

Marty shook slightly at the mention of his mother.

"But you saw Mr. Byrd?"

"Sure, he was on the couch. His back was bothering him a lot."

"Did you talk to him?"

Roch looked at Bridget.

"I guess some about how he was feeling," Bridget said.

"He wanted to know if we'd seen any bucks in the woods. I told him we saw a little three-point down by the creek."

"He was in pain?"

"Bad. I've never seen him that bad," Bridget said.

"Did you see him often?"

"No, just at these family reunions. Couple times a year."

"Was he drinking?"

The girls exchanged guilty looks.

"Tell me," I pressed, but there was silence. "Look, I don't want to play twenty questions. Just tell me what you know."

"I'm sort of freaking out over it," Bridget said, her cheeks flushed.

"Over what?"

"We gave him a small bottle," she admitted.

"A pint," Roch added.

"Tell me everything you remember about that." I wondered if the bottle in the cupboard was just a coincidence. Where was the pint bottle?

"He said he needed a drink, but that Paula was hovering around every time he got up. Asked us to get a small bottle from his luggage."

"Where was Paula?"

"She'd gone for a walk. I think out to their camper."

"She came to see me," Marty said in a small voice that caused all of us to turn toward him. The poor guy had lost his uncle, aunt and grandfather, and was at risk of having his mother taken to jail.

I turned back to the sisters. "Did he drink from the flask when you brought it to him?"

"Yep. He said his pain pills weren't doing shit and he took a big drink from the bottle."

"Kinda made me uncomfortable," Bridget said. Her hands were fiddling with the unusual necklace she wore. "I don't like seeing anyone in that much pain. Giving him alcohol just seemed wrong. I told him he shouldn't mix alcohol with his pain pills, but he said he didn't have any choice, since the pills weren't doing any good."

"What else happened while you were there?"

"Nothing," Roch said with a shake of her head.

"Were you all there?" I asked Andy and Cory.

"We waited on the porch while they went in," Andy said. Cory nodded.

"That's an interesting piece of jewelry," I said to Bridget.

"She made it," Cory said.

"Really?"

"Show it to him," Andy told her. "She's a real artist."

She took it off her neck and handed it to me. The work was incredible. The wood had been carved into a series of woodland creatures all interlinked.

"Was this carved from one piece of wood?" I asked.

"A friend gave me some maple. That's one of the pieces I made from it," Bridget said.

"I can't believe you took a solid piece of wood and made a necklace," I said, thinking how much Cara would love something like this.

"She's got her carving knives with her. You should come down to our camp and see her work," Andy said. Bridget and Cory gave him a look that I couldn't interpret.

My phone buzzed with a text alert. I glanced at it and saw a message from Dad reading: *on my way*. I didn't want to think about what had been the catalyst for the text. Dad usually only came to the most high-profile crime scenes. He didn't do that to be in the spotlight, but rather to take the pressure off of the lead investigator. There was nothing more annoying than to be dealing with a crime scene and have the press clamoring for information.

I thanked the young people for their time. Everyone except Marty assured me that they were more than glad to help. Marty remained sitting in the wooden rocker, staring off into the distance as the rest of them wandered toward the pond.

CHAPTER THIRTEEN

I knocked on the door. With Dad on the way I didn't have much time, but I wanted to lay eyes on Owen and determine his condition. I didn't need any more dead bodies.

Bernadette answered the door.

"I thought I heard you out here," she said. She was trying to sound like her usual upbeat self, but there was too much grief in her heart. She seemed more stressed than anything.

"I just wanted to check on your dad."

"He says he's okay." She moved back from the door, giving me room to come in. "I tried to get him to go to the hospital, but I should have known better. His middle name should be Mule."

"Can I speak with him?"

"He's resting right now," she said gently.

I thought about pressing her. If I'd known exactly what information I wanted from him, then I would have, but I had to admit I was just on a fact-finding mission.

"Do you know if he saw his brother yesterday?"

"Oh yes, they confabbed for about an hour yesterday evening. They asked Paula to leave, so she came down to my cabin."

"Do you have any idea what they talked about?"

She considered the question for a time before answering.

"I can speculate," Bernadette said. "They were probably discussing Paula. I don't have to tell you that there are going to be legal questions to answer in the near future, depending on what you and the State Attorney decide to do. Dad and Uncle Bruce would have been very concerned, not just about Paula and Marty's future, but about the family, our name and, maybe most importantly, at least to them, what Althea would think and do. Both of them have been tied to that woman for so long that they can't turn around without worrying what she'll think."

"Yeah, I've gathered that. I can see where they might think it necessary to have a brainstorming session. I'll need to talk to your father soon," I said with a heavy emphasis on the word "soon."

"I know. Just give him a little time to recover." Bernadette looked me straight in the eyes. "Is someone killing off members of my family?"

"I don't know. Coincidences *do* happen. It's possible that this is just a strange roll of the dice."

"What do you believe?"

"I had a bad feeling when the body count was two. Raising the count hasn't made me feel better."

"I'm glad. Because I think something strange is going on here. The only thing that would make this worse is if I had to convince the authorities to take it seriously."

"I can assure you that I'm taking the deaths very seriously." I looked at my watch. "In fact, my dad is paying us a visit. If the sheriff is coming out to the scene, then you know the department is doing everything it can."

"I like your dad."

"He's all right," I said with a small chuckle. "I better go and meet him. Take care of your dad and let me know when I can talk to him. Tomorrow at the latest."

I walked over to my car to wait for Dad. I hadn't taken two steps before I got another text: *what's the gate code?* I sent it, then leaned against my car, thankful that I'd parked in the shade. A few minutes later, Dad pulled up in his old van.

"Is he in there?" I asked.

Dad leaned out the window. "Yes, and he's more than a little whiffy. It was probably a mistake giving him part of my hotdog."

I looked in the window of the van to see Mauser sprawled out on the floor behind the front seat. Dad had taken out the middle seats and created a bed for the canine pasha to ride around in.

"He looks content," I commented.

"We were at the Friends of the Animal Shelter's summer camp." Dad looked as tired as Mauser.

"Sucker."

"The kids are okay. Even the one that kept asking every stupid question you could think to ask about a giant dog."

"There are no stupid questions," I reminded him.

Dad grunted and gave me a look that told me that, if I kept it up, I'd be doing the next demo for the kids. He rolled the windows down and got out. We leaned against the van and looked toward the pond and Bernadette's cabin.

"What's going on here?" Dad asked, waving his arm to indicate the rest of the farm.

"You know about the two killings on Monday. Well, last night Althea's son, Bruce, died. He's also the father of the woman who killed the husband who killed his wife." I gave him a minute to untangle my verbal knot, then told him what we knew so far about Bruce's death.

"Sometimes a cigar is just a cigar," he said unconvincingly.

"Says the man who hates coincidences more than I do."

"You got that right. What's your plan?"

"That depends."

"On what?"

"How much time you and our limited budget will give me."

"I'm impressed you're taking that into consideration."

"I didn't think you and Johnson were giving me a

choice."

"Like the man says, there are always choices. Look, from my point of view as sheriff, there are several angles to these cases. One, I don't like the thought that someone might be getting away with murder in my bailiwick. Two, it's going to cost the department to have you working these cases like they're clear-cut murders. Three, if they are murders and we don't treat them as such, it could blow up in our faces somewhere down the road."

"Soooo…?" I asked, watching Jessie, Debbie and Cleo come out of the cabin.

"Today's Wednesday. I'll give you through Friday. Pursue all leads and find nothing concrete, then you wrap it up until the autopsy and forensic reports come in. You find solid evidence, then we can renegotiate. I'll even give you some of Darlene's time if you need it." He held up a finger. "Mind you, not *all* of Darlene's time, just some of it."

"How are you going to cover for us?"

"It's summer, which means that patrol doesn't have to watch school zones in the mornings and afternoons, nor do we have resource officers in the schools. So I'll give a patrol deputy some time in CID covering robberies, and let Julio pick up a few of your assault cases."

"Friday?"

Down the slope, Cleo and the two women were walking toward the pond.

"Best I can do."

I started to thank Dad when I felt the van move violently. We both looked around and were just in time to see Mauser go nuclear. The dingbat had seen Cleo down by the pond and all reason had left him.

"Mauser, calm—" was all Dad got out before we witnessed the equivalent of a camel going through the eye of a needle. As we watched in shock, Mauser managed to squeeze, push and wrench himself out through the back window.

We were quickly in hot pursuit of Mauser, who was aided

by the downward slope of the land. Gravity helped propel his hundred-and-ninety pounds toward Cleo and the two women who were blissfully unaware of the incoming meteor.

We yelled to get their attention. All three looked up—the women in surprise and Cleo in delight. Cleo and Mauser knew each other and, even though he was a blundering clod and she was a gentle lady, they seemed to have a great time playing together. Cleo went down in a classic puppy bow, while giving a light bark of recognition. The goon responded with a ground-shaking woof and redoubled his efforts at reaching her before anyone could grab him.

I watched in horror as Mauser zoomed within inches of the terrified Debbie, who let out a classic movie heroine scream. Jessie was quick on her feet and managed to step between Debbie and the boomerang monster dog, who had circled around and was coming in for another pass. By this point, even the well-mannered Cleo couldn't contain her excitement at seeing her evil doppelgänger. Debbie was holding Cleo's leash and I reached her just in time to take it away before Mauser passed again.

The flying black torpedo was too much for Cleo, and she tried to follow him only to be brought up short by the leash I held tightly in my hand, which was now attached to an arm that was a good six inches longer than it had been before she yanked it.

I'll give Dad credit. He managed to get in front of Mauser and corral him. The beast's tongue was hanging down to his knees as he panted from the heat and exertion. Still, he bumped and nuzzled Cleo in excitement.

"It's... all... right," Dad told the women between heavy breaths as he tried to keep a hold on Mauser's collar.

"There's another leash inside," Jessie said, already moving in the direction of the cabin.

A few minutes later, both dogs were under control and everyone had caught their breath and relaxed a little.

"Debbie, this is Sheriff Macklin," I said, introducing Dad.

"Sorry about my appearance," he told her, tucking in his

shirt and holding his arms by his sides in an attempt to hide the large circles of sweat. He gave Mauser a stern look.

Debbie was looking back and forth between Dad and me with a questioning look on her face.

"He's my dad," I explained.

"Thank you for coming out here," Debbie said. "I don't understand what happened to Bruce."

"We're going to figure this out," Dad reassured her. "Larry's an experienced investigator, and I've given him the go-ahead to devote time and resources to the case." I took note of the fact that he didn't say they were unlimited time and resources.

"I know this is hard to consider, but do you know of anyone who might have wanted to harm your husband?" Dad asked.

I was surprised that Dad had chosen to ask such a question. I looked at his expression and saw only interest and concern. Dad had been a damn good investigator in his day. The kind of good that came from loving what he did. I realized how hard it must have been for him to restrict his interest in cases to what was appropriate as an administrator, rather than a lead investigator.

I could also see how his rank and seniority made it hard for Debbie to sidestep the question or take it lightly. "I'm not sure how to answer that," she finally said.

Dad looked down at the dogs, who were still panting and making googly eyes at each other. "I'm going to take Mauser over to the pond to cool off. Come with me and you can explain."

Jessie brought Cleo along to the pond. We watched the dogs splash and wallow in the shallow water while we gave Debbie time to consider her answer.

"What type of law did your husband practice?" Dad asked, prompting her.

"He was a real estate lawyer. In Atlanta. That's where we live." She made a most unladylike snort of derision. "He thought that would be far enough away from his mother to have some freedom. It wasn't, really, but at least him moving that far away spoiled some of her plans. She had wanted Bruce to be a lawyer and Owen to be a realtor so that they could help grow the family's land empire." She rolled her eyes. "Bruce hated all the pressure his parents put on him to help his brother buy and sell land. Bruce told me that when they were growing up, all his dad talked about was controlling an empire in North Florida. The old man even had dreams that one of them might become governor. Just crazy."

"What was the plan for Jack?" I asked.

Debbie looked at me quizzically. "Jack was before my time. They don't talk about him. Bruce told me before our first trip to meet his mother that I shouldn't ever bring him up."

"Bruce never talked about his brother?"

"Only once. He was really drunk. Some deal he was helping to broker had just fallen through. He came home and drank half the liquor in our bar. That's when he told me it was the anniversary of his brother's death."

"Jack drowned in this pond," I said, causing everyone to look at the pond as though they expected to still see his body floating there.

"That's right. Bruce said everything would have been different if his brother had lived. He claimed that Althea was tolerable to be around before Jack's death. Though I find that hard to believe," Debbie said with a hard eye-roll.

"What else did he tell you about his brother?" I pushed. Dad stood back, watching her. I knew how good he was at judging whether a person was lying a lot, a little or telling the truth.

"Bruce was pretty drunk, so he didn't make a lot of sense. He'd go off on how good Jack was one minute, and then the next he'd be rambling about what a spoiled brat he was. I admit, I was curious about Jack after Bruce made me swear not to bring him up. Best that I could figure out was that Jack had a lot of talent, but squandered it. I think Bruce was a little jealous of him. Kept talking about how much Althea loved Jack and just tolerated him and Owen."

"Did he say anything about how Jack died?"

"He said he drowned. Years ago, was all he said. One minute he'd talk about what an ass his brother could be, and the next he was saying how much he missed him. After half an hour, he started crying and got kind of crazy. I let it go and put him to bed. He slept almost all the way through the next day. That was the only time I ever saw him like that." Her voice sounded haunted. I didn't know if it was the memory of that night, or the thought that there would be no more nights with her husband.

"You still haven't said who might have wanted to harm your husband." Seeing that she had given us everything she knew about Jack, Dad returned to his original question.

"I guess that's obvious. There were a few clients who weren't happy with the way he represented them. Not too many. Bruce was good. When the client did what Bruce advised him to do, things worked out most of the time. At least the best they could."

"But some of his clients weren't happy?" I asked. She looked at me as if I'd asked what color the grass was.

"You deal with people, you're always going to get some who aren't happy with you. It's a fact of life. He dealt with big real estate deals where millions were on the table and sometimes he could turn the screws quite tight on the folks on the other side of the table. That's why his clients hired him. Bruce told me once that his clients expected him to leave the other side bruised and bleeding."

"And were there people who thought Bruce had cheated them?" I asked at the risk of getting another of her "you must be stupid" looks.

"He had a file with names. People who had made threats, that kind of stuff. Hey, I thought you said you didn't know what killed him?" Debbie seemed to have just realized that we were asking questions that pointed toward a belief that foul play may have been involved in Bruce's death.

Dad shook his head. "We don't know what happened. There's a good chance it was an accident, or just natural causes. We just want to be thorough." His voice was very calm.

"I don't know what to think. Tracy dead, Austin, and now Bruce. But you *know* what happened to Tracy and Austin."

"Those deaths are like your husband's. We know what they look like, but we can't be sure what actually happened. We'll have more answers when all the tests are done." That thought caused me to look at my watch. I wanted to be in Tallahassee for the autopsies. I had about an hour before I'd have to leave.

"But you're saying there could be something more… sinister going on?"

"I don't think there's anything to be alarmed about," I said, not knowing if this was true.

"If there is someone killing people out here, shouldn't we have some protection?" Debbie asked.

I hadn't wanted to go down this road. Truth was, if someone had killed these people, then I was asking the witnesses to stay in a place where they could all be in danger.

"I'm going home!" Debbie said, her eyes wide. I could see that flight was winning out over fight in her mind.

"We don't have enough officers to place one on duty out here 24/7," Dad said.

"I don't think any of us should stay!" Debbie insisted, her hysteria beginning to build. If I didn't do something, all of the witnesses were going to bolt for home.

"I'll stay here," I blurted.

Dad looked at me, his green eyes wide and a tight smile on his face.

Jessie had been standing near the water, watching Cleo splash about with Mauser, but I'd been aware that she was listening. Now I caught her looking over at us.

"You will?" Debbie asked, sounding suspicious but calmer.

"Yes. I'm sure there's somewhere I can bed down." I wondered what I was getting myself into.

"I know there are a couple more hunting cabins like this one," Debbie said. "Not that I've been in them." She scrunched up her face like she'd smelled something foul, then noticed the look on Jessie's face. "This one isn't that bad." She didn't sound sincere.

"I need to get Mauser home," Dad said.

At the sound of his name, the dog pulled himself out of the water and walked over to us slowly, with Cleo beside him. Without warning, both dogs gave tremendous shakes. Water flew as everyone tried to avoid the shower.

CHAPTER FOURTEEN

I followed Dad up the hill.

"What on earth were you thinking?" he asked me. "You're getting too close to this investigation. Hell, I don't even know whether I should say 'this' or 'these.'"

"Obviously, all three deaths have to be investigated," I said.

"Don't get smart with me. And don't think I'm paying you around the clock. The pay stops at eight hours unless you're chasing a suspect or being shot."

"Gee, thanks."

"One of the deaths was murder. No doubt about that. Someone killed Tracy. It was likely Austin. Someone clubbed Austin in the back of the head, which was most likely Paula. Though, from what you've told me, there's a slim chance that it might have been Marty."

"Exactly. I thought that was a possibility as soon as I saw the relationship between the two, and the way folks say Marty reacted."

"So how does that fit in with the death of Bruce Byrd?"

"Maybe he purposely overdosed. He might have learned that his grandson killed his daughter *and* son-in-law."

"As a father and a grandfather and, I might add, a lawyer, wouldn't he want to be here for them?"

"That's the hump I can't quite get over. Of course, depression isn't always logical."

"It's a stretch."

"Agreed. You asked about enemies. I'm not sure how a stranger could have snuck onto the property and killed Bruce."

"Not easily," Dad admitted. "Unless he had an accomplice here at the farm."

"I guess the accomplice could be a member of the family. The only people totally out of the circle are Sam the caretaker, Althea's nurse-slash-companion Ruby, and Andy, who's dating one of the young women."

We were about twenty-five yards from our vehicles when a small group began to form. As we got closer, I could see Ellie and Myron Morgan, as well as two other people who I assumed were Liam and Olivia Varney, though I hadn't met them yet. They all surged toward us as we neared the van.

"Is it true?" Ellie asked.

"Did someone kill Bruce?" the other man asked.

"We don't know anything yet," I said.

Dad was standing back with Mauser, a slightly bemused look on his face as he watched me being confronted by the angry citizenry. I knew he was thinking that this was what I deserved for stirring the pot.

"We're not staying here if we're in danger," Ellie said. Myron was standing behind her in moral support, but not saying a word.

"We have kids," Ellie and the other woman said in near perfect unison.

"I'm going to stay on the farm for the next couple of nights to make sure everything is all right," I assured them.

The group looked at me, trying to decide if my presence was enough to make them feel secure. I heard the van's side door open as Dad loaded an exhausted Mauser inside.

"He has the full support of the department behind him, and there will be plenty of backup if he needs it," Dad assured them. They took some reassurance from his uniform with its many stars on the collar.

"You'll guarantee our safety?" Ellie asked me point-blank. Her eyes were narrowed and focused like lasers on mine.

I thought about going into the usual spiel about how I couldn't guarantee anything, but instead I just said, "Sure."

They blinked at me

"I need to get my dog home," were Dad's parting words and he drove away, leaving me with the unhappy group.

"I need to ask you a few questions," I told Olivia and Liam. I figured I could squeeze out almost half an hour before I had to get on the road to Tallahassee for the autopsies.

They had just joined me, somewhat reluctantly, on the front porch of the main house when a shout came from an upper window.

"You! I want to see you right now!" said a shrill voice. I wasn't surprised when I looked up to see Althea Byrd standing by the window with a dark glower on her face. I waved up at her.

"I'll be right up." Turning to Olivia and Liam, I said, "I've got to go to Tallahassee, but I'll be back this evening. I'll want to talk to you then, or tomorrow at the latest."

"And you're sure it's safe for us to stay?" Liam asked. He was a small, wiry guy in his late forties, who matched my mental image of the person on the other end of every sales call I'd ever received.

"Yes," I said flatly before heading toward the house.

Then it hit me that I'd let Dad get away again without confronting him about the mysterious thing he wanted to discuss with me. I felt like I was losing control of everything. I didn't even have a handle on what I was investigating, and now I was going out on a limb with a camp-full of strangers and had given up my own bed for a bunk. *I'll just have to ride the wave and hope I don't drown*, I told myself.

Ruby was waiting at the front door.

"She's in a right foul mood," she said, pointing toward

the stairs.

I started to walk past her, but then a thought occurred to me. "Ruby, do you hold a nursing degree?"

"I do. I'm a registered RN in three states."

"Then why do you work for Althea Byrd? She has you acting more like a servant than a medical professional."

"Ha! I worked in a hospital for fifteen years. Every week we had new supervisors or administrators. Worse, I had a constant flow of nurses straight out of school that I had to train how to wipe their own butts. The pay was okay, but not great. I had to pay for my own room and board, but now, working for Althea, I live wherever she does. I have one boss, and a pain in the ass she might be, but at least she's the devil I know. The pay," she leaned in close, "is very, very good."

"Have you ever nursed any of the other members of the family?"

Her eyes grew suspicious. "I've looked after a few of the children and grandchildren when they were visiting and got a cold or the flu. Nothing more than that. What are you driving at?"

"Just trying to get a picture of everyone and the roles they play here on the farm."

"Where the hell is he?" said a loud voice from upstairs.

"Better go up. Her mood doesn't get better with time," Ruby warned me.

I went up the stairs, bracing myself for the confrontation.

"What's going on?" Althea asked me from her chair. "Was that the sheriff? Why didn't he come up and talk to me?"

"He had his Great Dane with him, and we were led to understand that you don't care for dogs in the house," I said in an attempt to derail her assault.

"You're right. I don't think that should be allowed. They're for working. Forget that. What happened to Bruce?"

Did I see the hard edges crack a little when she mentioned her son?

"We don't know for sure. Right now, it looks like a drug overdose."

"I told him to stay off of those painkillers." She ground her teeth for a moment. Whether it was in anger, frustration or grief, I couldn't tell.

I looked at my watch pointedly. "The autopsy will take place this afternoon and I need to be there. We're expediting this investigation and, with luck, we'll know more after the autopsy. At the least we should be able to eliminate certain possibilities."

"Like murder?"

"Maybe. From what I saw of the body, murder isn't likely."

"Three deaths in three days seems a bit much to swallow." I was impressed with the calm tone of her voice, though I probably shouldn't have been.

"I agree. That's why I'm here, that's why the sheriff was here, and that's why, with your permission, I'll be staying here for the next couple of days."

"You mean overnight?" Althea seemed genuinely surprised by my suggestion.

"Yes, if you'll let me."

"Of course, don't be stupid. There's another cabin behind the one that Dottie is staying in." She seemed to have a twinge of conscience. "I'd let you stay here in the main house, but I don't care much for company. Owen is about the only one I can tolerate."

"I'll be fine in the cabin."

"I'll tell you my thoughts," Althea said, then paused for dramatic emphasis. "Someone is behind all of this. I mean the murder of Tracy, the death of Austin and now Bruce. Mark my words. You just got to dig down."

"Do you have any suspicions?"

For the first time, I saw fear in her eyes. "I… don't know. I don't think it's one of us. Maybe it's a ghost."

I wasn't sure I'd heard her correctly. "Did you say a ghost?"

Her expression cleared. "It was a bad joke. Never mind. Just find out what's going on." She clenched her fists so tightly that her knuckles turned white.

I tried asking a few more questions, but all I got were snappy answers meant to show how stupid I was, so I gave up.

I was headed to Tallahassee by one o'clock and checked in with Cara on the way.

"I called about that refrigerator we looked at online last night," she said. "If we order it today, they can deliver it first thing Friday."

We debated over the cost for a few minutes, then I told her to go ahead with the order. It wasn't like a refrigerator was an optional appliance. Then, hoping she wouldn't be too upset, I said, "I'm not going to be home for a few nights."

"And just where are you going to be?"

I explained the situation and was met by silence. It didn't give me a good feeling.

"I'm going to stay with you," Cara said, her tone making it clear that she wasn't in the mood for an argument.

"No. You can't." I probably should have taken a moment to consider my response.

"Why not? I might as well be out in the woods with you instead of eating take-out at home."

"This is a murder investigation. Multiple murders, if you count Austin as well as Tracy." I also thought about adding the excuse of possibly primitive living conditions, but I knew it wouldn't work with Cara. Considering some of the adventures she'd had with her hippie parents, a cabin without running water wasn't going to scare her away.

"I won't get in the way. Besides, we've only been married a few months. I'm not ready to be apart from you yet," she said in the sweet tone that melted most of our infrequent arguments.

"Maybe," I said, already seeing the dam of my

determination dissolving.

"Good. I'll pack for both of us. I can look in on Ivy when I come in for work and Dr. Barnhill will be happy to keep Alvin for a few days."

I couldn't come up with a good excuse for why she couldn't stay out at the farm. Dad had already told me that I wouldn't be on the clock most of the time I was there, and Cara might even be useful to help wrangle witnesses and keep an eye on everyone.

I called Darlene next and brought her up to date on the investigation.

"You're camping out at the Byrd ranch? Is this a new thing, John Boy? You going to start moving in with the suspects every time we investigate a murder?" Her voice was gently mocking.

"Thanks for your support. Anyway, you're going to be moving on up to the big chief's seat, right?"

"I haven't even gotten an interview yet." She almost sounded forlorn, a rare condition for Darlene. I felt bad for giving her a hard time.

"If they don't hire you away from us, they're idiots."

"They're politicians, therefore, by definition…"

"Hey, watch your mouth. Technically Dad is a politician."

"Your dad is a fish of another color. Enough with the banter. What do you need me to do?"

"Come out tomorrow morning and help me sort out the rest of the witnesses. I could use a second opinion. Especially on Paula and Marty."

"Can do, Magoo. See you bright and early."

I gave her the code to the gate and, knowing her tendency for early hours, asked her not to show up before eight.

When I arrived at the morgue, I swear the receptionist looked up and mumbled, "You again?" before buzzing me through to the exam room. Once inside, I saw all three bodies laid out in a row on stainless steel tables.

"A triple header. You are getting to be a gold star client," Darzi joked. He was standing over the body of Tracy Stokes.

"I'll give you a gold star if you can find some real evidence for me," I said, not joking at all.

"You sound a little testy," Linda said. She was at the second table, working on Austin Stokes.

"These cases are driving me crazy. We've got three bodies, and for the first two we have witnesses. One of the witnesses even admits to killing the killer of the first victim. All neat and tied up with a ribbon. Then a third body turns up with no witnesses. Seems to be an overdose, but could also be a suicide. Yet, with each case and with all of the witnesses, I get an odd feeling. It's like each one is a puzzle piece, but I'm missing the lid of the box to see how they fit together."

"Very poetic," Darzi said. "But you should be careful what you wish for. The evidence might point in a direction you don't want to go."

"I'd be happy to go in any direction."

"If everything you look at seems wrong, then maybe it's you and not what you're looking at," Linda suggested.

"In the words of every crazy person ever, I'm not crazy," I told her.

"Have it your way. Let's take a look and see what we can find." She turned to Darzi. "Your buddies upstairs did a number on Mr. Stokes." She was looking at the surgery scars left after his organs were harvested. They'd been cleaned up, but not sewn up.

"I asked them very politely to leave the body in good shape. You can believe me, this is good for them. I've seen the sort of mess they can leave for the mortician."

I stood back and watched them work, hoping that they would discover the elusive clue that would tie everything together.

"Skin lacerations and post-mortem bruising of the neck are consistent with strangulation," Darzi said, examining Tracy's throat. He made some incisions. "Yes. The hyoid bone is fractured, which also appeared on the X-ray." He moved a small video camera in on the break.

"My victim has damage to his hands and lacerations that could have been obtained during a struggle. There is also bruising on the inner thighs, which would support the idea that he was straddling his victim as he strangled her and that she was putting up a fight," Linda said.

Darzi looked up. "You'll find my analysis of the wounds on the back of his head in the file. I've reviewed the X-rays, which only reinforce my conclusions." He turned to me. "The wounds on his head are what I would expect if your suspect's story is correct. The victim was looking down as the first blow was struck, and he began to rise up as the second blow caught him on the back right side of the head. The second blow was the strongest and caused roughly sixty to seventy percent of the trauma he experienced. Also, the wounds match up with the piece of wood identified as the weapon used in the assault."

They worked efficiently and bantered lightly. I mostly listened and hoped for something new, but everything was adding up. They called me over when it was time to roll the two bodies back to their refrigerated drawers.

"Where is all your help?" I asked. Normally there were a couple of interns available to help manhandle the cadavers.

"We had two of our interns—" Darzi started.

"Flake out," Linda offered.

"Exactly. Flake out on us. Since it's summer, we have not had an easy time filling our vacancies. In my day, students would have been fighting over internships. Now everyone wants to work in the big cities." He closed the door on Austin. The latch snapping into place sounded very final.

"Now for the last victim. I can see by your face that we haven't found anything you didn't already know. Maybe the cigar really is just a cigar," Darzi said as we moved to the last table.

"I'm growing tired of that cliché. I know I should be glad that the story is checking out, but still…"

"Do you have any evidence that the witnesses aren't telling the truth?" Linda asked as they got into place around the body of Bruce Byrd.

"No." I paused. "Though I probably shouldn't say that. There are inconsistencies in some witness statements that could be considered circumstantial evidence. If you use the word 'evidence' loosely."

"What do you find suspicious about this death?" Darzi put me on the spot.

"It was unexpected, assuming that the death was caused by an overdose of drugs that were taken accidentally or on purpose. Or someone else gave them to him."

"So accident, suicide or murder. Now, be honest with me. The fact that bothers you the most is that there were two prior deaths." Darzi nodded toward the coolers where we had just stowed Tracy and Austin.

"I'll admit that."

"Let's see what we can find."

He went on to describe the age, sex and other known facts about the victim for the recording software. As with the other bodies, there were X-rays of the victim on monitors above the table.

"There are no signs of trauma apparent on the X-rays," Darzi said as he clicked through the images. Occasionally, he would flip back and forth between a couple of images before being satisfied. He stopped on one that even I could recognize as Bruce's spine.

"You can see the compacted vertebrae. The seventh lumbar is where much of the pain was coming from. If nothing else, I can assure you that he was not faking."

Linda had started to examine the body, videoing anything that piqued her interest before she poked and probed at it. Several times, she took sterile adhesive tape and picked up hairs and other fibers off of the body.

Organs were examined, weighed and put back and samples were taken, all while Darzi dictated his findings.

"His breathing stopped. We can assume that it was

caused by a combination of alcohol and a quantity of drugs that he was not able to tolerate."

"He had an excessive amount of drugs in his stomach?"

"For someone who was not used to them, yes. Maybe ten pills. And with the alcohol, that could be enough to stop his respiration. Now, if he had a tolerance for them, then ten would not be an excessive amount. With these drugs, it is all a game of conditioning." Darzi's voice was irritated. "This family of drugs has a narrow window where they are useful. Unfortunately, they were sold to doctors and patients for years as a cure-all for pain. And it's not just the patients; I've seen more than a few doctors who've been addicted to them."

"You're talking to a deputy. I've seen what they do to good people."

Addiction could take a person and twist them into two people—one who wants nothing more than the drug, and another who wants nothing more than to be *off* of the drug. One would do anything to their friends and family just to spend ten minutes high, while the other would sometimes be driven to kill themselves to spare their friends and family from having to live with them.

"This man was no addict," Darzi pronounced. "At least not a chronic one. All of his organs are in good shape for a man his age."

"No one has suggested that he was an addict. He did complain that the pills weren't cutting the pain."

"Maybe he had become inured to the lower doses. Instead of upping the dose, he decided to consume alcohol along with the pills. That would be very dangerous. You take one pill, you get one dose. You take two pills, you get two doses. You take one pill with alcohol, and you might get the equivalent of two pills or five pills. Very unpredictable."

I should have felt relief. All three autopsies fit the prevailing stories of what had happened to each of the victims. Instead, I felt irritated. Maybe Linda was right and the problem was with me.

I left the morgue and headed back toward Adams County. It was close to six and I needed to meet with Dr. Horvath. We'd exchanged half a dozen texts, ending with a promise that I'd meet her at her house around seven, assuming she didn't get involved in any medical emergencies.

She lived in a rambling old farmhouse, not unlike the one on the Byrd farm. But while Althea's looked like a museum piece, Horvath's home looked like what it had been built to be. Chickens clucked in the front yard, while the world's laziest farm dog barely lifted his head from the front porch when I drove up.

I saw Horvath's Dodge dually parked by the barn. She was loading up the white boxes in the bed of the truck with supplies.

"Howdy!" she greeted me. "Just getting ready for tomorrow, or the middle of the night, whichever comes first. If I don't do the restocking as soon as I get home, I'll find myself without the one thing in the world I need. And the hell of it is, you never know *what* that one item is until you're knee-deep in horse manure."

The doctor worked with an economy of motion that reminded me of Dr. Darzi, or even Pete when he was teaching at the gun range.

"I also learned that if I didn't refill them in a specific order, I'd forget things." She latched the last box. "There. Any word on who grabbed my UPS delivery?"

"No. I thought I'd take a look and see if I could suggest anything to keep it from happening again."

"Come on, then." I followed her back out to her gate, where she'd placed a wooden box big enough to hold two men and still close the lid. "The UPS driver has the combination to the lock, but you can see that the creeps just pried it off."

"According to the report, it doesn't look like they got anything too valuable."

"That's what pisses me off. They didn't get anything worth the effort, but they inconvenienced me. I hate the business side of being a vet. I tried having a partner, but that was just as big of a hassle as doing the ordering and bookkeeping myself. Less work, but more aggravation. He wanted to have meetings all the damn time. Anyhoo, I have my drugs held at the UPS or FedEx office and I pick them up there. I guess these clowns thought I'd be dumb enough to have the good stuff sitting out here by the side of the road."

"Meth-heads aren't known for their brains," I said. "I can't suggest much except for some security cameras and a better box and lock. Though none of that is going to stop a determined thief." The truth wasn't always satisfying.

"I figured. Just makes me feel like sitting up all night with a baseball bat."

"If I thought you'd get them, I'd loan you the bat. Unfortunately, these types of robberies are usually random. Could've even been kids. You could have your stuff delivered to another address where someone is home. Maybe a friend or relative?"

"I thought about that. It'd just be more work and time, plus I'd be inconveniencing a friend. But I'll think on it."

CHAPTER FIFTEEN

"Should I bring some sheets and pillows?" Cara asked as she stacked supplies in the living room.

"Probably should to be safe. I'll fill an extra bowl of food and water for Ivy."

Ivy was staring daggers at me from the back of the couch. She recognized the signs of packing, and she didn't like the thought of being without her hot and cold running servants.

An hour later, Cara followed me in her own car through the gates of the farm. The sun was just setting behind the trees as we parked near the main house, leaving the sky filled with layers of vivid color.

"Wow. How much land do they own?" Cara asked as she got out of her car.

"Bunches and bunches. At least a thousand acres. I looked at their holdings on the property appraiser's list. It's in dozens of separate parcels. I quit adding it up when I got to a thousand."

"Must be nice."

"I don't know. The wealth hasn't made Althea or her family very happy."

"And this is just *some* of their land?"

"Yeah. They don't even live here. Althea owns land

throughout the Panhandle, but her main residence is in Lake City. The rest of the family is spread out across the Southeast."

We walked down to Bernadette's cabin. After greetings and small talk, Jessie walked us to our cabin, which was another hundred feet past theirs.

"I cleaned it up a little," Jessie said.

"That was really nice of you," Cara told her.

There were sheets and pillows, but I was glad we'd brought our own. The ones on the bunks looked like they'd been used by every hunter in Florida without ever seeing the inside of a washing machine. We fetched our stuff from the cars, then rejoined Bernadette and Jessie.

Cara and I settled down on the well-used couch that held the faint odor of dogs and beer. As our butts hit the cushions, Bernadette put bottles of a locally brewed beer called Bloody Adams in our hands. I wondered if the name was a joke on the number of murders in the county.

"So are you closer to an answer?" Bernadette asked.

"Short answer: no," I said. "To be fair, we won't know a lot until we get all the test results back, which could take months."

"Do you still think there's some kind of foul play going on?" Bernadette sounded like she was on stage at the Grove Theatre, where she was artistic director.

"In my heart, I feel like there is something wrong about the deaths. On the other hand, my brain's telling me to deal with reality, which is that, even if there is something strange going on, it's going to be very hard to prove anything unless some hard evidence comes out." I didn't mention the other way that the cases could be solved—confession. I didn't want it to get back to a possible perpetrator that all they had to do was keep their mouth shut.

"How many people are here?" Cara asked. She was petting Cleo, who'd climbed up on the couch, plopping her butt down on me while she put her head on Cara's thigh so she could have her ears stroked.

"Not counting you two, or Bernadette's mom and Debbie, since they're staying in town, there are nineteen," Jessie said. When she caught my look, she added defensively, "I'm not investigating anything, just collecting a few facts."

"Jessie and I couldn't help but talk about the murders," Bernadette said in her defense.

"Thinking and talking are fine. Just no doing," I warned. "Deputy Darlene Marks will be here in the morning to help finish with the interviews. How's Paula doing?"

"She's holding up."

"Darlene and I will conduct a formal interview with her tomorrow. Debbie and Karen are still at your house?"

"Of course. Mom tried to talk Dad into leaving, but he refused. Thank goodness. I told Mom that he's not up for a road trip right now. And he always has to do the driving. But she still badgered him. Mom has one concern—Mom. He had to put his foot down and tell her he was going to stay to make sure that Paula is okay. He told me later that he feels like he owes it to his brother to look after Paula and Marty now that Uncle Bruce is gone."

We talked for a while longer before Cara and I left to go back to our cabin. The night was warm and clear, filled with the sound of a thousand frogs.

"We can walk around the pond," I suggested, taking her hand.

"The pond where Jason drowned," she said in a horror movie voice.

I pinched her lightly. "His name was Jack, not Jason."

"Too soon?"

"Too soon for Althea. Twenty-five years and that wound is still raw."

"He was her child," Cara said, sounding sympathetic.

"More than that, he was her baby. She had Jack when she was forty-five. Back then, that was pushing the age for a woman to be giving birth. Sadly, I think Jack was the only one of her children she really wanted to have."

"That's awful."

"She had Owen when she was only sixteen."

"A woman can want a child that young. It might not be a good idea to have that kind of responsibility when you're a teenager, but that doesn't mean she didn't want the child."

"I'm not sure she was really in love with Ryan."

"They did all right."

"I can't shake the feeling that all of this is wrong. Something is hiding in the dark."

"I hope you don't mean literally, since we're here at Crystal Lake," she joked.

"This isn't *Friday the 13th* or *Sleepaway Camp*, even if our accommodations aren't much better. You know, you didn't have to come out here with me."

"I wasn't kidding when I told you that I wasn't quite ready to let you run off on your own yet. Give it a year and I'll be pushing you out the door so I can get some alone time." Cara squeezed my hand.

We looked up at the lights from the campers and other houses.

"Am I wasting my time *and* the department's time?"

"You're doing what you think is best. Would you be happy if you did anything else?"

"No. But I'm lucky to work for my father. Not because he's my father, but because he lets people follow their instincts."

"Only because he has people he can trust working for him."

"I saw Dr. Horvath today."

"About the burglary?"

"Not much I could tell her. With her keeping the box down by the road, there isn't a good way to protect it. I suggested that she have her stuff delivered to a different address, but she wasn't too keen on that idea."

"Did they get any drugs?"

"She has those deliveries held at UPS and FedEx." I put my arms around Cara and looked up at the stars. "You can see the Milky Way."

Cara pointed out the constellations she could recognize and told me some of the goofy names that her mother had given them. Then we headed back to the cabin to enjoy an evening without TV or computers.

"We agreed to only twenty minutes on the phone," Cara reminded me as we went inside.

"Scout's honor. I'm just going to text Darlene and check my email."

I kept my word. We were both tired and headed to bed after only an hour. We briefly considered trying to share one of the bunk beds, but with mutual shakes of our heads we decided it wouldn't be a recipe for a good night's sleep.

Morning brought an odd mix of the strange and familiar as we bumbled around the cabin, trying to stick to our usual routine but finding ourselves constantly having to improvise.

"At least there's indoor plumbing," I said.

"If there wasn't, then I would have just accepted the fact that we were going to be separated for a couple of nights. Did I ever tell you about the time Mom and Dad joined a group of fellow hippies trying to start a commune in Tennessee? That place had running water. It was called a creek. I was thirteen and not a very happy camper, literally. They gave up after six months. Turned out there were only three people doing any work—Dad, Mom and me."

"You're a trooper," I said, giving her a kiss before continuing my hunt for a cereal bowl.

We walked up to our cars together, where we found Darlene leaning against her car and drinking her morning coffee. Cara waved to her and headed off to work.

"Morning, sleepyhead. You're crazy-committed for sleeping out here," Darlene said.

"I just hope there's a separate section of hell for morning people," I yawned.

"It's all going to be part of the grand underworld experience," she said. "So what's the game plan, hunchmeiester?"

"I've gone along on some of your hunchier wild goose chases," I reminded her.

"You have. Never very happily, but you've usually gone along."

"I have to admit, this is probably the biggest longshot I've ever played." I brought her up to speed on the investigation, including the results of the autopsies.

"Wow! Most of the time you have at least *one* fact to anchor your theory."

"Not this time."

I pulled out a sheet I'd drawn up the night before with the names of everyone on the property and where they were staying.

"There are nineteen people. Sixteen relatives of one stripe or another, one boyfriend and two employees. Jeanette and Elijah are Ellie and Myron's children, and they're too young to be involved. Same goes for Olivia and Liam's son, Derrick. That leaves sixteen. The family members all share one motive—money. There's a lot of land and money in Althea's estate. Who inherits what? I don't know and I don't think most of them know. Even so, our murderer may figure that if he or she bumps off enough people, then their odds of making it in the will improve."

"There is a huge flaw in your thinking. Aren't Paula and Marty the only real suspects?"

"Maybe. Though they could be covering for someone else. I'm pretty sure they aren't telling the whole story."

"Pretty sure? Don't oversell your ideas," she said with an extra scoop of sarcasm.

Then I told her about Althea's dead son.

"And that fits in how?" She looked at me sideways. "Look, I'm not poo-pooing your case here, but... what?"

"Jack's death might not play a part in the current cases. However, it was the catalyst that sent the family down this road. Go talk to Althea yourself. Emotionally, she's still living in the days just after her son died."

"Okay, say I buy that. Althea is a hurt and manipulative old woman sitting on a pile of money. Why isn't *she* the target?"

"I keep going back to the money. Killing her might be the ultimate goal, but the murderer wants to eliminate other potential heirs before she dies."

"Or the husband killed the wife in a fit of jealousy, and the sister killed the husband in an attempt to protect her sister. A day later, the father dies of a drug overdose, which was either an accident or suicide."

"Yeah, or that," I said grumpily.

"Don't be irritated with me. You called me in this morning to act as a sounding board. You need someone to push back, 'cause you're way outside the lines on this one."

"I can't argue that point. One more day. If we find nothing, then I let them all go back to where they live and the whole thing will languish until all the test results come back."

"Deal. So who do you want me to tackle first?"

We went over the names and I asked her to talk to Ellie, Myron, Olivia and Liam while I chased some more wild geese.

CHAPTER SIXTEEN

I headed for town with the goal of getting as much background information on Althea and her family as possible. The first thing I did was stop by the office and visit the records department.

Beth Miller was generalissimo of records. She was also the best baker in the Southeast. Every deputy found an excuse to visit records a couple of times a week, just to have a taste of whatever treat she'd brought in. Today it was a coconut-almond dark chocolate cookie that could make strong men weak at the knees.

I ate one as I explained what I needed.

"Here are the names of the folks I want to look into. I doubt you're going to find anything too revealing. I also need any records relating to a drowning that occurred in 1992." I saw Beth frown when I mentioned the date. "I know you might have to dig back into the paper records for that."

"Some of the boxes got damaged last year when the roof caved in during the hurricane."

"I know. Just do the best you can. The victim's name was Jack Byrd, born in 1972. Check background for him too."

When I left the records division, it was with another

cookie wrapped up in a napkin in my pocket.

I cruised by my desk and was surprised to see Deputy Andy Martel sitting there.

"I got called in to cover some of Julio's cases and he said I could sit here. I guess he's taken on some of your battery cases. Said something about you being away at summer camp," Martel said with a good-natured smirk.

"I'm following up on multiple homicides," I explained.

"You sure they aren't multiple hunches?" I heard Pete ask. I turned around to see the big guy coming toward me with a box of donuts. "Want one?" he asked, opening the box.

I pulled out the cookie and showed it to him with all of the care you'd use when showing off a precious jewel. "I got it in records."

"I'll trade you the whole *box* of donuts," Pete said seriously.

"Forget it."

Pete sighed and offered the donut box to Martel.

"Sure, if I can't have a cookie," he said, and grabbed a cream-filled pastry.

"I hear you've dragged Darlene into your fantasy world of homicide down on the farm," Pete said.

"Let's sit down. I'll tell you the whole story and you can give me your expert opinion."

We went into the smaller of the two conference rooms where we could get a little privacy. Once we were seated, I went over all the details of the three deaths.

"You need to get into the drug drive-by market," Pete said when I'd finished. "I have one right now. No who-did-it? Just where-are-they?"

"I've had my share of those. In fact, I had one on the burner before this came up."

"Okay, let's look at what you've got. You've covered the basics. Logic dictates that Paula and Marty are either lying or they aren't. The real question is: how do you figure out if they're lying?"

"Nail, meet head. I don't know. Pressing them doesn't seem like the way to go. Especially if they're defending each other or someone they care enough about to go to jail for."

"You need to find some kind of leverage to open them up."

"That's what I'm thinking."

"I've learned over the last couple of years that you aren't as dumb as you look."

"Gee, thanks. You're my hero."

"I knew that. Go get me a cookie."

"Get your own. You could use the exercise," I shot back.

"Ouch! You wound me." Pete grabbed his chest.

I was about to make a smart remark when there was a knock on the door and Martel poked his head in.

"Johnson is looking for you and he doesn't look like he's in a good mood," he said to me.

I left them and headed for the lieutenant's office. When I got there, the door was open and I could almost see the steam rising off of Johnson's head.

"Get in here!"

I did and, before I could say a word, he launched into his tirade.

"Do you even know what the chain of command is?" he asked, not waiting for an answer. "You go behind my back and convince the sheriff to let you take *my* time for some investigation that you should be setting aside until you get the lab reports back."

"Your time?" I made the mistake of asking.

"You work in *my* division. Your time is my time. Got it?" This time he waited.

"Yes, sir," I said, and added some generous nodding. I'd never seen the man this hot under the collar.

"If you want to be some half-ass independent investigator, then you and the sheriff need to work that out. Do you understand I have set goals that I'm expected to meet?"

"I—"

"We're a unit and we work together or we don't work. This situation needs to be dealt with," Johnson said with a finality that I didn't like.

"I didn't mean any disrespect," I said, which was true. "I just need a day or two on this investigation."

"Son, the time to make your case to me was before you went around my back and talked to the sheriff."

A voice in my head told me that I should explain how Dad just came by and we got to talking and it had just happened. I told the voice to shut up before it got me killed or fired or both.

"I'll take this up with the sheriff. Dismissed!" Johnson said, burning a hole in my head with his eyes while he ground his teeth menacingly.

I turned and had to fight the urge to run out of his office. I knew he'd never been happy with the fact that I had a back door to the sheriff. And I had to admit that I'd used it more than once for things that should have been run by my lieutenant first. I wondered how Dad was going to handle the situation. One thing I did know was that he valued Johnson's contribution to the smooth and efficient running of the department.

Just one more thing to worry about, I thought as I headed for the front door. My best bet for getting out of trouble was to figure out what was going on out at the Byrd farm. I pulled out of the parking lot determined to stick to my agenda.

I had texted ahead to make sure that Albert Griffin would be home that morning. Mr. Griffin was the county's unofficial historian. When the local paper had folded, he'd collected all of the archives and organized them in an elaborate filing system in his old Victorian house.

As always, his welcome was effusive. Mr. Griffin pulled me inside and proceeded to alternate between quizzing me on what I knew about recent events and folks in the county, and giving me detailed accounts of anything he found fascinating.

"But you didn't come to listen to me ramble on," he

finally said.

"No," I agreed, stroking one of Mr. Griffin's many cats that had climbed into my lap. "I need to gather as much information about the Byrds as I can."

"Birds?"

"Sorry, the family. Althea and Ryan Byrd."

His eyes widened. "Oh *those* Byrds. They started their little empire here in Adams County, though they soon outgrew us. Interesting people in one way and boring as tears in another."

"In what way?"

"Business. All business. Ruthless. Ryan wasn't mean, just driven. And by driven, I mean he'd drive right over anything and anyone that got in his way. Not very sophisticated, though. I could tell you three or four occasions when people who were a little more savvy beat him at his own game. Ryan had no use for politics. I'm not sure if it was because he didn't understand how it worked, or if he just didn't want to take the time to deal with politicians. I tend to think it was the latter."

"You know what I'm dealing with?" I didn't doubt for a minute that Mr. Griffin had heard about the killings as soon as I had. He had more than a few friends who listened to their radio scanners religiously, and dozens more who worked for us or the ambulance service. Adams County was one hundred percent small town when it came to our grapevine.

"The family was prominently featured in the paper during the '70s and '80s. Typical big-things-are-happening stories. Ryan would buy this, or invest in that. He helped build the shopping plaza where the Supersave is."

"What about the drowning of Jack Byrd?"

"That was an interesting story. I was freelancing for the paper then and I covered it. Still remember watching them pull his body out of the pond."

"You were there?"

"Yep."

"Tell me what you remember."

"Best if we go pull up the editions of the paper."

I followed him to his filing room. As soon as we were there, I heard a noise in the south corner of the room.

"Is that one of your cats?" I asked.

"Don't shoot! It's me," I heard Eddie Thompson say.

"Eddie's using his newfound library skills to help label and organize the archive," Mr. Griffin said proudly.

"I'm doing more than that. I got him to install smoke detectors, and I was talking to a guy who writes grants for the library. He thinks we can get a grant to have all of this… what's the dang word… digitalized, that's it." Eddie was all smiles as he made his way through the filing cabinets toward us.

"I'm impressed."

"You should be. How's it going, boss?" he said, shaking my hand.

"I was telling Mr. Griffin that I need some information on a drowning that took place in 1992."

"What month?" Eddie asked eagerly.

"I don't know," I admitted.

"I believe it was March or April," Mr. Griffin said. "The air was cool, but not really cold. I'd say April."

"On it," Eddie said, weaving his way back through the cabinets. A minute later he shouted, "Here!"

We joined him as he pulled a file from a middle drawer.

"Does this have to do with those deaths out at the Byrd farm?" Eddie asked.

"Where'd you hear about them."

"A little bird. That's *b-i-r-d*," Eddie said.

"I bet it's spelled *J-e-s-s-i-e*."

"And you'd be correct. I warned you about her."

Eddie *had* tried to warn me. He worked with Jessie at the library, and he'd told me that she was a little crazy the first time I'd met her. When she'd started to insinuate herself into the case I was working at the time, I'd decided he was right. She'd been as much of a help as she was a hindrance, but it was a close thing.

"Y'all getting along?" I asked.

"She's all right." I thought I detected a slight blush to Eddie's cheeks.

"You're sweet on her," I joked. He just looked away.

"Let's see what we've got," Mr. Griffin said, ignoring us as he started flipping through the papers in the file. "The paper was down to two editions a week by the '90s. Lucky to manage that many."

He pulled out three editions. After showing me the pictures of several deputies standing around a body covered by a sheet, he began to read and was soon lost in the articles he'd written more than two decades earlier.

When he finished, he handed the papers to Eddie. "Would you scan these and send a copy to Larry?" Then he turned to me. "Let's sit down in the other room and I'll tell you everything I remember about Jack's drowning."

Once we were settled in the front parlor, Mr. Griffin described his involvement in the case.

"An old fella I knew who worked at the Byrd farm called me about the drowning. Must have been first thing in the morning, 'cause I remember that there was still a layer of fog on the ground. In fact, the caretaker said that's why they didn't find the body sooner, the fog was so thick over the pond. When I got there, a pair of deputies had just dragged the body out of the pond."

"Was anyone living at the farm at the time?"

"Ryan Byrd used it as a place to take clients hunting. Quail, dove and deer, mostly. I don't think anyone but the caretaker lived there year-round, even back then."

"What was Jack doing there?"

"My understanding was that he'd gotten into a fight with his parents and had come out to stay at the farm. He'd been living with them in Lake City at the time."

"How long had he been at the farm?"

"What the investigators were told was that Jack had left Lake City around eight the previous evening. According to

Ryan Byrd, the fight had started at dinner. Jack stormed out and didn't tell anyone where he was going. The caretaker claimed that Jack wasn't at the farm when he did his last round at ten o'clock. So the assumption was that Jack got there sometime between ten and midnight. The first time the caretaker noticed Jack's car was when he went out to feed the dogs at six the next morning."

"Who found the body?"

"He and the deputies."

"What time did he call the deputies?"

"When he saw the car."

"I'm confused. He sees Jack's car at the farm and calls the cops? Why? Didn't Jack have a right to be at the farm?"

"Sorry, I left something out. Jack had a right to be there, sure, but the caretaker didn't recognize the car. And usually the family let him know if one of them was coming out so he could turn on the water to the house. When he saw the car, he went straight up to the main house and saw that the door was half open. That's when he called 911, thinking there'd been a break-in."

"That makes sense," I said, as Eddie joined us in the parlor.

"When the deputies got there, they searched the house and found nothing. By that time, the sun was above the trees and the fog was starting to burn off. Someone looked toward the pond and saw Jack's body floating about twenty feet from the bank."

"They thought it was an accident?" I said suspiciously. I'd seen the date on the papers. The first story had appeared on March 21. The weather would still have been chilly.

"Well… that's what the official verdict was. I'm not sure anyone really believed it. The family had enough influence and there was enough ambiguity about the situation to allow for a probable suicide to be called an accident. Ryan Byrd had a reputation. If he didn't like something you did, he'd sue you. I don't think the county wanted to deal with that, so they let it go."

"I have mixed feelings about that sort of accommodation. On the one hand, it can be an act of compassion. But on the other hand, if there *is* some foul play, it can let a bad guy off the hook. What was the victim wearing?"

"Ha! You went straight to the heart of the matter. He was wearing shorts and a polo. That was what made most people think it was a suicide."

"Shoes?"

"He'd taken them off, which was what the people advocating for an accident pointed to as evidence that he was just taking a swim."

"But not many people take a swim in a polo shirt and shorts."

"People with a high blood alcohol level might," Mr. Griffin said.

"He was over the legal limit?"

"And then some. I don't remember the exact number. It wasn't marginal, but also not staggering. Maybe double. Something like that."

"Enough to make a person do dumb stuff, but not so much that they *can't* do dumb stuff."

"Exactly."

"Had he been in the house?"

"Now you're asking questions I'm not even sure I thought to ask back then. I didn't put it in the article if I did. And, before you ask, I'll tell you that any notes I took are long gone."

"Anything else you can remember about the case?"

Mr. Griffin thought for a moment. "I've got a subjective observation. I interviewed Ryan Byrd. I think he agreed to the interview as a way of getting his opinion out in front of anything that the sheriff's office might release to the media. He acted... strange. I think it says something that I remember how odd he acted after so many years."

"Odd how?"

"He kept mentioning the argument that they'd had at the

dinner table. The funny thing was, I asked a couple of times what the argument had been about and, each time, he told me that it didn't matter."

"Why do you think he kept bringing it up?"

"I thought about that. At the time, I just thought he was feeling guilty about having harsh words with his son before he died. Now I'm not so sure. It seemed like the fight argued more for suicide than for an accident. Though he did say that Jack would sometimes go swimming when he was upset. So maybe that's what he was implying."

"My father would always talk about how rebellious and argumentative I was after he'd hit me. I figured out that it was his way of justifying his being an asshole," Eddie said.

"Maybe it was more of a fight than an argument. I hope Beth can find the autopsy records. It could be interesting if there were any marks on the body other than what you would find from a drowning, accident or suicide," I said.

"You think the drowning has something to do with the recent deaths?" Mr. Griffin asked skeptically.

"Yes, no, maybe." I shrugged. "I'm fishing. I don't even know if Bruce Byrd's death was an accident or a suicide. It seems like we've come full circle. Now two of Althea's sons have died under questionable circumstances, separated by a thousand yards and more than two decades."

"I see your point."

"After Jack died, did you talk to Althea Byrd?"

"No. I asked Ryan if I could speak with her and he slapped the idea down hard. Told me he'd sue the paper if I attempted to contact her."

"Didn't that strike you as an overreaction?"

"I knew she was upset. A woman loses her child, by all accounts a child that she dearly loved, I wasn't surprised that her husband was being protective. Truth is, I felt like I was pushing the bounds of decent behavior by asking for an interview with her."

"I can see that. You can trust me when I say she is still touchy on the subject. Like you, I'm not surprised. Her family has confirmed that Jack was her favorite."

"Parents often feel that children they have late in life are special."

We talked for a few more minutes before I got up and headed to my car. Eddie followed me.

"I emailed you the scans of the articles," he said, giving me the feeling that he wanted to say more.

"Thanks. I'm impressed with the way you've straightened yourself out," I said, meaning every word. When I'd first met Eddie, I'd assumed that he would always be an addict on the make.

"I owe a lot to you and Mr. Griffin."

"You've more than paid me back. And, from what I can see, you've done a good job of paying Albert back as well."

Eddie was quiet for a moment, but as we neared my car he suddenly blurted, "It's not dangerous out at the farm, is it?"

"You dog. You *do* have feelings for Jessie. Have you all gone out?" I ribbed him.

"No, and don't give me a hard time. I'm still in my first year of sobriety and my sponsor doesn't think I need any complications right now," he said defiantly.

I turned and looked at him for a minute. "If you think I'm going to give you a hard time, you're wrong. You're doing a damn good job of remaking yourself and I know the twelve-step program has had a lot to do with the new you. Keep it up. Just... When you think you're in the right place... She's kooky, but she has a good heart."

"That's what I think," Eddie said.

And that's also how I'd describe you, I thought.

CHAPTER SEVENTEEN

I found Darlene at Olivia and Liam's campsite. They had pitched a five-person pop-up tent on the edge of the woods not far from the cabin where Tracy and Austin had been killed. The tent was tucked back in the shade of several thirty-foot-tall magnolias.

Darlene was perched uncomfortably on a camp stool. "Liam was just telling me that they were down at the St. Marks wildlife refuge when Tracy and Austin died," she explained as I walked up.

"That's right. Derrick has a fascination with alligators, so we took a day trip down to where we were sure we'd see some," Liam said.

"There were a whole *bunch* of gators!" Olivia said, sounding like the reptiles had been a bit much for her.

"Derrick loved it. We saw a couple that were ten feet or bigger," Liam said, then he paused guiltily. "I don't mean to sound callous. Doesn't seem right talking about what a great trip we had down to the coast when Tracy and Austin were killed."

"Somehow it just doesn't seem real," Olivia agreed.

"How old is Derrick?" I asked, wanting to keep them talking about themselves.

"He's eleven. Excited by everything."

"You said you left around eight in the morning," Darlene said, reviewing her notes for my benefit.

"That's right. We've been getting up early 'cause it's so hot. Not really very pleasant to hang around in the tent when the heat and humidity is so high," Liam said.

"What time did you get back?"

"We took our time. Had dinner and got back here around seven. Derrick was bushed. Who am I kidding? We were too." Liam sounded like a modern-day version of *Father Knows Best*.

"Did you see anyone before you left that morning?"

Liam's brow furrowed. "I don't think so."

"I saw Tracy when I went to the bathroom at their house." Olivia hugged herself and gave a little shake like she was cold. "I don't like to think about it."

"You used their bathroom?"

"There's a small half-bath with a shower off the back porch. They left it unlocked so we could use it. I went to grab a quick shower. Usually I get in and out without seeing anyone, but that morning when I walked in, Tracy was looking around for something. I asked her what she was looking for and she just said, 'Nothing,' like you do when you don't want help or don't want to be bothered explaining."

"Did she say anything else?" I asked, interested in this image of Tracy four hours before she'd been killed.

"No."

"What did she look like? Was she dressed? Did she look like she'd been up all night?"

"She had on a nightshirt. Just that. Maybe… you know, panties, but nothing else. Like she'd just gotten out of bed."

"Did she have shoes on?" Darlene asked.

"No. She was kind of shuffling around the way you do when you're not quite awake."

"What else did you see or hear while you were in their house?"

"Nothing, really. Maybe… I don't know. I was in the shower and thought I heard someone yell."

"Think. Was it one word shouted, or more like a sentence?"

"It was hard to hear. I think it was more like someone yelling a question at someone else. That's what I thought at the time."

We talked about that trip to the shower for a few more minutes, but Olivia couldn't remember hearing or seeing anything else while she was in the cottage.

"I may have missed this, but I'm still trying to sort out all of the different relationships. How are you related to Althea?" I asked.

"I'm the grandson of Rachel Byrd, Ryan's sister. Ryan Byrd was my great uncle," Liam said.

A young boy came running over to us from the direction of the main house. He was dark haired, thin like his father, and wearing swim trunks with a towel hung off his shoulders. When he saw Darlene and me, Derrick put on the breaks. He sidestepped us and went to stand next to his mother.

"How was the pond?" Olivia asked him.

"Great! But I didn't see any alligators."

"That's a good thing," his mother said, giving him a hug.

"Cleo had to go back in the cabin, so I had to get out of the water."

"Did you thank Aunt Dottie for watching you?"

"Another lady was there too. I think her name was Jessie," he said, still breathing heavily.

"Go get out of those wet clothes," Olivia told him.

He looked at us curiously.

"I'll walk with you to your car," Liam said, standing up.

Once we were out of earshot of the tent, he said, "We haven't told him about Tracy and Austin."

"And Bruce?" I asked.

"Actually, we did tell him that Bruce had died. It was kind of hard not to since we were here when the ambulance came. One of our neighbors had a heart attack last year, so we'd already gone through the process of explaining death to him, at least in ten-year-old terms."

"When was the last time you saw Bruce Byrd?"

"Dinner Sunday night. I wasn't real close to him." Liam sounded hesitant, like there were aspects of their relationship that he didn't want to go into. That just made me curious.

"Was there a particular reason y'all weren't close?" Darlene asked, beating me to the punch.

The question was met with silence from Liam.

"There's any number of other people around here that we can ask. You may as well be the one to tell us what was going on between you two."

"Nothing was going on. It was ancient history. Just… I was a kid. But it soured any chance we had to get along."

"Wouldn't you rather we hear it from you than someone else?" Darlene pushed.

Liam stopped walking and gave a sideways glance at the cottage that still had crime scene tape across the doors. I wondered what he'd told his son about the tape.

"I was fourteen. We were here for the Fourth of July. Fourteen, for Pete's sake."

"Go on," I said gently.

"It was nighttime and everyone was down by the pond for the fireworks display. Owen had brought some pretty impressive rockets and stuff, so the whole family was down there except Tracy and me. We were sitting behind the main house, looking down on everyone. We'd been making eyes at each other all weekend, and that night she'd snuck some beers out of her father's cooler. We drank them and watched the fireworks. One thing led to another and we snuck off to one of the hunting cabins. We'd just gotten into some pretty heavy petting when Bruce found us." He stopped talking, his mind full of memories.

"I guess he was pretty steamed," Darlene said.

"Not the half of it. He blew his friggin' top. Told us we were committing incest. He actually took off his belt and chased me out of the cabin. Managed to get a couple of good licks on me too. We were just young and distant cousins." His eyes pleaded with us for understanding.

"He never forgave you?"

"He got Althea to tell my parents to leave. He wouldn't even let us wait until morning. I felt awful. My parents were humiliated. I hated him for years."

"But you're here now. And you brought your family. What changed?" I asked.

"My parents died." He saw my face and shook his head. "Nothing sinister. Just bad luck. There was a car accident when I was twenty-five. Dad was killed instantly and my mother lingered on with back issues for a few years. I think it was her pleading with Althea from her deathbed that changed things. I was invited to a few functions and I ignored them for a while. But when I got the fourth invitation eight years ago, I just decided, what the hey? I wasn't going to let some stupid thing I did as a kid spoil the chance for Derrick to meet and spend time with the rest of his family. I already felt guilty for keeping Cory away from them for so many years."

"How has it been?" Darlene asked.

"Better now, but it was rough at first. Mostly just awkward. At least with everyone but Bruce. He never said a word to me after that night."

"That is one impressive cold shoulder."

"Everyone says he took after his father. Had his own sense of right and wrong and nothing could change his mind."

"Did anything happen between you two this weekend?" I asked.

"No. The usual frosty treatment from him, that's all."

"Does your wife know why he wouldn't talk to you?"

"Of course." Liam looked shocked that I would suggest anything else.

"What was your relationship with Tracy like?"

Liam's face turned red and anger flashed in his eyes. "I

hope you aren't suggesting that we continued to have a... romantic relationship." I tried to look innocent and shrugged my shoulders. "We did not! We were just stupid kids, that's all. We talked about it a couple of times. She told me it traumatized her to see her father act like that. Tracy told me that she felt like Bruce never fully trusted her again."

We asked him a few more questions, then let him get back to his family. Reliving old tensions had taken a toll on him. He walked with slumped shoulders and a slow gait down to the tent.

"What do you think?" I asked Darlene when he was gone.

"Family secrets. They can fester."

"Maybe jealous Austin got worked up over the past, or even a current, affair between his wife and Liam. There was a big fight and Tracy and Austin ended up dead. The rest of the family feels guilty about what happened, so they cover it up for Liam and his family's sake."

"Seems like a stretch that they would take a chance of Paula getting convicted of murder in order to protect Liam."

"Maybe. Maybe they also thought it sounded less scandalous. You know, less incest-y."

"So then Bruce refuses to go along with it and Liam kills him?"

"It makes a strange kind of sense."

"Except for that trip down to the wildlife refuge."

"True, except for that. If their alibi checks out, then it would be hard to see how he's involved. Would you..."

"Sure, I'll check out his alibi. I've got a friend who works as a ranger down there."

"I brought lunch," I said with a grin as we reached my car.

"What?" Darlene asked suspiciously.

"Tex-Mex delight picked up from your favorite taco truck."

"Tell me you didn't leave it in your car."

"I'm not that stupid. No, I left it at the cabin where Cara

and I are staying. In the refrigerator," I emphasized.

"You're smarter than the average bear. Lead on, MacDuff," she said, and followed me down to the cabin.

"Decorated in early *Texas Chainsaw*," she observed when we were inside. I turned on the window air conditioner and stood in front of it for a few minutes, letting the air dry my sweat stains.

We divided up the food, warmed it in the junior-size microwave and settled in for a late lunch. I told her everything I'd learned from Albert Griffin that morning.

"You realize that this is an investigative pit. The deeper you dig, you just wind up with more dirt," Darlene told me.

"I won't lie. It does feel that way."

"I didn't learn anything that you don't already know. I talked to about half the people on the list. I didn't see any red flags from Myron and Ellie. If there's a chance of breaking this open, it's going to come when we interview Paula or Marty."

"I agree. What did the caretaker, Sam, have to say?"

"He backed up Bruce and Owen. They went out and checked on the dogs before going into the woods and tending to their feed plots. He came across as neutral. Just a man who works here. Ten years, a professional with a degree in forestry. Worked for the state for a few years out of college before deciding that the pay sucked and taking this job."

"Same impression I got. The alibis are killing us."

"Do you think Paula will let us interview Marty?"

"I don't know. If we push her too hard this afternoon, she'll probably shut down. That would include doing everything she can to close off our access to Marty."

"So why not flip it around and talk to Marty first?" Darlene suggested.

"Makes sense."

"Then how much pressure we bring to bear on Paula will depend on what we learn from Marty."

"Exactly. Great minds think alike," I said, finishing my

iced tea.

"This great mind has an interview for the chief's job," Darlene said.

"Oh no. Seriously, you can't go work for the city."

"More money, more responsibility and a nice title to go on my CV."

"I know," I groaned, wanting to talk the job down but knowing that it wasn't fair. "Do what you have to do. When is it?"

"Monday. My source tells me they've set up interviews with five candidates."

"I'm going to vacillate between wishing you luck and trying to figure out a way to sabotage your interview."

"That's what friends are for," Darlene said with a bright smile.

Paula agreed to let us talk with Marty as long as someone else from the family was allowed to sit in. I was sure that she wished her father could have been there to help navigate the legal angles, but in the end Bernadette agreed to sit in as Marty's advocate.

"You realize I'll put a stop to it the minute I think you're pressuring him or taking advantage of his naiveté," Bernadette told us point-blank.

"Fair enough," I agreed.

We decided to conduct the interviews in the dining room of the main house. Marty, sitting across the table from us with Bernadette to his right, looked like he hadn't slept since Monday. Who could blame him?

"Marty, I just want you to go over everything that happened Monday as slowly and as completely as you can. We're going to record this interview so no one will be mistaken about what is said."

"All right," he said softly, his eyes down and looking at a spot about halfway across the table from us. His voice was strained as he described finding Austin strangling Tracy and his mother attacking his uncle.

"Did your mother make a phone call after Austin was unconscious?" I asked.

"I think so."

"Who did she call?"

"Uncle Bruce."

"Was that before or after you called 911?"

"Before."

"Do you know what they talked about?"

"She was just crying a lot. Trying to tell him what happened."

"Why didn't *she* call 911?"

"I don't know."

"Who told you to call 911?"

"I don't remember. Mom and Grandpa, maybe Myron too."

I noticed that he was uncomfortable talking about the phone calls, so I had him repeat his answers a couple of times. Marty was laconic, but cooperative. We let him go and asked Bernadette to tell Paula that we were ready for her.

Paula looked dreadful. There were dark shadows under her eyes and her hair was greasy and unwashed. Her hands were shaking a little. She appeared to have aged ten years in three days.

"How is Marty?" she asked before we had a chance to pose a question.

"He was okay," Darlene said.

"He hardly speaks to me." A tear rolled down Paula's cheek.

"Marty is going to need time emotionally to deal with the events he witnessed. He's had his world turned upside down. I'd suggest you encourage him to talk to someone," Darlene said gently.

"I already have the names of a couple of counselors that friends have suggested. I didn't have any choice."

The last part of her statement confused me. "What didn't you have a choice about?"

"Hitting Austin. He was killing Tracy."

"Take me back to when you entered the cottage."

Paula told essentially the same story she had on the day of the murder.

"Tell us what you did after you hit Austin the second time," I encouraged.

"Some of it is fuzzy. I couldn't think. Seeing my sister under that man. I know I pulled on her and she was… gone. The horror of looking at my sister's face. I blacked out for a minute or two." Paula began to weep.

Darlene brought her a glass of water and a tissue.

"Did you do anything with Austin?" I asked, once Paula had regained some of her composure.

"Like what?" She seemed puzzled by the question.

"Feel for a pulse. Try and stop the bleeding. Anything."

Paula blinked twice, staring at a point over my shoulder. "I never thought about him at all," she said bluntly.

"What did you do next?" Darlene pushed.

"I called Daddy."

I wanted to ask her why she hadn't called 911, but I didn't want to put her on the defensive. We just needed to hear what she did rather than try to convince her that her impulses were wrong.

"What did you tell him?" I asked.

"That Tracy was dead and I'd killed Austin."

"Are you sure you said that you killed him?"

"Yes."

"How did you know he was dead?" I didn't point out the fact that he *hadn't* been dead yet.

"I meant to kill him," she said flatly, causing me to look into her eyes to see if they were dilated. I was thinking that she looked and sounded like someone on drugs. I wouldn't have blamed her if she'd taken a sedative. I was pretty sure that any doctor would have prescribed them for her after what she'd been through. However, her eyes were clear, yet distant, like a part of her mind was somewhere else because it was too painful to be in the present.

"Did you tell your father anything else?" I asked.

"I told him I needed help."

"What did he say?"

"He told me to call 911. I told him again that Tracy was dead and that's when he asked to speak to Marty. Daddy got Marty to call an ambulance."

We asked a few more questions about Tracy and Austin, but she didn't add anything of substance to what we already knew. So we moved on and asked her about the night her father had died. Again, nothing new came out. Paula seemed even more foggy about that day, which made sense. She had still been in shock from Monday. I couldn't blame her, but it also didn't help us. Hell, for all we knew, it was an act. I didn't really believe that Paula was playing us, but I couldn't prove she wasn't.

CHAPTER EIGHTEEN

By the time we were done with the interviews, it was close to four o'clock. I was getting ready to suggest that we head back to the cabin to discuss what, if anything, we'd learned, when Ruby appeared at the doorway.

"Mrs. Byrd would like to see you," she said, looking at me. I turned to Darlene and Ruby added, "Her too."

We went upstairs to find Althea in her usual chair. I wondered how mobile she was. Could she walk unassisted? Did she need a walker or a wheelchair? I hadn't seen either one, but maybe Ruby kept them out of sight.

"Learn anything?" she asked without waiting to be introduced to Darlene.

"Deputy Marks and I have been conducting a number of interviews and background checks," I said stiffly. I was irritated by her attitude, or maybe I was just getting frustrated with my own lack of progress.

"Seems to me that you do a lot of talking and not much doing," Althea groused. "There."

She pointed to a table by the door, where I saw a folder lying on the marble top.

"That's my will. I figure you're wondering about it."

Darlene was closer to the table than I was, so she reached

out and took the folder. We all waited in silence while she flipped through it.

"Seems pretty standard," Darlene said.

"Everything is split evenly between my children. 'Course, there's only one left now." I doubt she'd have admitted it, but she choked up for a moment before she could continue. "There's a provision for the grandchildren, and a little bit for the cousins and other sundry hangers-on. Even-steven, but they'll still fight over it like the rats they are. I figure you've been thinking that the money might be a motive. Maybe. There's certainly more for those who remain, that's the truth. I don't have much use for my family, but I don't like the thought that someone is out there killing them off. Especially on my property while I'm sitting right here."

"Like I told you before, if someone is committing murder, we'll catch them."

"If you don't, then I'll find someone who will," she growled.

From the look she gave us, it was clear that Althea considered the meeting over. I wasn't ready to go quite yet.

"Can you think of another possible motive for the killings?" I asked, staring at her.

"No."

"How about Jack's death?"

As soon as the name was out of my mouth, I saw her face turn red and her expression grew furious. "I don't know what you mean by that," she said through clenched teeth.

I thought about pushing her. I was right on the edge of telling her that I thought Jack's death was suspicious, but I stopped myself. Althea could order me off of the property, which would make things very awkward. With three ongoing death investigations, she couldn't keep us away, but she could hinder our access not just to the property, but to the witnesses. I was sure that if she told them not to talk to us, most of the family and employees would be glad to clam up.

"I'm just being thorough," I said nicely.

Darlene and I said our awkward goodbyes, then escaped

from the house.

"That's a freight train in a wig," Darlene said with a shake of her head, once we were off the porch. "Why do you think she showed us the will?"

"I think she's scared. Not for herself. But for all of her tough talk, I think she really does care about some, if not all, of her family."

"She sure got hot when you mentioned Jack."

"There's something there that she doesn't want exposed. Whether it has anything to do with the recent deaths, I don't have a clue."

We stopped by Darlene's car. "Your thoughts on Paula and Marty?" I asked her.

"Marty's hiding something to do with those phone calls."

"You noticed that too."

"When you mentioned 911, his eyes started darting around like he expected you to pull out the handcuffs right there."

"Paula?"

"Strange. I didn't get deception as much as confusion."

"You think she's blocking out her memories?"

"Or she saw or heard a piece of the puzzle that she can't fit in with what she thinks happened."

"Looking at the whole picture, what's your take?" I asked, hoping for a different perspective.

"Still just random acts. Austin attacked Tracy and then Paula clubbed the shit out of him. A couple of days later, Paula's father dies of an accidental or suicidal overdose of prescription medication."

"Odds that it didn't happen that way?" I asked.

"Eight out of ten, it went down just the way everyone says."

"The trouble is, I can't let it go." I shook my head, puzzled over my own intransigence.

"Don't make us do an intervention," Darlene warned.

"No promises." I took a deep breath. "One more day. Nothing turns up, I'll come home with my tail between my legs."

"I'd say that's a reasonable plan. I'll check up on Liam and his alibi."

"Thanks."

There was a rumble of thunder in the distance that caused both of us to look toward the southern horizon. Dark clouds were moving up from the Gulf for one of our usual summer afternoon thunderstorms.

After Darlene left, I went down to the cabin and logged onto my laptop. Among the emails was one from Beth in records. She'd sent me a link to a secure folder where she'd placed all of the background information she'd gathered.

A quick review told me that there weren't any bombshells in the documents. I would have liked to run everyone's credit histories, but I'd need some evidence before I started digging into the witnesses' personal finances.

Witnesses. I couldn't even really call any of them suspects. Except for Paula. But she wasn't a suspect either. She was a perpetrator, and she'd never denied killing Austin. *This is crazy*, I told myself.

That's when I got the phone call from Dad.

"You need to know how thin the ice is that you're standing on," he said.

"Okay." I could tell by his voice that he was deadly serious, so I quashed the jokes that had come to mind.

"Johnson called me around noon to give me an ultimatum. I can't continue to cater to your habit of going around him to get what you want."

"Come on. You were already out here and—"

"I told him I'm as much to blame as you are. Past and present. What I hate is that he's right. It's not fair to him or to you."

"I haven't meant to be disrespectful."

"I know that. I think *he* might even realize that. But what I *can* tell you is that he means what he says. I'm not going to risk losing a man as good as Lt. Johnson. To be honest, he's on the short list to replace Major Parks when the day comes."

"I didn't mean to cause you any problems."

"You have through tomorrow. If you can get some proof that there's more going on out at the Byrd farm than meets the eye, you take it to Johnson and he'll decide how to proceed."

"Understood. Does this have anything to do with what you've been trying to talk to me about?" I asked.

There was a long pause on the other end of the phone before he answered. "No. We'll discuss that later." Before I could ask anything else, he hung up.

By the time Cara got back from work, I'd convinced myself that I was only going to do a minimal amount of digging the next day. If nothing turned up by noon, I'd call it done and let the State Attorney decide what to do about Paula.

"It's going to pour down rain," Cara said when she came through the door. "Ah, home sweet home."

She gave me a big smile and I pulled her in for a kiss, timing it with a flash of lightning that was followed seconds later by a roar of thunder that signaled the approaching storm's arrival.

"You're in a good mood," I told her.

"How's the investigation going?"

"It's not. But that's okay. I've been chewed out by Lt. Johnson for going around the chain of command, and Dad let me know in no uncertain terms that it has to stop. So I'm on notice to finish this up or convince Johnson that it's worth pursuing. Unless something slaps me upside the head, this will be over tomorrow."

"Good for you. So there isn't a Jason or a Freddie stalking the woods of Camp Byrd?"

"I think I was just seeing every discrepancy as a lie and any coincidence as evidence of a nefarious plot."

"Nice. So now we can cuddle up in our cabin and enjoy the thunderstorm."

We enjoyed the hell out of it for a little while as inches of rain came down, making a thunderous din on the metal roof. We started on one of the bunk beds, but ended up on the floor in a tangle of blankets and naked limbs.

Later, we sat eating sandwiches and drinking beer as the last of the rain drizzled down. In the west, the sky was clearing and bright orange and red colors flared through the window.

"I talked to Dr. Horvath," Cara said with a twinkle in her eyes.

"About what?"

"Running the business side of her practice."

"Really?" I wasn't sure about this, but it was clear that Cara was excited and I didn't want to rain on her parade.

"When you told me she'd been robbed, and then how much she didn't like doing all the ordering and everything, I thought, 'Hell, that's what I do for the clinic. I could handle hers too.'"

"Can you?"

"Sure! Once I get everything organized, it won't be that bad."

"Dr. Horvath was interested?"

"She was excited and really liked the idea of turning over all the stuff she hates to someone else to deal with. I can save her money too."

"You didn't oversell it, did you?"

Cara gave me a look that made me worry I'd been too critical, but she turned it into a smile. "How much you want to bet that I can do it? I know I can save her enough money to pay my fees and leave her with money left over."

"Fees?"

"You didn't think I was doing this out of the goodness of my heart, did you? I told her we could agree on the exact amount after I've had a chance to look at her books and the rest of her business."

"Wow! That's all I can say."

"Wow, good?" She brought her face in so close that our noses were almost touching.

"Wow, great. I'm impressed." I meant it and kissed her to prove it.

A minute later, she brought up the one thing that was tugging at the back of my brain.

"Did you ever find out what your dad wants to talk to you about?"

"No. I tried to bring it up after he read me the riot act, but he just shut me down. As soon as I close up shop here, I'll corner him and find out what all the mystery is about."

There was a knock at the door and I opened it to see Jessie holding half of a cake.

"Bernadette thought y'all might like some. Her mom made it and sent it over. It's really pretty good. Caramel apple upside-down cake or something like that."

"Looks good. You want a piece?" Cara asked, taking the cake from Jessie.

"I already had one. Thanks."

"Have you been keeping your promise?" I asked her.

"Pretty much. I can't help listening and looking, though."

"Can't argue with that," I told her. I thought about Eddie's apparent infatuation with her and wondered if it was mutual.

"How's Eddie doing?" Cara asked as though she'd read my mind.

"He's a freak, but I kind of like that," Jessie said, and her eyes went to the ground. I figured Eddie had a chance.

After Jessie left, we sat on the couch with the windows open and listened to the frogs chirping in the pond. The spooky call of a Great Horned Owl shocked them into silence for a split second, then the chorus started up again.

"This does feel a bit like a scene from *Friday the 13th*," Cara joked.

"Oh my God! We had sex! We're doomed!" I joked, pulling her over on top of me.

"I don't think the rules apply to married people."

"You're right. No one in those movies is ever married," I said, hugging her tightly.

"They're all under twenty," she laughed. "Not old like you."

"Why, I ought to…" I gave her a serious kiss. "Enough. It's time for this deputy dog to go to bed."

I slept the sleep of the just until my phone went off at four in the morning. When I saw that it was Bernadette, I was instantly wide awake.

"Bernadette, what's wrong?"

"Dad's missing."

"What do you mean by missing?"

"He went off looking for those two hunting dogs he brought with him and he hasn't come back. We tried his phone and it goes straight to voicemail."

"I'll be right there."

CHAPTER NINETEEN

Ten minutes later, I found Bernadette standing in the doorway of her cabin, a flashlight in one hand and a phone in the other.

"Why did your dad go looking for the dogs in the middle of the night?" I asked.

"They're a friend's dogs. Besides, they're pretty valuable."

"How long has he been gone?"

"We're not sure. The dogs probably got out during the storm. Dad texted Mom about it at nine o'clock. She wasn't paying much attention, but I'll cut her some slack 'cause she's having to deal with Debbie, who's been inconsolable."

"We'll find him," I said, trying to be reassuring.

"I should have been keeping a better eye on him," she fretted.

"What's been done so far?"

"Jessie and I have looked around. He's been staying at the main house and we went up there, but Ruby says they haven't seen him since they went to bed at ten. Mom thinks he got himself so worked up worrying about the dogs that he couldn't sleep. He's like that."

"Is anyone else helping you look?"

"Sam. I got him up. He said he'd take the ATV and

search the trails for him."

"Good. Where do you think your father would go to look for the dogs?"

"That's just it. The dogs are wearing GPS collars. He can track them on his phone, so he might have just headed off into the woods after them."

"At night?"

"He's a hunter. He was a *great* hunter when I was growing up. That's one of the reasons he did so well selling land. He had a reputation. If he told some rich guy from Tampa that they were looking at prime hunting land, they had every reason to believe him. Ten years ago, I wouldn't have worried about him. He could go out hunting coons at night and never get lost. But now…"

"If he's got his phone to track the dogs, then he can call if he gets lost or just use the GPS to find his way back here," I suggested hopefully.

"I don't know. He's not answering his phone and, honestly, he's not very tech savvy. Hell, *I'm* not." She was tearing up out of fear and frustration. "For all I know, Dad might not have charged his phone in days. What if he got out in the middle of the woods and it died on him?"

"We'll find him," I said again. "You say he's an experienced outdoorsman. The weather is warm. He'll be fine." The nagging voice in the back of my mind was asking how it was possible that yet another unfortunate event had struck this family. I tried to focus. "I don't think a bunch of us going off into the woods right now is going to help. Let's get a few more of the adults up and we'll search the areas around all the buildings. Let's eliminate the possibility that he's fallen somewhere near the house."

"What about a full-scale search?"

"If the weather conditions were hazardous, then we might need to start searching before daylight. But we would be trampling any tracks that might be useful when the sun comes up. Sam is searching what he can on the ATV, and I'm sure he's stopping every so often and listening for your father. If we have a bunch of people traipsing through the forest, that would just make it more difficult to hear your father if he's calling for help."

"I guess that makes sense," Bernadette said, though she clearly didn't like it.

"Did he take a gun with him?"

"I don't know."

"Go see if you can tell. There's that case filled with some nice shotguns up in the main house. Maybe he took one of those."

"I'll check."

"Also try and figure out what he might be wearing." Giving her some jobs to do would help to focus her mind. "I'll go around and knock on doors."

I went to Olivia and Liam's camp. The young folk were in tents right behind the family's. I thought some young ears and eyes might be of help. Besides, it would be best to get them on board now rather than have them find out when I wasn't around. I didn't want them running around messing up evidence if this turned out to be a long-term search.

I woke Liam first and tried not to make too much noise. There wasn't any reason to stir up Derrick and Olivia. I needn't have bothered. As soon as the words were out of my mouth, everyone was awake.

I stood outside Liam's tent and waited for everyone to put on some clothes. In the glow of my flashlight, I could see movement from the two tents for the young adults. I could guess what was happening. No doubt they were supposed to be divided up, males in one tent and females in the other. I suspected they weren't maintaining that order and were hurrying to regroup themselves before anyone noticed.

"Owen is missing. He went out looking for his hunting dogs approximately four hours ago," I told the group when they had all gathered in front of the tents.

"You mean the old guy went out into the woods in the middle of the night?" Liam asked, sounding shocked at the idea.

"We think he was following the dogs' GPS signal on his phone."

"I guess Bernadette's already tried calling him," Liam muttered to himself.

"We can go look for him," Cory and Andy said, almost in unison. Cory was already ducking back into their tent to get flashlights.

"Hold up. If we don't find him soon, we'll probably bring out a search party in the morning. What we don't want to do is take a chance of messing up the trail. Until the sun comes up, we're going to stay near the house and cottages."

"He could be hurt," Rochelle said.

"Sam is searching the trails that he can access on his ATV. There's not a whole lot more we can do while it's dark," I explained.

"What good is it to look around the houses?"

"He could have fallen or passed out. He wasn't doing well the other day," I reminded them.

Andy and his gang had their flashlights in hand and set off to check the immediate area. I asked Liam to explain the situation to Ellie and Myron, while I went back to Bernadette's cabin to find Jessie.

"Do you know where the dog pens are?" I asked her.

"I do. Cleo and I stay clear of there 'cause the dogs start barking and howling whenever they see her. They probably think she's a deer." Cleo was lying on the couch looking unhappy with all of the middle-of-the-night kerfuffle.

"I want to take a look at the pens."

They were located clear on the other side of the property, near a massive pole barn that housed a couple of tractors, as well as an assortment of farm implements. Without the barking of the dogs, it took Jessie a while to locate the kennels in the dark. There were about a dozen open runs.

"There's the run they were sharing," she said, pointing to one on the end which had a couple of aluminum bowls and other evidence that dogs had recently been kept there.

I got down close to the door of the run. They all had concrete floors and were constructed out of chain link. There was a roof that had been built against the pole barn that afforded the kennels protection from rain and sun. As I looked at the door, it was clear how the dogs had wiggled out.

"See this?" I pointed to an area where the chain link had come loose.

"How did that happen?"

"Good question. The front panel was wired to the sides here and here." I pointed out two places where a loose wire still hung on the links.

"Did a dog do that?"

"To my eye, these look like they've been cut. But see here. It looks like one of the dogs might have been chewing on the fencing and left these marks." There were a number of scratches and gouges that might have been the result of an animal tearing at the metal.

"What do you think?"

"Like everything else in the last week, I can't say for sure." I almost growled in frustration. "I just want one solid piece of evidence to hang my hat on."

"That's a ridiculous phrase."

"I don't think so. It means I want a hook. Makes perfect sense to me."

"Whatever," Jessie said contemptuously, proving once again that she had an uncanny ability to irritate me.

"Come on. Let's head back up to the house."

When we got there, several members of the family were milling about. I looked up at Althea's room and, sure enough, the lights were on. I wondered how long it would be before I received another summons to the royal bedchamber.

"Has anyone found anything?" I asked.

There was general headshaking all around. In the distance, I saw Andy, Roch and the other two looking around the old summer kitchen. Marty was sitting in the dark on the porch. The group looked like they were talking with him. I wanted to know what they were saying, but I knew that if I went over there, the dynamics would shift and all I would hear was what they wanted me to hear. I took a deep breath and made a decision.

"How well do you know Andy and that bunch?" I asked Jessie.

"We've hung out a little since I've been here."

"I'm not asking you to spy for me, but would you mind going over there? Listen to what they're talking about with Marty, then let me know," I said so quietly that no one else could hear.

"Sure, I'll go spy on them," Jessie said with a smirk and sauntered off toward them. I sighed and turned back to the others.

"Anyone who wants to go back to bed, you can. We won't be doing much more until the sun comes up." I looked at my watch. "Which won't be for another couple of hours."

Liam and Ellie started back toward their respective campsites. Bernadette was about twenty-five yards away, talking on the phone. I assumed she was talking to her mother and was proven right when I got near enough to hear her side of the conversation.

"No, Mom, don't come out here now. Wait until morning. I know. Yes. You've been drinking. I know, I'm a smart-mouth. That doesn't change the facts. I understand that you've been cooped up there with Debbie. That's another reason you shouldn't come out here tonight. Do you really want to wake her up? Well, you can't just leave her alone. I know she's not your responsibility. Everyone appreciates what you've done. I know that Dad is your husband. We've done everything we can at this point. They'll mount a big rescue party tomorrow." Bernadette noticed me standing nearby and dramatically rolled her eyes skyward.

"I'd like to talk to her," I said and Bernadette whispered her thanks.

"Mom, the deputy who talked to you the other day, he wants to ask some questions. Yes, he's right here." She handed me the phone before shaking her arm to get the blood circulating again.

"Mrs. Byrd, I want to ask about the last contacts you had with your husband."

"Oh, please don't say that. I hope they weren't the last contacts," Karen said with a slight slurring of her words.

"I'm optimistic," I said, not wanting to promise too much. "Did you talk to your husband this evening?"

"Once. He was very upset about those damn dogs."

"What time was the call?"

"Maybe nine, around then."

"Try to remember what he said."

"He didn't say anything that would tell you where he is now. What does this have to do with finding my husband? Do you think he told me where he was going to go?" Her voice was a mix of alcohol and hysteria.

"I'm just trying to be thorough. Please, if you can remember, I'd like to know what he said. Maybe there's a clue we can use."

"He just said he was worried about the dogs. The dogs belong to his friend. Valuable. He told me they're worth thousands. Though it wasn't the money. He couldn't face his friend again if the dogs were lost."

"If they're hunting dogs, aren't they pretty good about coming back?" I knew a lot of guys who had hunting dogs, but I didn't know much about running them.

"These dogs are real young. That was the reason Owen brought them with him. I don't think he thought they'd be lost forever, just long enough that he'd have to admit to his friend that he'd lost them. Really, the dogs were just part of it. He's broken up about his brother and what's happened to his nieces. He told me he'd have to get Paula out from under all this mess. I... think... he was close to a nervous breakdown," she stammered.

Thinking about his physical collapse on Wednesday, I

didn't doubt that she was right.

"Did you have any contact with him after that?"

"Contact? He sent me a couple of texts."

"Can you read them to me?"

"They don't say much. I'll have to figure out how to talk on the phone and look at the texts. Hold on." I could hear fumbling and a few slurred curse words until she managed to put the phone on speaker and pull up her text messages. "First one says: *I'm tracking them on the phone. Frustrating.* I texted back that he should ask Sam to go after the dogs and he responded: *Don't want to bother the man. They'll be fine until morning.* I just said good. Then about eleven he texted and said he wasn't able to sleep and was going after them. I said that was stupid. He texted: *I can do this. Easy following the GPS.* I asked him to let me know when he got back. That's all."

"And that was the last you heard from him?"

"Nothing since. I've tried calling a dozen times. Finally I called Dottie." She was crying now.

"The weather is very mild. He'll be fine. Probably his phone's battery just died."

I went on to assure her we'd get some search and rescue teams out at first light. The fact that Owen wasn't in the best of health would make my argument for that easier.

CHAPTER TWENTY

I went to my car and used its laptop to pull up the property appraiser's website and look at maps of the property around the Byrd farm. There was a wildlife management area adjoining the east side of the farm and two timber tracts that covered thousands of acres to the west. My best guess was that Owen Byrd could have been lost somewhere in about ten thousand acres. I was putting a lot of faith in his woodsman skills.

If there isn't foul play involved, of course, my annoying little voice said. I banged the steering wheel with the palm of my hand and cursed the voice. This was maddening. Maybe the Byrds *were* just cursed. *That would explain everything,* my sleep-deprived mind agreed.

Half an hour before the sun came up, I called Dad.

"This can't be good," he answered.

"You got that right. Owen Byrd is missing."

"Which one is that?" I couldn't blame him for having a hard time keeping track of all the players.

"He's the last remaining son of Althea Byrd." I went on to describe the events of the night.

"I thought you were staying out there in order to *prevent* any more bad stuff from happening?" Dad grumbled. "Get off me. I've got to get up." I knew the last bit was directed at Mauser. I'd had my own experiences with the world's largest bed hog.

"We're going to need some deputies on the ground. If you'd call up the search and rescue volunteers and make an official request for assistance, that would be a big help."

"Johnson."

"I don't have time—"

"And I don't want to argue about this anymore. There is a chain of command and Lt. Johnson is who you need to call first. Didn't we just talk about this yesterday?"

"Yes, but this is special—"

"And that's the problem. The reality is, a lot of what deputies do is life and death. Forget it. Call him or not. Work it out. I don't want to lose either one of you. And you're probably both right. So grow up and figure out how to make it work."

"Understood," I said through clenched teeth. It didn't make me feel one bit better that he was right.

I called the lieutenant, hoping he was an early riser.

"Johnson," came his usual greeting.

"I'm at the Byrd farm. Owen Byrd is missing," I said and went on to explain what had happened.

"He's lost in the woods and had a physical breakdown the other day? He's a senior whose health puts him at added risk. Issue a silver alert, then contact search and rescue."

He was being civil, so I thought I'd push the envelope a little. "Could you contact Leon County and see if we can have some time with Air One?" I asked.

The silence stretched out long enough to make me nervous, but then to my surprise, he said, "I'll call."

I felt like we'd made progress. "Thank you. I wouldn't be pushing this investigation if I didn't believe that there's something malicious behind all of this," I said as firmly as I could.

There was more silence on the other end of the line, then Johnson finally said, "Then fight for it. Even if you have to fight me." With that, he hung up.

I made a few other calls, then got out of the car and walked down to Bernadette's cabin. I was going to appoint her the official family liaison. For everyone's sake, I thought her mother should be kept as far away from the farm as possible. A loose cannon like that could do a lot to hinder a search effort.

"Tell me this isn't connected to my uncle's or cousin's death," Bernadette said as she let me into the cabin. She looked so tired that I had second thoughts about my plan to have her spearhead the family's interests.

I told her that the sheriff's office was going to send in as much cavalry as we could, which perked her up some.

"We can do this. I'm sure Dad is fine," she said, almost like a yoga mantra.

"Do you feel up to being the point person for the family?"

"Who else could do it?"

"Thank you. If it gets to be too much…"

"I'll help her," Jessie said from the small kitchen, where she was feeding Cleo. Having spent so much time around the bullish Mauser, I was always impressed with Cleo's manners. She sat politely, waiting for Jessie to tell her it was okay to eat. Only a single strand of drool stretching down from her jowls testified to how much she wanted her breakfast.

"You'll want to post yourself up at the main house where you can be more accessible. The search and rescue teams will set up in the parking area."

"The sooner they start looking, the better."

"I want to talk with Sam."

We found him at the pole barn, pouring gas into an ATV. There were two others nearby that he was also getting ready.

"I figured we could use all the four-wheelers we got," he said as he lifted the can away from the fully gassed machine.

"Have you looked at the dog pen?"

"Yep. I don't believe it."

"I could see marks where the dogs could have chewed their way out," I said, playing devil's advocate.

"No way. We've kept dogs in those pens for ten years. Ever since I came to work here."

"I understand these are young dogs who haven't been here before."

He looked at me like I was an idiot.

"Okay, then, what's your thought?"

"Somebody let them out," Sam said flatly.

I wanted to cheer that someone was finally seeing this from my perspective, but then I reminded myself that Sam had a motive for suggesting there might be someone else involved. If the dogs had gotten out, then he could be blamed for not keeping a good eye on them. His insistence on a culprit might have just been a way of deflecting guilt away from himself.

"Let's set aside how the dogs got out. Where do you think they would go?"

"They might chase the scent of a deer. They're being trained to track deer. After the thunderstorm, the air would have been wet, which helps to carry and hold the scent."

"You think the dogs will come back?"

"I'd have expected them to be back by now. But since they're young, you never know. They can go for miles, and there're still some pretty thick areas where we've got trees down from last year's storm."

"Why do you think Owen went after the dogs by himself?"

"He's stubborn. A good man and a good hunter, but he overestimates himself. He's crapped out on hunts a couple of times in the last few years. Still thinks he's forty years old."

I told him that search and rescue would be arriving shortly.

"I know all the trails. I'll take them anywhere they want to go," he said. "There's no reason we shouldn't be able to find him."

I wondered what shape Owen would be in when and if we *did* find him.

My phone rang. "You've got incoming. They're going to need you on the radio," a dispatcher told me.

When I got to my car, I saw Cara walking up from our cabin dressed for work. Without saying a word, we hugged each other close.

"Tell me this isn't connected," Cara said.

I threw up my hands. "I don't know."

"Just seems crazy."

"Maybe he'll be found safe and sound and all this will be—" My radio blared.

"I'd better go," Cara said. "Let me know if I can do anything. I can bring food from town if y'all need it."

The call on the radio was from the first of the search and rescue volunteers. "We need the gate open." I gave them the code, thinking that I needed to ask Sam to rig the gates open. We'd have people coming and going all day.

By nine o'clock we had several teams out in the field. Each one was led by someone well versed in tracking. The point was to make sure that any virgin trails were covered for clues before they were roughed up by volunteers.

Leon County gave us two hours with their helicopter. At ten-thirty, one of the teams on foot found the dogs. They were tired, but happy when they were brought back to the kennels by Sam. I met him there, and we gave the dogs a good once-over.

"They're fine," he said, ruffling the ears of the larger of the two dogs. "Good all-round dog. Hunting, herding, you name it."

I looked at the dogs, light brown except for the black around their muzzles. I would have taken them for mixed breeds, but I remembered that Owen had called them Black Mouth Curs. Both were wearing orange collars with small boxes attached that were maybe three inches long.

"That's the GPS transmitter?" I asked, pointing at one of the boxes. The dog lolled its head happily and tried to lick my hand.

"Yep. Those are good ones."

"How do they work?"

"They connect to your phone. The old ones just used a receiver, but with these you can track them on Google Maps."

"What if you don't have a cell signal?"

"Doesn't matter. Once you connect, it works without using cellular data."

"What's the range?"

"Line of sight, it's supposed to be eight, nine miles. Around here you get two or three miles."

"I guess you couldn't track where the dogs have been?"

"Not without Mr. Byrd's phone. He connected it with the dogs the day they got here. We took them out for a little test run. Dogs did great. Though it took us a while to get everything connected. I like the old ones. Less gadgety, if you know what I mean?"

We headed back to the RV that was being used as search headquarters. Phillip Pope, a short, broad-shouldered man in his late forties, was overseeing the operation. I'd worked with him a few times. He was a retired fire chief who knew what he was doing and could dole out compliments as quickly as he could reprimands. He wasn't stingy with either.

"Macklin. Your man must be pretty far off the beaten path," he said as Sam and I walked up.

"No luck?"

"We're bringing in the first teams for a break. Hot as blazes today." To emphasize his point, he ran his hand across his forehead and shook off the sweat.

I watched as two groups of volunteers came out of the woods and headed our way. I saw that Andy, Roch, Bridget and Cory had joined one of the teams. They seemed in better spirits than the older people they were with. When the teams got to the RV, Phillip explained that they had an hour and needed to make use of it, getting water, food and rest before they went back out.

Andy came over to where Sam and I were standing.

"We aren't really tired." He looked back at the others for confirmation. "We were wondering if we could take the ATVs out." He saw my expression of concern and read my mind. "We'll just stick to the road and the larger paths. I've got a few ideas from our hikes."

Phillip was standing nearby and had heard Andy.

"I'm okay with it. Just as long as they don't get off into the woods."

Sam pointed out two of the ATVs that were parked near the summer kitchen cottage.

A few minutes later I saw them riding toward the east where the woods were denser. They passed another group of searchers coming in, and I was surprised to recognize Darlene with the group.

"I don't know how I let you talk me into these things, Davey Crockett," she said, panting a little.

"You could have taken off your Kevlar vest first," I pointed out.

She panted some more. "I'm done for the day. They needed someone along as their evidence collector. Truth is, I didn't see much in the way of evidence. We picked up one Twix wrapper, but I think it'd been there for several days."

"You're my hero," I said and got the finger in return.

"You sure the old guy wandered off?" she asked me.

"As sure as I can be. His car's here. The dogs were loose and Karen, his wife, got a text saying he was going out to look for them."

"The spouse is always the prime suspect," Darlene reminded me, taking a bottle of water from a cooler.

"I don't think that's the case here. Besides, he might have done just what you said and wandered off."

"You don't think that for a minute." She lowered her voice and leaned in so no one else could hear. "You expect him to turn up dead, another victim of the Byrd curse."

"I don't need your sarcasm," I scolded.

"I checked and Liam's alibi holds up. My friend said that

someone signed the visitor's book with their name and address, and a ranger working the register in the gift shop recognized the picture of Liam that I texted over."

"I'm not surprised. That would have been a tough alibi to sustain if it was false. The boy and his mother would have had to support it." I realized that I'd forgotten to ask if Cory had been with them. I'd just assumed that he had stuck with his friends. I'd gotten to thinking of them as a group rather than as individuals.

Darlene moved to a spot in front of a fan under the RV awning.

"We can go inside," I offered.

"I'll be fine just as soon as I collapse from heat exhaustion." She took a deep swig of water from the bottle before pouring the last inch over her head. "Not pretty, but I'm not kidding about the heat."

When she was less red in the face, we made our way over to my car where we climbed in and I turned on the air conditioner.

"Okay, suspicious Sidney. What's your current breakdown of the situation?"

"Last night I was willing to call it all a series of most unfortunate occurrences."

"But now you've lost another man and you're back to thinking it's murder most foul."

"I wouldn't put it exactly like that. Finding Owen would help."

"If he's alive and well and just wandered off into the woods, are you going to abandon this whole Don Quixote crusade?"

"Yes, until the lab reports come back, at which time I'll reassess the cases."

"And if he's found dead?"

"I guess that would depend on the cause of death. Obvious murder would put me on track to investigating everything that has happened out here as a possible serial event."

"And if he died of natural causes?"

"I'd lean eighty for twenty against abandoning the investigation until I find out more from the lab reports."

"You're lucky that Austin didn't have a lot of family, otherwise they'd be breathing down your neck to press charges against Paula."

"I'm laying that at the feet of the State Attorney. We've already had one conversation. He's good with me just providing him with the facts and my conclusion and he'll make his own determination."

"The lieutenant will be glad when you turn this over."

"He actually wasn't too much of an ass this morning."

"I've got a clue for you. Johnson gets up at four every morning and goes for a run. He's a morning person. He's in his best mood right after he gets back from his 5K."

"The man's a machine," I said respectfully. I knew he always ranked in the top five when we had our physical evaluations. I sighed. "You know what's really been pissing me off about this thing with Johnson?"

"That he's right?"

"You didn't have to agree so fast."

"You've been using your dad for years. It doesn't bother most of us, 'cause you're right most of the time, but, honestly, you've gone to the well a few too many times."

I was just about to make excuses for my past behavior when I heard a shout from one of the volunteers.

Darlene and I got out of the car and jogged over to Phillip's RV, where a woman was telling him that someone had found Owen Byrd.

"He's alive, but needs medical attention." The woman had eyes of steel and the way she snapped out the words made me think that she and Lt. Johnson probably had similar stories to tell.

"I want to see him," I jumped in before Phillip had a chance to ask any questions.

The woman gave me a *who-the-hell-are-you?* look.

"This is Deputy Macklin," Phillip explained. "Can he be

transported?"

"We have a vehicle en route to his location. The man who found him says that he's disoriented and unable to walk." She broke from her official voice and added, "Sounds like he's had a stroke." She turned to me. "They'll bring him here to the ambulance." She pointed to the ambulance that was already parked two cars away from mine.

"How long before they bring him out?"

"They just headed out to the location, which is about a mile and half east of here. He was found just off the road in a boggy area."

"I'll notify the family," I told them.

I found Bernadette sitting on the front porch of the farmhouse with Cleo resting her head on her thigh.

"They found him," I told her when I was close enough to be heard without shouting. "He's alive."

Bernadette started crying. "Thank God! I was so scared. I've got to call Mom."

I put my hand on her arm. "They think he's had a stroke."

"Oh." I watched as she tried to process the new information. "Then I better see him before I call Mom."

We walked over to the ambulance. The sky was overcast now, cutting some of the heat, but not the humidity. Cleo walked beside us, interested in all the people but focused on Bernadette.

Within ten minutes, a truck came out of the woods with two EMTs riding in the bed. Behind the truck were the ATVs driven by Andy and Cory. Roch was riding behind Andy while Bridget rode with Cory.

The truck parked next to the ambulance. The EMTs jumped down and started to ease a stretcher carrying Owen Byrd out of the truck. His eyes were darting around and his expression was confused. His clothes were covered in mud and leaves.

"Dad!" Bernadette shouted as she moved beside the stretcher. The EMTs were experienced at dealing with concerned relatives and gently nudged her out of their way as they carried him to the ambulance.

"Will he be okay?" she asked one of them.

"We can't say. Looks like he's had a stroke. The doctors at the hospital will be able to tell you more after they've examined him."

"I want to ride with him," Bernadette insisted.

"Yes, ma'am."

"I'll look after Cleo," I said.

Cleo gave Bernadette a gentle bump with her head. For a second, Bernadette turned to her and rubbed her ears gently before wiping away her tears and getting into the ambulance.

CHAPTER TWENTY-ONE

Andy, Roch, Cory and Bridget came over to me as the ambulance pulled away.

"He seemed in pretty bad shape when we found him," Andy said, concern in his voice.

"How did you find him?" I asked.

The other three were petting and making over Cleo.

"We were taking turns stopping and listening like they told us to do. Roch heard him."

"My hearing is really good. It was just a soft kind of moan," she said.

"How far off the road was he?"

"Not far. Fifty feet or so. He was bogged down. It was swampy and he was kind of held up by a cypress tree. If he'd fallen over, he could have drowned," Andy said.

"Lucky he didn't get bit by a water moccasin," Cory added.

"Did you mark the spot where you found him?"

They all looked at each other.

"We didn't think about that," Andy said, seeming a bit embarrassed that they hadn't.

"It's okay. You did the right thing by focusing on getting him medical attention. Follow me down to Bernadette's cabin. I'm going to leave Cleo there, then I want you to take me out to the spot where you found him."

I didn't know exactly why I wanted to look at the spot, but I knew that in a couple of days it might be heard to find again. Memory could be very tricky, even for twenty-year-olds.

They followed on the ATVs as Cleo and I walked ahead.

Jessie had been helping with the search and saw me heading down to the cabin with Cleo. She jogged to catch up, exchanging greetings with Andy and crew.

"They found him?"

"Yes. I'm heading out to look at the spot now. Can you watch Cleo?"

"Of course."

Cory and the two women agreed to stay with Jessie and Cleo while I took the other ATV and followed Andy into the woods.

While we bumped along the grassy trails, I tried to put this new incident into perspective. Was this just what it looked like? Even I couldn't come up with a way to twist it around. So why was I riding out to look at the spot where Owen had been found? For a sense of completion, maybe. Or I was going around the bend and seeing conspiracies and crimes where there were only accidents and bad luck.

Andy slowed to a stop and turned off his ATV.

"I'm pretty sure it's right up there. I don't want to add more tracks. It was muddy from last night's rain, so the area around the spot is already kind of messed up."

"Good thinking."

We got off the vehicles and I followed him sixty feet farther down the trail.

"We were trying to stop every hundred yards. Roch heard him when we turned off the four-wheelers. I didn't even hear it when she told me there was a sound. I couldn't hear the moaning until I got up here. I don't even think it was in response to us calling."

"How far off the trail was he?"

"Fifty feet, maybe. That way." Andy pointed out into the palmettos and pines on the south side of the trail. The ground was soggy. From the looks of it, there was probably water standing any time we weren't in drought conditions. "You want to go over there?"

I looked at the thick undergrowth and wished that I was wearing snake boots. "Yes," I said reluctantly.

I could see the spot where others had slid down off the raised trail. I stepped down and felt the water seep over the tops of my shoes, trying not to think about how many water moccasins there probably were in that swamp.

Andy pointed the way to a spot where there was a pond filled with cypress knees.

"He was right here." Andy pointed to the base of a cypress tree that looked to be one of the largest near the pond. It was easy to visualize poor Owen Byrd collapsing against the tree, where the cypress knees would have kept him propped up.

"He was a lucky man. Fortunate to have fallen here and very lucky that Rochelle heard him."

I heard a clicking sound and turned to see Andy pointing his phone at me.

"I hope you don't mind. This is one of the most interesting things that has ever happened to me. I guess that sounds stupid and callous."

"Maybe a little, but I think you can be forgiven. What do you do?"

"I'm in graduate school. I'd tell you my major, but it's sort of in flux. My undergraduate degree is in political science. That's the graduate program I got accepted into. But now I want to change it. Tough, though, after putting in so many hours and so much money. Of course, the money is all in the form of student loans."

"That's hard, but if you don't think you want to make a career of it, then it's better to change now than have regrets thirty years from now."

"That's what I'm thinking. I'm considering switching to

psychology. How'd you get to be a deputy?"

I was looking around the tree. I couldn't see any personal effects or any signs that Owen had been there. But what had I expected?

"My father is in law enforcement. Actually, he's the sheriff."

"Of this county?" Andy sounded amazed. "It must be weird to work for your dad."

"It can be a… challenge. What's your father do?"

"I don't know. He's dead. I never met him."

"I'm sorry."

"Don't worry about it. I managed. Though it's been tough. It's only been recently that I've finally felt like I'm getting my feet under me."

We started back to the trail. Looking around, I could see how easy it would be to become lost out here. I wondered if Owen had been lost *before* he had the stroke.

"Did you find a phone with him?"

"I didn't see one."

Maybe it had been in his pocket. I'd have to ask Bernadette. Owen's phone might answer a few questions. Or he could have dropped it out here, in which case it was probably lost forever.

When we got back to the parking area, only a few of the search and rescue folks were left and they were busy packing up supplies and equipment. I thanked Andy for taking me out to the spot where Owen had been found.

"Here, I'll send you that photo," he said, taking out his phone. In a second I heard my text alert. "You can send it to your wife." Andy smiled, then took off on the ATV.

I texted Bernadette and asked her to call me when she had an update on her father's condition. While I had the phone out, I texted the photo Andy had taken to Cara, knowing she'd appreciate it. I also gave her an update on the current situation.

"What's up, shortcake?" The voice caused me to jump.

"Don't sneak up on me like that," I told Darlene.

"Get your nose out of your phone. What are you going to do now?"

"I was just wondering the same thing."

"I know what the boss's advice would be."

"And I tend to agree. I have no proof…" I stopped when I saw Myron and Ellie walking toward me. Their kids were about four paces behind them, picking up pinecones off the ground and throwing them at each other.

"We'd like to leave," Myron said without any preamble.

"I can't stop you."

"So it's okay?"

I wanted to tell him that we needed him and his wife to stay put a while longer, but there was no way I could justify that. I was forced to come to terms with the fact that there was no investigation beyond Paula's justifiable homicide. My quixotic search for a killer was over.

"Yes. I have your phone number. I'll call you if I need more information. There's a possibility you might be required to come back and testify before a grand jury."

"Are you going to charge Paula?" Ellie asked.

"That's up to the State Attorney. With the evidence I have now, I would recommend that charges not be brought. But take that with a grain of salt. Until the lab reports come back, I can't make a final determination," I said diplomatically.

"Like you said, you've got our number." Myron nudged his wife and tipped his head to the side, indicating his desire to head back to their RV. They turned and pushed their kids along ahead of them.

"He sure seemed ready to get the hell out of Dodge," Darlene said, watching the family as they started to pack up their camper.

"Can you blame them?"

"You going to break camp?"

"Soon. I think I'll go down and talk to Liam and Olivia. Let them know they can go."

"I'm going back to work before I get a nasty call from

Johnson."

"I'm expecting one at any moment," I said with a grim smile.

I found Liam and Olivia breaking down their tent.

"Myron texted and said it was all right to leave," Liam said defensively.

"You're free to go. Not that I was holding you here."

"Now he tells us," Liam said to Olivia, who had her hands full of tent poles.

"I do have a couple more questions before you go."

They looked at me like I was a robocall on their phone. "What?" Liam asked.

"When you went to St. Marks, did Cory go with you?"

"Cory quit going on family trips when he was fifteen."

"Do you know what he did while you were gone?"

"Ask him. He's been hanging with Rochelle and Bridget," Olivia said.

"And that boyfriend of Rochelle's," said Liam. "What's his name? ...Andy."

"He seems like a nice enough guy," I said, wanting to see their reaction.

"I wouldn't disagree. We've been trying to talk Cory into taking college seriously and Andy's a pretty good role model for that. Kid is smart. Don't tell Cory we said that," Liam said.

I didn't know why I cared where Cory had been. It was just a loose end I wanted to tie up.

Liam dropped into a chair that hadn't been packed away yet. He looked at me. "You know, this week has ruined a lot of lives." His tone clearly suggested that his was one of them.

"How was your life hurt?"

"Beyond losing people I cared about, I lost the chance to truly become a full member of this family, to reclaim a... place within it. That's why we come to these get-togethers. Tracy is gone; Bruce is gone. I doubt Paula will ever be the same again. That old bat in the tower... Well, this will probably kill her, or at least suck out any humanity left in her. And Owen… I'll be surprised if he recovers."

"I don't know—" I started to say that you couldn't be sure. I'd seen a few stroke victims as a deputy, and they often had remarkable resilience. But he didn't give me the chance.

"He probably had that stroke last night. He went too long without treatment." Liam was wallowing in self-pity built up over many years.

"We need to get home," Olivia said in a voice as desperate as his. "Derrick!" she yelled.

"Coming!" he responded from the woods.

"Everyone going home?"

"You'd have to ask them. Cory said they might stay a couple more nights, then go down to Panama City. It *is* summer break." Liam stood and folded his chair.

"You said he doesn't go on trips with you anymore, so why did he come here?"

"He and the girls are good friends." He saw my look and gave me one back that clearly said: *Don't go there.* I looked away. It wasn't any of my business anyway.

I left the campsite and saw Bernadette's SUV heading down to the cabin. Jessie was driving.

"Bernadette asked me to pack up," she explained when I joined her.

"Is she still at the hospital?"

"They have Owen in ICU and are still waiting on a specialist to look at him." Jessie looked older, or maybe just more mature. "She wants me to go to her house and try to keep Debbie from hurting herself."

"Is Karen at the hospital?"

"Yes. Debbie went with her for a little while, but she said she couldn't stand it and left. Said she was going back to Bernadette's house."

"It's good of you to help them."

"I don't know how much longer I can. My job at the library is part time, so my hours are flexible, but I can't afford not to work for very long."

"How are Bernadette and her mother holding up?"

"I think they're both going a little crazy after everything that's happened. Now with Owen in the hospital…"

I told her I'd help her pack. When she opened the cabin door, Cleo was as excited as I'd ever seen her. Not as rambunctious as Mauser, but more than her usual, dignified self. I wasn't surprised that all of the fear, grief and chaos of the last week was having an effect on her.

"Can I ask what's going to happen now?" Jessie said as she packed up the food from the refrigerator.

"I think we know what happened. There are inconsistencies, but that's not unusual." I went on to tell her what I thought would happen to Paula, which was nothing. A long period of uncertainty while the case was mulled over, but in the end I didn't even think it would make it to a grand jury.

"That sounds fair," Jessie said, then turned to me. "You thought something else was going on, didn't you?"

"I did. I might have just been seeing conspiracies where there were only misremembered events and mistakes made in the moment."

"Is that what you really believe now?"

I sighed. "There comes a time in an investigation when you have to go with what the facts are telling you, whether you want to believe it or not, and whether or not you have an odd feeling about the case. Law enforcement officers have done some bad things when they ignored the facts in favor of their gut instinct."

Jessie seemed to think about this for a minute. "I can see that. I was watching one of those shows where they reenact air disasters. I don't remember all the details, but in this one the pilot ignored what the instruments were telling him because he felt like the plane was going up instead of down. They said that pilots can even be flying upside down, but they don't feel like they are and they refuse to believe what the instruments are telling them."

"Exactly. I'm not going to beat myself and other people

up because I have some gut feeling."

Half an hour later, everything was loaded and Jessie brought Cleo out to the SUV.

"Let me know if I can help. I'd like to," Jessie said. I could tell she wanted to say more.

"I'm going to look into the options to get you into the academy. Promise. I'll call or text when I find out what can be done."

"Thanks."

"By the way, what were Andy and the others talking to Marty about this morning?"

"Nothing really. I think they were just trying to get him to… come out of his depression. I heard Bridget tell him that everything would be fine. He mumbled something about how everything was screwed up, then Andy said he needed to think about his mother. There was more like that. They seemed to be being supportive."

"Okay, thanks." All of that fit in with my general impression. "Let me know if Bernadette needs anything. I'll come by the house and talk to Debbie. She's probably anxious to know when Bruce's body will be released by the coroner."

"I think they're going to wait until they know about Owen. Bernadette said he'd never forgive them if they buried his brother without him."

CHAPTER TWENTY-TWO

After Jessie left, I wandered up the hill, thinking that I'd check on Paula. On the way, I got a text from Cara mocking the picture Andy had taken of me in the swamp. She asked how things were going and I told her that we'd most likely be sleeping on our own beds tonight.

Paula was sitting on the porch of the main house. As I approached, she turned toward me and wiped her eyes.

"You still here?"

I shrugged. "I was going to ask you the same thing."

"The land is so beautiful. I've always loved this farm. Sitting here on the porch, I can imagine being in a world where we just work the land and grow our families. I can see the world I want, so why can't I live it? What curse has fallen on our family?" She looked at me.

"I don't have an answer. I've seen the hand of God or fate smack people down hard in my job. Good people, bad people. Doesn't matter. All I can tell you is that this is life. Why your family has suffered so much in the last week, I can't tell you because no one can."

"It hasn't just been the last week. It seems like our family has only had brief moments of happiness." Her jaw tightened. "I know that we brought a lot of it down on ourselves. I watched as my grandfather drove himself and his sons mercilessly in the quest for money."

"What about Jack?"

"Oh, Jack was different. He was never interested in law or real estate. And he loved arguing with his older brothers… about everything."

"Why do you think Althea doted on him?"

"Part of it was 'cause he was the baby. But that wasn't all of it. I think a small part of her relished the fights. She liked to see him piss off his father and brothers. Why are you asking questions about Jack anyway?"

"An unexplained death at a farm where there have been several other unusual deaths. Just seems like a road that ought to be traveled."

"Nothing unexplained about Jack's death. He went swimming and drowned."

"In the middle of the night?"

"That was Jack. I would have thought it more suspicious if he'd died in some mundane way. The man never did anything that was expected of him."

"Did you know that he'd had a fight with his father the night he drowned?"

"No, but I'm not surprised. If they were in the same room, they were fighting."

"There's fighting and then there's fighting. Did they have violent arguments? Or were they just heated discussions?"

Paula scrunched up her face in thought.

"I'd say they varied. I wasn't around much toward the end. I was married and had my own life. But I do remember Mom talking about it a bit. She got on the outs with the family pretty early on, so she had a lot of sympathy for Jack, who seemed to be an outsider with everyone in the family except Gran." She paused. "I should tell you that she was a lot different before my grandfather's death. She wasn't the hard-ass she is now. Hard to believe seeing her now, but she was a nice grandmother. But she changed after Jack's death, and even more after her husband died and she took over all of the business interests."

"She didn't handle any of the business side when Ryan was alive?"

"She did a lot of the grunt work. Don't get me wrong, she was as much an empire builder as Gramps. But he made all of the decisions, especially the hard ones. He decided when someone was going to be evicted or sued. At least that's what everyone saw. Gran appeared to be the passive partner in the business. Daddy said that he thought he was going to be running the family business after his father died. Instead Althea jumped in with both feet and went at it with teeth and claws. Ruthless, just like Gramps."

"What caused Ryan Byrd's death?"

"Massive heart attack. Doctor said his heart literally burst."

"When was this?"

"Fifteen years ago. He and Althea were at dinner in Lake City. Paramedics were on the scene in minutes, but there was nothing that could be done. See what I mean? A curse. Maybe where he was concerned, it was more like karma. But Tracy? She'd made some bad decisions, but did she deserve to die?"

I didn't want to get into another philosophical discussion or cause her to fall further into a morbid state of mind.

"How's Marty doing?"

"Okay. But he's good at hiding his feelings. I had a hard time when his father left us. Marty just folded up into himself. I'm worried about that now. Of course, if I don't have to deal with a bunch of legal issues, that will help." She looked straight at me.

I felt like she was trying to manipulate me, which I didn't appreciate. "What exactly did Marty see on Monday?"

"He saw enough," she said cryptically.

"If the events happened the way you described them, then the more I know, the better off you'll be. I'd like to speak with Marty again."

"My father was not big on talking with the police

voluntarily."

"Few lawyers are."

She gave a dramatic sigh. "He needs to talk to someone." She stood up. "I'll get him."

A few minutes later, Marty came out onto the porch with Paula behind him.

"I'd like to talk to him alone," I said in my best non-threatening voice. "I give you my word that the conversation will be off the record."

The truth was that a good defense attorney would be able to shred it anyway. Police interviews were expected to be recorded and conducted in a manner that suggested no coercion took place.

Paula thought about it for only a second before speaking to Marty. "Is that all right with you?"

"Yeah," he said tersely.

His mother went back inside, leaving us standing on the front porch.

"Why don't we sit down?" I suggested. Without a word, he dropped into one of the wooden rockers. I scooted another one away from the wall and sat down facing him. "I know that the last week has been traumatic for you. I just want to go over the account you gave of the events surrounding your aunt's and uncle's deaths."

He flinched. "I told you everything."

"That's fine. I'd just like to go over it again."

Nothing. He just kept looking at the floor.

I asked my questions and received flat answers without any elaboration. When we got to the point where his mother went out on the porch to call her father, I tried to force him to be more detailed.

"She called your grandfather. Did you stay in the house?"

"I guess so. Maybe I followed her out on the porch," he said, the muscles in his arms visibly clenching.

I leaned toward him. "What did you do before you went out on the porch?" I pressed.

I thought for a moment that he was going to answer, but

instead he stood up so abruptly I had to rock back to keep him from bumping into me.

"I've got to go inside."

I stood and blocked his way. "You're hiding something, Marty. If it's to protect your mother, I understand. But listen. If everything else happened like you said, then there's nothing to worry about. At most, your mother will get probation." I didn't know that for a fact, but I felt certain enough that it felt like the truth.

Marty tried to walk around me, but I had him blocked against the porch railing.

"If it's to protect yourself, we can work together and figure this out. If you made a mistake, everyone will understand. Anyone in a stressful situation like that could do something they later regretted."

He looked up at me. I could see that I had come close to the mark. Yet still he held back.

"Tell me," I urged.

"I... I... maybe." Then he pushed past me into the house.

"This secret will eat you alive if you don't tell someone," I said to his back.

When he was gone, I pursed my lips and muttered a curse under my breath. I'd been so close. Why had I let him get away? But what else could I have done? Throw him on the ground and sit on him until he broke down and confessed?

Paula came out of the house, wearing a concerned expression.

"Did he say anything?"

"Nothing he hadn't told me already."

But that was a lie. Nonverbally, Marty had admitted he was hiding the fact that he'd seen something or done something in the interval between his mother stepping out of the cottage and him going out on the porch.

"I don't know what he could tell you that I haven't. We were together the whole time."

I didn't push the point. She probably just didn't consider

the time between her leaving the cottage and Marty following her outside important. The interval was probably no more than a minute or two. What could he have done in that time? Anything he might have seen would've most likely still been there when we arrived. Unless his grandfather had interfered with the crime scene. A possibility I hadn't considered. Maybe that was why he had killed himself.

"Are you going home?" I asked her.

"Not yet. There are funerals to arrange. I've already chosen a funeral home. Debbie hasn't been of any use. I can't even be mad at her. She seems... really torn up by Daddy's death. Of course, Gran has been on top of everything. I'll let her have her way on most of the details." She shook her head and gave me a little smile. "I'll let her pay for everything too."

I pulled out a couple of my cards. "Here, give me a call if you think of anything else. I'd appreciate it if you gave the other one to Marty."

I started to walk away before I realized that there was one other person I needed to talk to before I left.

"I guess I ought to see your grandmother," I said, dreading the confrontation yet wanting to put some closure on this whole strange odyssey.

"If you're sure."

As soon as I was inside, Ruby appeared from the back of the house.

"Yes?" she said.

"He wants to see Gran," Paula said firmly. Ruby gave her a look that was cold as an iceberg in Antarctica. *No love lost there*, I thought.

"Mrs. Byrd isn't feeling very well today," Ruby said, alternating looks between me and Paula.

"If that's the case, I can—"

"No. She'll want to talk with you," Ruby said, and turned for the staircase.

Again I was ushered into the bedroom suite. Again she was sitting in the chair that threatened to swallow her. But there was one change. Althea Byrd looked humbled. Her eyes were not as quick to search mine out and challenge me. Her voice not as hard. There was even a slight tremble as she spoke.

"So this was all just crap that happens. My life," she said with more melancholy than anger.

"Austin killed Tracy; Paula killed Austin. I can't tell you whether your son, Bruce, killed himself or died of an accidental overdose."

"What does it matter?" she muttered.

I didn't like seeing her so downtrodden. She'd been mean-spirited before, but there'd been a strength to her that had to be admired. In her former state, she'd given me hope that we could be as iron-willed in our elder years as we were in our youth. Now all she promised was the despair of a life filled with disappointments.

"We won't push the issue. We'll call it an accidental death."

She waved me away. "How is Owen? No one will tell me."

"I don't know. I'm waiting for Bernadette to call. She's at the hospital."

"Damn fool. Running out in the woods after hunting dogs. They aren't even his dogs!" With her anger came a bit of her old vigor.

"The stroke could have happened anywhere and at any time," I said, defending the man.

"Owen was always going off half-cocked. Jack…" She started to sob. "I've become the one thing I've always despised: an old fool. Dreaming of the past instead of the future. No children now."

"You have your grandchildren and other relatives," I said in a lame effort to comfort her.

"No. Dottie's all right, but the rest? They could be strangers for all they mean to me."

"You must miss your husband," I said, not knowing why I said it.

As soon as my words registered with her, she seemed to convulse as though I'd hit her with an electric cattle prod. She shot fire at me from her eyes. "I miss nothing about that man. Look at the spawn he left me with. The venom in my life all comes from his fangs."

"There must have been some good times," I pushed. I didn't know if I was doing it to keep the spark alive in her, or if I was trying to learn the truth about their relationship.

"Yes. The day Jack was born," she spat.

I considered my next words carefully. Her irrepressible love for this child when she seemed to have so little interest in her other kids had caused my curiosity to flare. I decided the best way to broach the subject with Althea was to be blunt.

"With all due respect, may I ask what was so special about Jack?"

She looked up and over my left shoulder as though she could see him standing behind me.

"Jack, my boy. My baby. Everything about him felt special to me. He was so different from his father and brothers. Never a care in the world. He was like an Irishman on St. Patrick's Day." She paused. "I know just how stupid this sounds, but you'd have to have met him to understand. Every time he walked in the room, he made me smile. Don't get me wrong. That Irishman comparison bore out in more ways than one. He loved to argue with his father and brothers. He got to be an expert at goading them. Made me laugh out loud, 'cause each and every time he made them furious. Once they were all worked up, he'd just leave. Walk out while they were still sputtering." She smiled and shook her head.

"What did he want to do?"

"He did some theatre. And he wrote. He was good. Needed more discipline, but he could turn a phrase."

"He'd had a few drinks the night he drowned," I said softly, thinking the man had to have some vices other than being querulous.

She gave me a hard look for criticizing her baby. "He wasn't a drunkard, if that's what you're getting at."

"Not at all. Just trying to get a complete picture of the man."

"Man. That's the right word. Not a businessman. No, sir, he was a real man. Living life like it was meant to be lived. I was proud of my son. The others knuckled under to their father at the first look from him. Jack never bowed down. He was tough."

I wasn't getting anywhere. She was besotted with her dead son. I certainly wasn't going to get an unbiased picture of what the man had been like. Instead, she painted the picture of a playful, talented rogue. *Who had Jack been, really?* I thought. Then my inner voice shot back with, *What does it matter?* It didn't. I looked at the sad old woman and decided that I couldn't do anything to help this family.

"I appreciate your time. Call me if you need anything."

"Funerals. At my age, you get tired of funerals. Now I've got to go to my son's and granddaughter's. Maybe another son's." Her voice trailed off.

I left her buried in her chair with her eyes closed. Ruby glared at me as I came down the stairs.

"She's not well, you know."

"I won't be bothering her anymore."

CHAPTER TWENTY-THREE

Outside, the sun was blistering hot, but it was past three so the temperature was past its peak. A soft rumble from the southwest promised afternoon thunderstorms and cooler air.

I drove down to the cabin so I could pack up our stuff. When I got out of the car, I heard another rumble that wasn't thunder and looked to the top of the hill to see Andy and his gang riding the four-wheelers toward the barn.

Is there anything else I can learn from them? I asked myself. *The best thing you can do is pack your stuff and go home*, my self responded. I could get a good start on the final report this evening and then be back at work Monday to unburden all the folks who'd been picking up my slack while I chased wild geese.

"No more nights at the farm," I told Cara as I drove away.

"That doesn't break my heart. The new refrigerator came as promised."

"Life in the fast lane. I'm sure Ivy and Alvin will be glad to have everything back to normal."

Then I thought about Dad. As my mind let go of the Byrd cases, it immediately looked for something else to obsess on and Dad's mysterious little secret was the obvious choice.

"I'm going to run Dad down and find out what he's been avoiding telling me," I said with determination.

"Is that a good idea? I mean, if it's something you aren't going to like, wouldn't it be best to let him bring it up? You'd probably have a better chance of changing his mind that way. Instead of… ambushing him."

"I'm not ambushing him. I'm just tired of playing I've-got-a-secret."

Though Cara was probably right. I was already getting worked up just thinking about whatever it was Dad wasn't telling me. Good sense would have dictated that I give him time to bring it up, or at least get a good night's sleep before poking the bear.

"I'm just sayin'," Cara warned, knowing it was no use trying to talk me out of the confrontation.

I was about to call Dad when my phone rang. It was Bernadette. I took a deep breath and answered the call.

"It's not good," she said. "It was a major stroke." I could tell she was fighting back tears.

"I'm sorry."

"I keep thinking how tough it's going to be on Mom. He's probably going to live, but don't know how much he'll recover."

"Your grandmother asked how he was."

"I'll call and talk to Ruby. As much as Gran complained about Uncle Bruce and Dad, I think she really cares."

"She does," I said, then let it go. "Is there anything I can do for you?"

"No. Jessie's helping with Cleo. Debbie and Mom can sort of lean on each other. At least I hope that's how it will work. Has everyone left the farm?"

"Everyone except Paula, Marty, the four young people and your grandmother and Ruby."

"That's probably best."

"I've decided to suspend any further investigation pending new evidence."

"You think the… deaths of Tracy and Austin happened the way Paula said?"

"Basically. And Bruce's death will be written up as an accidental overdose."

"What a mess. Right now, I'm just overwhelmed."

"You need to get some rest."

"I will."

We hung up and I called Dad.

"I heard you found Owen Byrd," he said.

I gave him a quick recap and an update on Owen's condition.

"That's rough," he sympathized.

"I thought we could talk. I can meet you," I offered.

"Oh…" There was a long pause.

"Where are you?"

"I'm on my way to the house. Mauser has his annual with Dr. Barnhill," Dad answered, sounding unusually cagey.

"Fine, I'll meet you there and go with you."

"I…"

Before he could say anything else, I said goodbye and hung up. What could have possibly been causing him to act so weird and out of character? I was determined to find out.

I got to his house just as he was pulling into the driveway.

"The appointment is at four, so we have to hurry," he told me, getting out of his truck.

Jamie, Dad's dog sitter, opened the door and Mauser strained toward us at the end of his leash, excited to see both of us at once. Jamie had helped to bring some discipline into Mauser's life, but the big mutt still had moments when he just lost his mind.

"Okay, big guy," Dad said to Mauser with a fatherly tone that I'd never heard growing up. He took the leash and loaded Mauser into the van while I got in on the passenger side.

"Okay, so talk. What horrible message do you have to deliver?" I asked once we were headed toward town.

Dad stared out the window. "I don't want to tell you like

this," he said grumpily.

"No. You've been doing this for almost a week now. Out with it. I'm a big boy. I can handle it."

He was silent for several minutes, staring straight out the windshield and chewing on his lip.

I'd had enough. "What are you going to do? Fire me?!"

"No, nothing like that." He finally looked over at me. "Okay. I'll tell you." Then he went back to staring out the windshield.

"Yes?"

"I've asked Genie to marry me."

"And?"

"That's it. We're getting married this fall."

"That's great!" I said, wondering what was such a big deal about it. They'd been dating for more than a year.

"I thought you might be more upset. I know when I first started to—"

"That was ages ago! I admit, I was pretty immature about the relationship at first. But… I think she's nice. And I really like Jimmy." Jimmy, Genie's son, had Down syndrome. He was only a little younger than me and was able to be independent with the help of a group home. "Y'all getting married will be good for everybody," I said sincerely. "And I think Mom would approve."

Dad looked over at me and gave me a quick smile that disappeared just as fast. I thought about asking him who the best man was going to be, but I figured it'd be Mauser.

Cara met us outside the clinic, which had become protocol since the time that Dad had brought Mauser in the front door only to send a cat waiting in the lobby into orbit, where Mauser had been quick to join him. They'd had to spend half an hour getting the animals under control and cleaning up the wrecked displays of pet food. Mauser loved cats and had just wanted to play, but most cats had no desire to get close enough to him to find this out.

"Come on, buddy," Cara said to Mauser. She was his second favorite human and he leaned happily into the ear massage she gave him before calmly following her through the back door of the office.

"Let's talk out here," Dad said.

"Haven't we covered everything?" I said with a smile.

"Personal business, yes. I just want to make sure that you're turning the Byrd farm case over to the State Attorney." It was a statement, not a question.

"As soon as I write up the reports, and with the caveat that the lab reports for the three bodies won't be complete for a couple of months."

"Good. Make it right with Lt. Johnson," he said.

"I thought I had."

"When I brought up your name this morning, he still looked like he'd swallowed a porcupine."

"I'll get back to my other cases first thing Monday morning."

"I've been putting pressure on the division commanders, so he has a right to be out of sorts about anything or anyone that's keeping his division from covering its workload."

"I heard you the first time. I'll admit that I might have let my suspicious nature get the best of me on this one. But you have to agree that three deaths in three days, plus a disappearance, are pretty unusual."

"This. This is exactly the problem," he said, frowning.

"What?"

"You trying to convince me that you were justified in the amount of time you spent on the cases."

"How so?" I still didn't know what he was talking about.

"Don't try to convince *me*. Johnson is the one you have to convince. Chain of command is his problem with you."

I took a deep breath and attempted to swallow my pride. He was right. "I get it."

"I hope so. The day will come when I'm not the sheriff. The election last year could have gone against me. You can't continue to use me as a crutch. Johnson is doing both of us a favor by demanding that we act like sheriff and deputy and not father and son when we're on the job."

"Agreed."

Honestly, I'd never felt like I got much preferential treatment as the sheriff's son. But I had enough self-awareness to admit that I'd always held the Go-to-Dad card ready to use when I needed to push an investigation beyond where I thought Johnson would allow me to go.

By the time they finished weighing, poking and prodding Mauser, it was late enough that Cara could leave. So I rode back to Dad's house with her, saving me a trip for ice cream to reward Mauser for not actually destroying anything during his appointment.

Alvin, our Pug, had been coming to work with Dr. Barnhill, so he was riding home with us tonight. With the Pug sitting in my lap and looking thrilled to be riding shotgun, I told Cara about Dad's wedding plans.

"That's fantastic!" Cara gushed. "I can't wait to talk to Genie about it. She and Jimmy are so nice. I think your dad will be really happy."

"Even I can't think of a downside."

"And you thought he was going to fire you!"

"No, I didn't. He was just driving me crazy with his secret squirrel routine."

"If I remember correctly, you did get your panties in a wad when you found out they were dating."

"Ancient history. By the way, I'm going to swing by the office on my way home."

"Go by the store and stock up so we can test out the new refrigerator. Something for dinner would be great too."

As soon as I was back in my own car, I called Lt. Johnson and told him I was coming by his office.

"See you then," was his curt reply before hanging up.

I swung by my desk to check how high the pile of reports waiting for me had grown. There was a comprehensive note from Julio covering what files he'd handled and which ones were waiting for my return. He'd also managed to find the two suspects in the shooting I'd been hunting for on Monday before all the mess with the Byrds had come up.

I knocked on Johnson's door shortly after five-thirty.

"Come in."

"Lieutenant, I just wanted to give you a complete update on the Byrd cases."

He seemed to consider this for a moment before nodding toward the chair in front of his desk.

I gave him a detailed account of the investigation and ended with, "I'll be back in the office at eight on Monday to start following up on the other cases that have been assigned to me. There are a couple of issues left open on the Byrd case. The reports, obviously. I'd also like the opportunity to re-interview Marty Reece at some point in the future. I feel like he's hiding something. Having said that, it won't in any way interfere with my regular caseload."

"Glad to hear it." Johnson's expression was neutral.

I debated whether I should rehash the issues that had been coming between us. I decided that the atmosphere couldn't get any cooler than it already was.

"I also wanted to say that I've never meant any disrespect to you now or in the past when I solicited advice or permission from my father. My only motivation has been to solve the cases I've been given to the best of my ability." I cringed inwardly, waiting for him to explode.

He looked at me without so much as blinking for almost a full minute.

"I appreciate your candor. But do you realize how insulting that last statement was? It implies that I am an impediment to you solving your cases."

He paused and I immediately wanted to interject a defense of myself, but decided it wouldn't be wise.

"Some people think that an officer who insists on his subordinates following the chain of command is being autocratic. Is that how you feel?"

I could see the blood rising in his eyes and decided it was safest to leave that question unanswered.

"When you go outside the chain of command, you make the officer you circumvent irrelevant. Do you see that?"

"Yes, sir."

"You also put more work on your father's shoulders. You know that he's under a lot of stress right now. Do you think that's fair to him?"

This left me feeling like an ungrateful ten-year-old. "No, sir."

"Do you think I'm incapable of understanding the complexities of your cases?"

"No, sir."

"In the future, you will come to me when you have a problem or want some leeway to investigate one of your cases. If you think you need to talk to your father about a matter related to your job, you will come to me and ask for permission to speak to him, just like every other person who works under me. Understand?"

"Yes, sir."

"Are we on the same page?"

"Yes, sir."

He stood up, which I took as a sign that our meeting was over. I had turned and was heading for the door when he spoke again.

"It's to your credit that you came to me so we could clear this up."

I turned and gave him my best man-to-man look. "I'll be here bright and early on Monday. I'm determined to make it a fresh start."

"I'm counting on it," he said in a way that implied I'd better be, for my sake.

I was feeling good and thinking that I was off the hook when Johnson said, "We don't have to wait until Monday to start our new relationship. The Sheriff's Explorers are meeting at eight tomorrow morning. I'd like you to come in and talk to them about the duties and responsibilities of an investigator. Show them the difference between what they see on TV and what it's actually like to work cases."

He was behind me, but I was sure that I could feel him smiling at me. I respected the young people in the Explorers, but I'd never considered myself very good at relating to kids. However, I knew I deserved this and that it wouldn't kill me to put in some time working with young people who dreamed of being our future deputies.

I saw my Saturday disappear before my eyes as I realized that healing my relationship with Johnson was going to come at a price.

"Great. I'll look forward to it," I said with a wave over my shoulder.

Even with the early appointment with a room full of teenagers, I left the office feeling at peace. I'd settled most of the pending issues in my life and was looking forward to putting my head down and cruising for a while. I made a quick stop at the store, then picked up a pizza.

The smell of pepperoni, sausage and mushrooms filled my car, pushing my appetite to a ten on the hungry meter as I drove. Cara met me at the car and helped carry the groceries so we could fill the new refrigerator.

"I'm looking forward to a quiet weekend," Cara said as we finished admiring the new appliance.

"About that," I said, and went on to explain that a Saturday sleep-in was off the table for me.

"It won't hurt you to give back a little," she said, doling out treats to Alvin and Ivy.

"Easy for you to say. You don't have to get up at the crack of dawn to face Johnson's junior cadets."

Cara and I savored the greasy pleasure of pizza in front of the TV, with the furry kids crashed on the carpet in front of us.

"When I'm done, I'm going to work on my proposal for Dr. Horvath," Cara told me.

"That works. I want to take one more look at the Byrd files."

"You're done with the investigation, right?"

"I still have to write up my final report, and Darlene sent

over her reports on the interviews she did. I just want to review everything."

"You said something about Marty too."

"He's hiding something. I know that. Thing is, he's a shy, sort of withdrawn kid. Maybe 'sensitive' is the right word. So it might be something simple like… I don't know, he moved the two-by-four or saw his mom make an inappropriate gesture."

"Inappropriate gesture?"

"Like shooting a bird."

"You're kidding?"

"Seriously. I was talking with a defense attorney a couple of weeks ago, and he was defending a woman who had been attacked by a man in a parking lot. Broad daylight. They caught the attack on CCTV. The guy came up to the woman and talked for a minute or two, then when she turned to her car, he grabbed her. What he didn't know was that she had a knife in the shopping bag she was carrying. As he tried to drag her toward his car, she had the presence of mind to go limp. When she went to the ground, she grabbed the knife out of the bag. It was a gift that she'd had engraved, and she was just able to pull it out of the box."

"Lucky her."

"Exactly. She stabbed him repeatedly until he fell to the ground. What you can clearly see on the camera footage is that, after he's down and she gets to her feet, she yells at him and shoots him the bird several times. She was so hyped up on adrenaline that she didn't have any memory of having done it."

"Wow."

"The attorney was worried that, if the footage was seen by a jury, she'd be found guilty of manslaughter."

"Even though she'd been attacked?"

"Her yelling at the man while he was bleeding out on the ground and flipping him the bird looked really bad."

"What happened?"

"The police and State Attorney didn't press charges. It

was a clear case of self-defense. The point is, people do things in the heat of the moment that they can be very embarrassed about later. A quiet person like Marty might feel very guilty for a moment of madness."

"I can see that."

"But… I don't want to let it rest. I'm going to ride him a little bit. I think with some pressure, he'll tell me what he saw or did. And if it *is* something innocent, or at least not criminal, I'll be doing him a favor. Getting it out now could save him years with a therapist later."

"Fair enough. Read your reports. I'm going to work," she said, and took our plates into the kitchen.

I went to fetch my phone, which should have been in its holder attached to my belt on the pants I'd thrown over the corner of the bed. The holder was there, but the phone wasn't. I looked on the floor, the couch, the kitchen counter, the bathroom counter. Nothing. Cara got involved and I tried calling my phone. Still nothing. Fighting panic, I went out to the car and found… nothing. I came back inside and was about to call the pizza joint when Cara found my phone between the mattress and the footboard of the bed.

"The ringer was off," she said, handing it to me.

"I forgot to turn it back on after my meeting with Johnson."

I took the phone and settled down with my laptop at the dining room table.

I started with the first two deaths. I went through the crime scene pictures and the list of evidence collected. I reviewed a few texted notes from Shantel, then staring at my phone made me think. Something was missing.

We'd collected Austin's, Paula's and Marty's phones. I remembered spending time looking through Paula's texts to see if she'd exchanged any heated messages with Austin or texted anything incriminating to Tracy. If she'd stated in a text or an email that she wanted to see Austin dead, that would have changed the investigation considerably. But there had been nothing, and nothing on Marty's phone either. Austin's phone had revealed several heated exchanges with Tracy, which just reinforced what we were told had happened. But now, for the first time, I was wondering why we hadn't found *Tracy's* phone.

"Wow!" I said out loud.

"What?" Cara asked. She was sitting on the floor with her back to the couch and her laptop and papers spread out on the coffee table.

"I overlooked a piece of evidence," I said, frowning at my laptop where I had half a dozen documents open. I flipped through them again, just to make sure I hadn't missed anything.

"What?"

"The woman who was murdered, her cell phone. It wasn't at the scene. I didn't notice, so I didn't ask anyone about it." I was irritated at my incompetence, though I was pretty sure why I'd screwed up. Even with my suspicions, I'd been convinced that Austin had killed Tracy. So the details of her murder seemed less important. I hated the thought that I hadn't taken hers as seriously as the other deaths.

"Maybe she didn't have one. As hard as that is to imagine," Cara suggested.

"No, she had one. I even know the number since we have Austin's phone, and there were thousands of texts and phone calls to her on his phone. I'm an idiot. That first day, it would have been so simple to just call her phone while we were in the cottage. If it had been there, we probably would have heard it ring."

"Unless she had it on silent like you just did."

"True."

"Somebody probably has it. They might not have thought it was that important."

"Son of a bitch!" I said, rising out of my chair. "That's what Marty did!"

"What?"

"Every time I'd bring up the phone calls that he and his mother made, he'd get nervous and evasive. I thought it was about the calls. It wasn't. He was upset that I kept talking about phones." I was pacing between the kitchen and the living room now.

"He took it?"

"Maybe. Probably."

"Why?" Cara had stopped working and was watching me.

"Who knows? He might have a completely innocent reason. Maybe he picked it up with the intention of using it to make the call to 911, found it was dead and stuck it in his pocket."

"So why didn't he tell you about it?"

"He's immature. Even for his age, he's immature. He might have been scared that taking the phone made him guilty of something. Or he thought it made him and his mom look more guilty. Protecting his mom could be a big motivation for him."

"Could he be guilty of more than just stealing the phone?" Cara stood up. I could tell she was being drawn into the mystery.

"Perhaps. If there was something on the phone he didn't want us to see."

"Like calls to him."

"Yeah, like that."

I looked at my watch, then stopped myself. There was no urgency to this. I didn't need to confront Marty in the middle of the night. Besides, he was a minor and, if I seemed too aggressive, his mother could start putting up roadblocks that would eat up time and money getting through.

"You want to ask him about it now," Cara said, reading me like a book.

"I'm afraid that would be counterproductive. Paula said they're going to stay a couple more days, so I'll just go out there casually tomorrow after I spend the morning with the Explorers. If I approach Marty nice and easy, I might be able to get the answers without too much trouble."

"You don't want to subject him to any more trauma if it's an innocent mistake."

"Exactly."

I went back to my laptop and looked at Austin's phone log. I made a note of Tracy's phone number, which could come in handy if Marty gave me the run-around.

We both worked through the rest of the evening with minor interruptions from Ivy as she tried to type her own report on my laptop, and Alvin as he tried to nest on Cara's lap.

At midnight, we went to bed. I was hoping for quick sleep, but my mind immediately started arguing with itself. Half of my brain thought the Byrd cases were wide open again, while the other, saner half advised staying on course, going slow, and seeing what developed. Eventually, I fell asleep, only to be awakened at four in the morning by my phone vibrating on the nightstand.

CHAPTER TWENTY-FOUR

For a second I thought about ignoring the call. Instead I looked at the number and saw that it was Paula Reece. *What now?* I thought as I answered.

"Please, please! Marty's missing," she said, giving me flashbacks to when Owen had disappeared.

"Wait. What do you mean by missing?" I was still trying to get my brain in gear.

My question led to a full minute of Paula wailing on the other end of the line. Cara was awake now and leaning on me with a concerned expression while I tried to get Paula to calm down.

"I… can't… find… him," she stuttered between sobs.

"Okay, calm down. Maybe he went down to one of the cabins. Or he might have gone to see Bridget and Rochelle," I suggested.

"No. I've already asked them. They haven't seen him."

"Okay. Call 911 and get a deputy to come out to take a report. We'll see where we go from—"

She interrupted me. "No, no. He'd hate that."

She was probably right. Teenagers hated to start a fuss. Cops coming out to the farm, blue lights flashing and a big search could push Marty away.

"I'll come out there," I said, wondering what I was getting myself into now.

"I'm coming too," Cara whispered.

"No."

"What?" Paula asked.

"Nothing. I'm on my way."

As I hung up, I told Cara, "You aren't going."

"I can help calm Paula down. You heard her." Cara had a point. Trying to do anything with Paula in hysterics wasn't going to be easy. "Really, it's no big deal. I'll just ride along and stay with Paula while you look for Marty."

If Cara was there with Paula and I *did* find Marty, I might have some time alone with him to ask about the phone.

"Okay," I said reluctantly. I still didn't like the idea of her going out there with me at the crack of dawn.

Twenty minutes later, we were driving through the dark toward the Byrd farm.

"Do you think he ran off?" Cara asked me.

"I don't know. If he has a secret and thinks I might be getting close to it, he could have spooked and run."

"You don't think he'd..." Cara said, no doubt thinking what I was thinking.

"I hope not. But who knows."

The yard in front of the main house was almost empty of cars when we pulled up. I saw lights on in Paula's cottage and the glowing embers of a campfire down by the pond.

Paula ran toward us as we got out of the car. A full moon bathed the yard in a pale blue light.

"I've tried his phone a million times. I keep texting him, but he doesn't answer." Paula sounded wild and desperate. One thing I didn't doubt was that her fear for Marty's safety was real.

"You remember Cara," I said. They'd met on Wednesday night when Cara and I had been walking around the farm.

"I'm sorry," Paula said, putting her hands over her face and crying again.

"Let's go inside. I want you to tell me everywhere you've

gone and everyone you've talked to since you found out Marty was missing."

Cara put her arm around Paula and led her back into the cottage. Once inside, we sat down at the kitchen table and I pulled out my small notebook. I also took out my phone, thinking it would be a good idea to record the conversation.

"I've woken everyone up. Nobody's seen him."

"When did you notice he was gone?"

"Around midnight? I went to look for him. I thought he was reading in his room."

"Which is where?"

"The small room in the loft," she said, pointing vaguely toward the stairs.

"Is it unusual for him to go out at night without telling you?"

"Yes! He'd never sneak out. When we're at home, he's very good about telling me where he's going. I don't think he's ever stayed out past midnight."

"Did he say or do anything unusual today?"

"No…"

"Talk to me," I urged her.

"I don't know. So much has happened. He's been acting withdrawn since… the deaths of his aunt and uncle. But isn't that normal?" Her eyes pleaded with us to understand what she and her son had been through.

"Everyone reacts differently to violence. I wouldn't be surprised if your son was traumatized by the events he witnessed. That's why we need to find him."

"So why aren't you out there looking?" she screamed.

I heard a soft knock at the front door.

"Stay with her," I told Cara, and went to see who it was.

Andy stood in the doorway with Cory a few steps behind him.

"I wanted to let her know that we looked around all the buildings, but couldn't find any sign of Marty," Andy said. I caught a whiff of beer from his breath, but in no way did he appear intoxicated.

"When did you last see him?"

"I guess yesterday morning. He hasn't really been hanging out with us that much. Not that he wasn't welcome. He just seemed… distant."

I invited them in so I could close the door and keep the mosquitoes and other night bugs from flying in.

"You say you searched around the buildings. Can you think of any particular place he liked to go?"

Andy shrugged. "This was my first time meeting him. Cory, did Marty have a favorite spot on the farm?"

Cory looked a little nervous, though it might have just been the fact that he was up at five in the morning. "No, but I'll think about it. He's been… quiet like you said."

"Okay. Thanks," I told them. "We may have to get a real search party going after the sun comes up. You might want to get some sleep if you can."

"Sure. If there's anything we can do…"

Andy turned and put his hand on Cory's arm, guiding him toward the door. It was subtle, but there was a strange vibe between those two. I followed them to the door and, after they'd gone, I went to a window and watched them walk away. Andy leaned in close and whispered to Cory. When he finished, he leaned back and laughed.

I turned from the window and was surprised to find Cara standing right behind me.

"What's wrong?" she asked.

"Those guys were acting strange. I can't say for sure, but I feel like they know more than they're saying."

We walked back over to Paula, who looked dazed.

"Do you know why we didn't find Tracy's phone on Monday?"

"Tracy's phone?" She seemed surprised and perplexed. "What does that have to do with Marty?"

"I think he might have done something with her phone," I said bluntly.

"I can't imagine."

"Did you see the phone during the… incident with Tracy

and Austin?"

"I don't know. I don't remember seeing it, but it might have been there. Probably was. Tracy was on it all the time either texting, checking Instagram or talking."

I started to ask another question when Paula got a funny look on her face. "What's the matter?" I asked.

"That morning. After she'd been so frosty toward me at breakfast, at first I thought I'd call and apologize for pissing off Austin. I thought I could do a quick apology and then see where things were between us. But for the first time ever, Austin answered Tracy's phone." Paula looked confused by the memory. "I remember now. I think that's why I wanted to go to their cottage. He answered the phone, then handed it to Tracy. She didn't sound like herself. Nothing I could put my finger on, but she was... tense. I should have remembered this earlier. Of course, I was hungover from the night before, along with everything that came after..."

"You think he took her phone?"

"Or was looking at her texts and calls. They both could be jealous and controlling."

"Do you think something on the phone might have angered Austin enough to cause him to kill her?"

"Yes. In the past, both of them had flown off the handle when they discovered the other had done something behind their back."

"Can you think what he might have found?"

"No. But Tracy didn't tell me everything."

"Why would Marty take her phone?"

"I don't know. He liked Tracy. Maybe he wanted to protect her reputation."

"May I search his room?"

"Yes."

I followed Paula upstairs to the small loft bedroom. The room had the feel of a bed-and-breakfast. There was nothing personal on the walls or nightstand. The bed was a twin, its sheets in disarray.

I wanted to dial the number for Tracy's phone, thinking

it could fast-track the process. But if it wasn't in the room and Marty had it with him, the ringing might spook him. I could imagine him ditching it out of fear of discovery, or something even more dramatic. Best to just search the room.

I pulled out a pair of rubber gloves that I'd stuffed in my pocket. As I slipped on the gloves, I saw Paula's eyes go wide. After thousands of TV shows and movies, everyone associated the blue rubber gloves with murder, surgery and crime scenes. Never anything good.

"I just want to make sure that I'm taking every precaution," I told her. I don't think my assurances made her feel any better.

I started with Marty's backpack and small duffle bag, but found nothing. The rest of the room was pretty easy to cover since there weren't many personal possessions. The wardrobe was empty except for a change of sheets, and there wasn't a closet. The only other furniture was the bed, nightstand and a large bookcase with bric-a-brac and an odd mix of books that had no doubt been left by various relatives over the years.

I was almost ready to give up when I came across an envelope stuffed between a couple of well-thumbed Leon Uris paperbacks. There wasn't any writing on the envelope, nor was the flap sealed. Inside were two pills. They were Percocets, though there was something odd about them. One blue pill was faded, while the other had a large chip out of it and was completely white. *Maybe they're old*, I thought.

I turned to Paula and asked, "Have you seen any signs of drug addiction in your son?"

"I… like what?"

"Sleeping more than usual. Hyperactivity. Eyes looking unfocused or dilated. Any other change in his behavior. Maybe more secretive than usual." As I spoke, I realized some of that was just typical teenage behavior.

"I thought he was a little more excited before we came. Honestly, I was surprised he wanted to come since he's not much for outdoor activities. Marty would rather read and play games than hike in the woods. But I know his grades are as good as ever. He's set to graduate with honors from high school with a year of college credits."

"Do you know his password?" I set the pills aside and picked up his tablet from the bed. There was an anime image on the screen and a password prompt.

"No," Paula said softly.

Unlike on TV, it was almost impossible to guess a person's password. I set the tablet down.

"Can you tell if anything is missing?"

"Just the clothes he was wearing, his wallet and phone." She looked uncertain. "Is that good?"

"It doesn't look like he intended to be gone long," I said, stating the obvious and not answering her question.

"You were camping out originally, right?" I asked as we went down the stairs.

"Yes. I'd rented a camper. After… everything happened, we moved in here. Myron took the camper back for me."

"Is there anywhere else that your son spent time?"

"When we first got here, he was hanging out with Bridget and the other kids."

"You mentioned Bridget earlier. Do you think there was anything between them?"

"Funny you say that. When he said he wanted to come, I wondered if he had a crush on her. They first met at a Christmas party at my dad's a few years ago and they've kept in touch. I didn't see a problem with it. She's older than him, and they're only second or third cousins or something. So he hung out with them a bit when we first got here. Until… Tracy was killed."

"How far do you think his interest in Bridget went?"

"I might have stated it too strongly. He likes all of them. Marty's talked a lot about Andy since we got here—"

Before she could finish her sentence, there was another knock at the door.

This time, Andy was on the porch, alone and looking nervous.

"I think I need to talk to you," he said.

"Come in."

"Maybe out here." Andy looked past me at Paula. "Just you."

I stepped outside and closed the door.

Andy shuffled his feet back and forth, looking up and down.

"What is it?" I encouraged him.

"Yeah, all right. First, I mean, I know he's underage, and we should have told someone but… Can you give me, like, a promise that we won't be in trouble?"

"Not without knowing what you're talking about," I said reasonably.

More shuffling.

"We didn't give him anything. Everything he took, he brought himself. Except for the mushrooms. Those he found here."

"Are you talking about drugs?"

"Sort of. I guess."

"What does that mean?" I pushed him.

"Getting high. Not much drugs. Just, like, mushrooms. I think he might have taken some pills too."

"When?"

"A couple of times with us." He hurriedly added, "Before that woman and guy were killed." He paused. "But he might have done some more since."

"Why do you think that?"

"Tonight, he came down to the campfire. We were all just drinking some beers and talkin'. You know."

"And?"

"He made a pass at Bridget. She didn't mean to be… harsh, but she kind of slapped at him. He was pretty upset."

"You think he might have gone off to get high?" I didn't like the direction this was headed.

"I've seen him get upset a few times since we've been here. Each time, he went off and got high."

"You know where he might be?"

"I was afraid to say anything before."

"Why didn't you go after him?"

"'Cause he got a little weird when he got high. I didn't want to find him… messed up. Especially since he was pissed at all of us after Bridget slapped him down."

"Do you know where he went?" I asked again.

"It's the spot where he found the mushrooms, a clearing maybe a mile away. They've been letting cattle graze in the area. I can show you."

"Wait here."

Paula was standing near the front door when I went back inside. "What does he know?"

"He just has an idea. I'm going to check it out."

"I want to go too," Paula said, her voice rising an octave

"No. I'll check it out and be back soon." If we found Marty and he was… messed up, I didn't think it would help to have his mother there.

"I want to go!" she insisted.

"Andy's going to run me out there. I promise we'll be back soon."

Cara, having heard everything, had moved up behind Paula. "I'll go," she said.

Paula turned and looked at her. "Would you?"

I wondered why it would matter to her if Cara went with us. I decided that Paula had recognized the nurturer in Cara. If Paula couldn't be there, then she at least wanted another mother-figure present if we found her son.

"Of course. If he's out there, we'll bring him back safe," Cara reassured her.

CHAPTER TWENTY-FIVE

"You shouldn't go," I told Cara once we were outside.

"I promised."

I should have argued against it when we'd been inside, but I hadn't wanted to get into a heated exchange with Paula. I decided this was the lesser of two evils and let it drop.

When we were off the porch and out of the glare of the cottage lights, I could see Cory and Andy sitting on the ATVs.

"They're running a little low on gas," Andy said. "We'll fill them up and be right back."

Cara and I waited in the dark. On the horizon, I could see a small tinge of light. In another half hour, we'd be able to see without flashlights.

"Sure I can't talk you out of going?"

"No. Does Andy know where Marty is?"

"I don't know." I explained about the pills I'd found in Marty's room and the story Andy told about the mushrooms.

"That's why you don't want me to go along," Cara grinned. "You know my mother's affinity for mushrooms and you're afraid a little of that rubbed off on me." Her hippie mother did indeed hunt mushrooms of all sorts, and had once accidentally dosed me with one of the happier varieties left in a salad bowl.

"You don't want to remind me of the time your mother tried to killed me."

"You know it was an accident."

"I should have—" I didn't get to finish my rant as Cory and Andy came back with the grumbling ATVs.

Cory got off the second one and handed helmets to Cara and me. We climbed on and Cara put her arms securely around my waist.

"Follow me. It's about a mile out," Andy shouted to us.

Andy started slowly, making sure that I was following behind him. The lights pierced the night, illuminating progressively smaller trails through the uplands and swamps. After a few minutes, he increased his speed. The trail was rutted, and it was all I could do to keep from jarring the teeth out of both of us. I wanted to tell Andy to slow down, but I didn't have any way to communicate. I flashed my lights as he moved farther ahead. I felt like I was on the edge of losing him as we made several turns, both right and left through the dark.

Just as I thought we had to have gone at least two miles, he turned off into a field that ran uphill. When I crested the hill, I saw the lights of his ATV turning onto another trail. I made it to that trail in time to see his lights disappear to the left. I wanted to stop or turn around, but I had a tiger by the tail. If I lost him, I knew it would take me a long time navigating with my phone to make it back to the main house.

Suddenly the ATV started to sputter. I turned up the throttle, which just made it worse. Then the engine coughed once and died.

"What's wrong?" Cara asked.

"I don't know. We have plenty of gas," I said, tapping the gauge. I tried starting the ATV again. The engine caught, then died again. A dozen more twists of the key didn't change the outcome.

"It's dead?"

"Apparently," I said with a frown. We got off the ATV, laying our helmets on the seat. I had a bad feeling about this.

"Why was he going so fast?" Cara asked, voicing just one of the things that was bothering me.

"I think he wanted to lose us."

Now that the lights of the ATV were off, it was clear that dawn was fast approaching. I pulled my phone out of my pocket and was glad to see that we had a strong signal. I pulled up the GPS.

"Where are we?" Cara asked, looking over my shoulder.

It took a minute or two, but finally I said, "Good news. Looks like he was just taking us in a big circle. The houses should be right over there." I pointed toward the east, where the sky was much brighter now.

"Over that hill?" Cara asked with a heavy dose of skepticism in her voice.

"According to my phone. Looks like there's about half a mile of woods between us and the houses."

We started walking. I put the phone away since I felt confident that I had a good feel for where we needed to go.

"Why would Andy try to lose us in the woods?"

"Andy has shown more than a little interest in the investigation. He and the others were the ones that found Owen. I should have been more suspicious of that."

"Why would they want to take Owen out in the woods and leave him? That makes less sense than doing it to us."

"And why find him? Maybe it's a form of Munchausen by proxy."

"What?"

"You know, when a woman makes her own kid sick to get attention. Or like when a nurse makes a patient go critical so they can save them and look like heroes." Saying it out loud, it didn't make a lot of sense. How would Tracy and Austin fit into something like that? Or Marty taking Tracy's phone, if he even had?

Thinking about Tracy's phone caused me to take out my own and check our position. "That's weird," I said, concerned.

"What?"

"I must have gotten off track. According to the GPS, we need to go more that way." I pointed to a position that seemed farther east than last time.

"That can't be right," Cara said with a firm edge to her voice.

"That's what the GPS says," I argued childishly. I held out my phone.

With a scrunched face, she studied the map as the blue dot representing our position pulsed. She closed the app and opened it again, then looked at it and repeated the process.

"The app is screwed up," she finally pronounced.

"Can't be."

"Close the app and open it again. Each time I did it, it showed us in a different place."

Not believing her, or not *wanting* to believe her, I went through the process myself, which only proved she was right.

"That's crazy," I said, staring at the phone.

"I'll check mine." Cara dug her phone out of her pocket. "It's not working!" She sounded shocked.

"Did you charge it?" I said, which got me an *are-you-kidding?* eye roll.

"I'm going to call Darlene. She'll be awake."

"Hello!" said a perky male voice.

"Who is this?" I asked, confused.

"Ouch, I'm hurt. And I just saw you half an hour ago."

"Andy?" I said, looking at my phone which confirmed I should have been talking to Darlene. "How did you get Darlene's phone?" I asked, a cold chill running down my spine.

"Look, if you don't want to talk to me, call someone else." He hung up.

I hit the speed dial for Pete, not caring if he was awake or not.

"Hello, again!" came Andy's chipper voice after two

rings.

I hung up and dialed 911.

"Hanging up on me isn't going to get you anywhere," Andy said when he answered.

"I don't know what kind of trick this is, but let me tell you, you're going to find yourself in some serious trouble if you don't come back and get us right now."

"No. I think you need to cool off first. In fact, the first step to finding your way out of the swamp is to throw your gun away."

"That's not happening."

"Then we have nothing else to talk about," he said and hung up on me again.

Cara looked concerned, but not frightened. For my part, I was feeling both fury and fear. Fear for us, fear for Marty and fear for anyone else who crossed this psychopath's trail.

"What kind of game is he playing?" Cara asked.

I was staring at my phone, trying to figure a way out of this.

"I don't know, but I'm betting his plan doesn't involve anything good for us."

"What about Marty? Do you think he's involved?"

I considered that. "No. I think he knew what was going on, and they may have involved him in it, but I don't think he was committed to whatever their plan was or is."

"They?"

"Yes. Cory has to be involved too. I imagine they sabotaged our ATV when they went to fill it up."

"What's going on with your phone?"

"My uneducated guess? I'd say it's been hacked." And I had a sinking feeling I knew how.

I chose a speed dial number at random.

"So you have it all figured out," Andy said in greeting.

"What?"

"The phone hacking, of course. And Marty's unwillingness to be involved. I really thought that Bridget would be able to hold him together better. He just doesn't have the stomach for it."

"You've been listening to us," I said, beginning to realize the full extent of the hack.

"Easy-peasy. Amazing the information you can find on the dark web these days. So, no, I can't take the credit. I just paid someone for the program."

"It was embedded in the photo."

"Congratulations! You beat level one and get to go for a bonus round."

"You've been eavesdropping on me."

"And good thing I've come into your life. I'm surprised you haven't died of boredom. I would have thought that a deputy's life would be more interesting. You're only surpassed by your wife, whose existence seems to consist of catering to animals and dreary coworkers before she comes home to your snoresville life."

"I sent her the picture."

"Of course. That's why her phone isn't working. I just turned it off. You know, I didn't want to have to use this on you. If you'd done what everyone was telling you to do and left the case well enough alone, I'd have never activated the virus. But you didn't leave me any choice."

"Okay, where do we go from here?" I asked, wanting to buy some time and figure out his plan.

"You can start by throwing your gun in the pond to your left," he said, startling me. Then I figured out he must've been using the phone's camera. I looked at the phone, trying to decide how best to thwart him. I didn't want to break it. Being able to communicate with Andy gave us some control of the situation.

"Do you have anything that would stick to the camera lens?" I asked Cara, bringing my mouth within an inch of her ear.

She looked in her pockets and gave me a big smile as she pulled out a couple of sticks of gum. Dr. Barnhill gave gum to the younger pet owners at the clinic, and Cara often came home with sticks in her pockets.

I took the pieces and quickly chewed one, managing to stick it over the lens.

"That was silly and pointless," Andy told us. "You're just wasting time. Throw your gun into the pond," he said firmly.

I decided to try a bluff. "Okay. I've done it."

"I'm not sure if you're stupid or think I am. Now take your gun out of your holster and throw it in the pond, or you can just rot out there."

"Can he see us?" Cara whispered in my ear.

I looked around and shrugged. I pulled my Glock out of the holster and held it up.

"Good, now throw it in the pond."

"How do you know I haven't already thrown the gun away?" I said, figuring it was time for direct questions.

"'Cause I can see you. Duh."

I wondered if my phone had another camera I didn't know about.

"Do you hear that?" Cara asked. She was looking around above her. "That buzzing noise."

I listened and could just hear a slight buzz. In seconds, it was louder and we looked up to see a drone flying about fifty feet above us.

"My eye in the sky." Andy's voice rang triumphantly from the phone.

I pointed the gun at the drone and fired a couple of shots, but it was almost impossible to hit as it moved. I'd need a dozen shots and a lot of luck. As it was, I had two magazines with seventeen rounds each, minus two now. I wanted to save what I had left. I knew I might need them to signal a rescue party or to defend us from the raving lunatic who'd led us out there.

"Okay, Andy, I get it. You have us where you want us. So what's this all about? Where's Marty?"

"You've got more to worry about than Marty," he said ominously. "Throw the gun into the pond and save us all a lot of time."

"I could care less about your time," I told him.

"You know, there are other things I can do. You should have learned by now that I can go after anyone I want."

"You killed Tracy and Austin?" I asked incredulously.

"In my own way."

I thought about how he had manipulated us and Marty, and who knew how many other people. "You got Austin to kill Tracy," I said in realization.

"Ding, ding! Ten thousand bonus points for the deputy."

I saw it now. "You hacked Tracy's phone and used that control to make Austin jealous enough to kill her."

"You really are pretty sharp. Which just means I can't let you live."

I put my gun back in its holster and hoped that he hadn't figured out a way to attach a bomb or a gun to a drone.

"I wouldn't do that," he said. "I told you to throw it into the pond."

I looked at my phone, weighed the pros and cons, then tossed *it* into the pond.

Cara gasped and the drone buzzed angrily as Andy made it dive and swing by us in several vicious passes.

"You need to toss your phone in too," I told Cara.

"But…"

"If we keep it, then he can listen to us and track us. The phone is useless to us."

She took one last look at it, then threw it into the pond.

"Wish we could get rid of that," I said, nodding toward the drone.

"What now?" Cara asked.

"All we have to do is figure out how to get out of here." I tried not to think about the Google satellite view on the property appraiser's website that had shown me tens of thousands of acres. If we went in the wrong direction, we could be lost for a long time. "At least the sun is up."

"We need to go in that direction," Cara said with an amount of certainty that seemed unrealistic.

"How do you know that?"

"Trust me."

"I know from our hikes that you have a pretty good sense of direction, but this is a little different," I said a bit condescendingly.

She frowned at me. "Mom and Dad had a very bad habit of leaving me in the care of their hippie friends. More than once, I was taken on walks in the woods with supposed adults who'd then get high as kites. Learning to get myself unlost was a survival skill I learned early."

I looked at her and thought of all her stories about growing up in communes out in the middle of nowhere. I started to believe.

"But how can you tell where we are? It's light now, but it was dark when we left the cottage."

"Have you ever heard of a song called *Follow the Drinking Gourd?* It was a sort of code for escaped slaves. They knew that the North Star was the pivot for the Big Dipper, or Drinking Gourd as they called it."

The drone buzzed over us a couple of times, just as a reminder that we weren't out there on a nature hike. I kept half an eye on it, hoping it would swoop in close enough that I could swat it down. It was a large one and would probably hurt my hand, but it would be a major coup to rid us of Andy's eye in the sky.

"So you saw the North Star?"

"It was on our left at first. We went east when we left the house, then south before turning east again. We're southeast of the house and cottages."

"Wow, I knew there was a reason I married you."

"Now all I have to do is figure out why I married you," she shot back with a big smile. A little levity helped to offset our uncomfortable and possibly dangerous situation.

"You married me for my good looks." I started walking in the direction she had indicated.

"Good for you. Keep believing in unicorns."

"Don't pick on me. I get enough of that from Darlene."

We had been walking for about twenty minutes when I realized I couldn't hear the drone anymore.

"We may have lost it," I said as we came to a swampy area filled with cypress trees and islands of palmetto bushes.

"I don't think their batteries last that long," Cara said, trying to decide how to get around the low area without taking a huge detour. "It's a toss-up whether it will be quicker to go east or west. West would probably be best, since we have to go a bit west anyway."

I slapped at mosquitoes as we went. "I should have put on some bug spray," I grumbled. Then I heard a buzzing that wasn't a bug. The drone was back. I looked up. "That's not the same one."

"Great, so he has two."

"He must have sent one back to recharge while he follows us with the other. I hate smart criminals."

We had come to a small clearing where a few large bushes with purple berries were growing. Cara went over to one of them and started picking leaves.

"I don't think we need to start eating plants yet," I said.

"This is a beautyberry plant. The leaves contain a natural mosquito repellant. Crush them and rub it on your clothes, and put some of the crushed leaves in your pockets." She saw my expression. "Last time I visited Mom and Dad at the co-op, they had a lecturer who talked about the uses of native plants."

I did as I was told. It helped. We made it around the swamp and Cara got us back on what she thought was the right course while the drone continued to follow us.

"There's some bad news we need to discuss," I said to Cara's back.

"What?"

"The drone. He knows where we are and will know a lot better than us when we're getting close to the homestead. He's not going to let us just walk out of the woods."

"You think he'll try and kill us."

"Not just him. I'm sure that Cory is in on it. Probably Rochelle and Bridget too. Last but not least, they might still be using Marty. So it could be five against two, with them having air support and better intelligence."

"Better intelligence, but we're smarter."

"I wish you hadn't come out with me tonight."

"And wouldn't that have been great? You'd be lost out here in the woods for who knows how long," she said with a small chuckle.

"Do you have any idea how close we are to the houses?"

"I could make a number up, but no, not really. When do you think Andy will make his move?"

"Make his move. You sound like some hard-boiled detective," I joked. "I like it. Very sexy."

She glared at me. "When?"

"Soon. I don't think he'll want us to get too close. At a distance, any gunfire will just sound like it could be anywhere on the property. I've heard some every day I've been out here. Sam said there's a hunt club with about a hundred members that uses the property."

"Is anything legal to hunt now?"

"It's always open season on invasive species like feral hogs and coyotes. Plus, they have a berm where folks can come out and sight in their rifles or practice."

"So no one will come to our rescue?"

"We can't count on it. Thought eventually someone will come looking for me."

I looked at my watch. It was already nine o'clock. We'd been out there for more than three hours. I smiled a little when I thought about how angry Lt. Johnson must have been when I hadn't shown up for the Explorers meeting.

"How soon?"

"I don't think anyone is going to get too worked up until this afternoon at the earliest. Johnson is going to be pissed off that I missed the meeting this morning, but I imagine his way of coping will be thinking of all the ways he can get me fired."

"Getting fired doesn't sound like the worst outcome at this point."

"Stop," I said, reaching for her hand.

"What?"

"We really need to come up with a plan. We don't want to just walk into an ambush."

I sat down and looked up at the drone hovering a hundred feet above us.

Cara saw the scowl on my face and asked, "What are you thinking?"

"I'm not happy about it, but I think we need to split up." I didn't like the idea one bit, but we had to do something and our options were very limited.

"Why don't we just stay in the woods? We can even head back the other way, pretend that we're lost. Maybe Andy will get tired of following us with the drone. Eventually, the sheriff's office will send help."

"I don't think Andy will just let us wander around until someone finds us."

"You have your gun, and we can last for a couple of days, easy."

"Maybe. But he knows where we are. Whenever he gets tired of waiting, he'll just try hunting us down. We wouldn't know when he was coming. Andy and his cohorts can sleep and eat until we're too exhausted to put up much of a fight."

"We could lose the drone at night."

"You're probably right," I said, not relishing the idea of staying out there any longer than we had to. "What are the odds he'd have an infrared set up on one of the drones?"

"I saw one of those in an episode of *Finding Bigfoot*."

"And while most of those shows are ridiculous, that type of technology is readily available."

I started to say something else when I heard a bullet whiz past my head, followed by the loud report of a gunshot ahead of us.

CHAPTER TWENTY-SIX

I dropped flat to the ground and yanked Cara down with me, then fired one round in the direction where the shot had originated. Not because I thought I might hit whoever was shooting, but as a reminder to them that we were armed and willing to defend ourselves. I hoped it would make them think twice before attempting to rush us.

"New plan," I said. "We don't split up. We've got to make a run for it. I'm guessing the houses are up ahead, which means we have to move toward the person who shot at us. Good news is, they're rotten hunters or one of us would be dead by now. Move and keep low."

We were lucky to be in an area of longleaf pine habitat. The undergrowth was made up of large sections of palmetto, interspersed with open areas of wiregrass.

"We should be able to stay concealed in the palmettos." *Just don't think about all the rattlesnakes*, I told myself as we started crawling forward.

I tried to move diagonally so that whoever was shooting would have a harder time figuring out where we were. "Let me know if we get too far off course," I told Cara. I didn't want to miss the cottages.

"Damn that drone," I muttered as we crawled. "With that

thing hovering around, we might as well be carrying a flag."

Then I saw a ravine to our right. Ravines were unique to this part of North Florida. Creeks cut deep rifts into the native limestone. The rich, damp slopes of the ravines allowed thick growths of magnolia, American beech and oak trees to flourish, protected from the fires that periodically swept through the longleaf forest. I thought I recognized this ravine from the Google photos as one that ran just south of the cabins. The pond near the cabins had been formed by a small dam across the creek that flowed through the ravine.

"If we can get to the ravine, we'll have a lot more cover and might even be able to lose the drone. Run when I give the word."

I saw Cara nod, her body going tense.

"Now!" I yelled and started sprinting for all I was worth. I went first to draw fire and it wasn't long before the rifle spoke. I slowed down so Cara could pass me. With her in front, I could make sure she got to cover safely. Another round whizzed by my ear. Lucky for us, it's not easy to hit a moving target at a distance.

We made it to the ravine and slid a hundred feet down to the creek. The drone was right behind us, but I was delighted to see it hit an oak branch and spin out of control. I couldn't hear or see it anymore after we got to the creek and started running. The water was only ankle-deep, but the sandy silt sucked at our feet as we splashed along. Soon, however, I could see where the creek flowed out into the open field near Bernadette's cabin.

"I want you to stay in the woods," I told Cara between breaths. I was panting heavily in the heat and humidity.

"No," she said, not breathing as heavily as I was.

"I don't have time to argue."

"No, you don't," she agreed.

"Listen to me," I pleaded. "You need to stay concealed. I'll go up and get help."

"Two of us have a better chance."

"Damn it! Don't argue."

"I'm not."

I knew it wasn't any use. We were already ten feet from the clearing. I stopped for a minute to catch my breath, scooping up water and pouring it over my wrists and neck to cool myself down. Cara did the same. I wanted to argue again for her staying behind, but there wasn't any point.

"At least do this. I'm going to make a dash for the hill. Wait until I get twenty feet out in the open. If I'm shot, go back and try to circle around. Remember, running out to help me would be a death sentence for both of us."

I gripped both her arms in my hands and looked her square in the eye, imploring her to do as I asked. She gave me a single nod. I kissed her and turned for the clearing.

I broke cover and ran up the hill, the muscles in my legs screaming. I huffed and puffed in the heat and humidity, wondering if I'd die of a heart attack before anyone had the chance to shoot me.

I heard another gunshot and saw a clod of dirt fly up ten feet in front of me. My lungs were fighting for air. I was aiming for my car and its radio when I saw movement over my shoulder. Cara had caught up to me, and I nudged her toward the main house just as one of the drones buzzed down toward us. When I saw that, I headed for the house too.

I pulled out my gun and looked for a target, making sure that anyone close by could see that I was armed. That might keep them from being too bold. We reached the steps of the main house as another bullet whined past us, throwing splinters as it hit the doorframe. Close behind us was that damn drone.

Once we hit the porch, I reached out and held Cara back just enough to let me get to the door first. I didn't slow down, lowering my shoulder so I'd hit the door close to the catch. I smashed through it, being careful to hold my gun out and keep my finger out of the trigger guard. Cara was right behind me.

With my shoulder throbbing, I stumbled to my feet and headed for the dining room where I'd seen the large cabinet full of firearms. I used my Glock to smash the cabinet glass, then handed it to Cara.

"There could be someone in the house, or they might come through the back door. Don't hesitate," I told her, then grabbed a 12-gauge side-by-side and opened drawers until I found a box of birdshot. I shoved several shells into my pocket and opened the gun, pushing a shell into each chamber before snapping it shut.

"See if you can find some 12-gauge slugs," I told Cara as I headed for the front door. I quickly found what I was looking for. The drone was hovering just feet from the porch. Before I'd even reached the door, I raised the shotgun swiftly. I saw it start to turn and I figured the operator must have seen what I was carrying. But he wasn't quick enough and I gave the drone both barrels. With immense satisfaction, I saw the contraption fly into a thousand pieces.

I closed what remained of the door just as a rifle round drilled a hole in it. Cara was coming up behind me and I pulled her to the floor.

"I found these." She gave me a box half full of slugs.

"Perfect," I said, wiping sweat from my face. I shucked out the empty shells and replaced them with slugs. A 12-gauge shotgun slug was capable of smashing through concrete block.

"How many are there?" Cara asked.

"Hard to say. At least two. One was operating the drone, while someone else was shooting at us. And there's probably at least one more. I don't think the first shots in the woods were fired by the same person who's shooting at us here. Which means we need to move quickly."

"What about Paula?"

"We can't worry about her right now. Either they've done something with her already, or she's hunkered down." *Or she's on their side*, I thought. "But while I can't do anything about Paula, I *can* go upstairs and check on Althea."

As I started to turn from the door, I looked outside to see Cory running toward the house.

"Stop!" I shouted.

His answer was a scream and a gunshot that went high.

"Get back!" I told Cara.

I heard Cory pound up onto the front porch. As soon as he hit the door, I let loose with one barrel from the shotgun. The slug smashed through the oak door and on through Cory. Both door and man dropped in the foyer in a mix of blood and splinters.

"Upstairs," I told Cara, and we made our way to the stairs as quickly as we could. Once we were on the second floor, I told Cara, "Stay here. Don't let anyone come up the stairs. I'm going to clear the other rooms." I also wanted to find a phone, but first I needed to check on Althea.

Her door was closed. I tried the handle carefully. If there was a bad guy or gal inside, I didn't want to warn them. I quietly replaced the spent slug in the shotgun, took a deep breath, then opened the door and rushed in.

A shot rang out. I swung my gun in the general direction of the shot and saw Althea sitting there with a small derringer in her hand. It was pointed my way and her hand was shaking.

"It's me," I told her. "Deputy Macklin."

"You aren't going to take him!" she shouted, and tried to shoot me again, but the two-shot pistol was empty. Ruby's body lay at Althea's feet, a smashed cell phone nearby. "She was going to call the cops."

"Are you mad?" I shouted at her, appalled.

"You aren't going to take Jack's son! Andy told me this morning." Her eyes were wild and unfocused.

I pulled the tie-backs off of the window drapes and used them to bind the raving old woman's hands. Then I left her and cleared the rest of the rooms on the second floor.

I started going from window to window, trying to see if anyone was attempting to rush the house. Fortunately, the grounds were clear around the house and cottages. Then I saw movement on the second floor of the converted summer kitchen. I wondered if it was Paula, but then a rifle stuck through the window and, just before the shot was fired, I recognized Andy. The bullet hit the window and sent glass flying at me. At least I knew where he was. I hoped that Paula was okay, then remembered Althea and hoped that Paula wasn't on his side.

Cara was backing her way down the hall toward me while she kept my gun aimed at the stairwell. I told her about Althea.

"What was she talking about?"

"I'm not sure. Trust me, she's gone around the bend. Andy's over in Paula's cottage."

As I spoke, another shot rang out from the same window. The distance was about fifty yards, well within range of a shotgun slug. I moved over to the other side of the window, so I wouldn't appear at the same place I'd been earlier. I took a deep breath and rose up, firing the gun. One slug tore a hole in the window frame of the cottage and the other exploded the window.

There was no sign of Andy. Backing up, I could look out on the parking area while staying out of sight of the cottage. I reloaded the shotgun as I looked at my car. *So close*, I thought.

"You can't take the chance," Cara said, knowing what I was thinking.

"I don't have much of a choice."

"We can wait it out up here. Someone will come looking for you."

"You can wait. I have a duty to protect others. Paula and Marty may be innocent and in danger. Sam could be injured. The sooner help is on the way, the better for everyone."

Cara looked at me. "I want to tell you that I don't care about anyone else."

I kissed her. "I can make it. I'm going to rely on you to make a bunch of noise."

"Are you sure?"

I took the shotgun and switched the slugs out for a couple of the birdshot shells I had in my pocket. "Sit down here. When I tell you, I want you to just shoot out the window. Don't worry about aiming at anything. Here are some more shells. Shoot four rounds, then reload and just sit here with the gun pointing down the hall. Anyone who's not a friend comes up the stairs, shoot them. It has some kick."

"I've fired a shotgun," Cara said, but her voice was shaking a little.

I looked out the window. While we'd been plotting our next moves, a car had driven up and parked next to mine.

"Change of plans," I said as I saw Lt. Johnson get out of the car in full uniform.

I grabbed the shotgun and aimed it at the cottage where I'd last seen Andy. I wanted to get a shot off to warn the lieutenant before he got too far from the concealment offered by his car. I fired a round of birdshot at the window of the cottage. Johnson dropped to the ground, then scurried back to his car. I waited for a shot from the cottage, but none came.

Standing back so that I didn't expose myself, I shouted down to Johnson. "It's Macklin. There's a shooter in the cottage."

Johnson had drawn his gun and was crouched behind his car. He pulled out his phone as a shot was fired from one of the first-floor windows of the cottage. I saw the impact of the bullet on Johnson's windshield. He never flinched and finished with the call, which I assumed meant the cavalry was on the way. Then Johnson moved to the back of his car and went prone to fire a couple of shots at the cottage window.

I could see movement at the window, but Andy was staying back behind the windowsill. I put a couple of slugs in the shotgun. They probably wouldn't go through the multiple two-by-fours of the window frame, but they could penetrate the wall. Some of Andy's body had to be behind the wall beside the window. I decided to teach him a lesson about the difference between concealment and cover.

I raised up and rested the shotgun on my hand, which I steadied against the windowsill. With only a bead sight on the end of the barrel, the shotgun's accuracy wasn't guaranteed, but it wasn't a great distance. I knew I should be able to make the shot. As soon as I saw the thinnest shadow at the edge of the cottage's window, I pulled the trigger. A satisfying hole was punched through the wall about five inches from the window frame. I saw Johnson look up at me. I waved for him to keep down. We waited.

After several minutes of silence, I signaled to Johnson that I was coming out. I traded guns with Cara and hurried down the stairs, running out the back door and around the far side of the house. I didn't see anyone.

As soon as I started toward the cottage, Johnson saw me and stood up, staying behind the car where he could best cover me. As I got closer to the cottage, Johnson broke cover and headed for the other side of the cottage.

Inside we found Andy on the floor, bleeding profusely. He was alive, but barely conscious. I could hear sirens in the distance. I left Johnson with Andy while I cleared the rest of the cottage.

After the other deputies and two ambulances arrived, we searched and found Paula and Marty being held in the small house where Tracy and Austin had died. Bridget and Rochelle were brandishing knives, but dropped them as soon as we arrived. Once they heard that Cory was dead and Andy was wounded and in custody, they surrendered and went into victim mode. They both swore that they had been forced to participate. We handcuffed them, read them their rights and stuffed them into a patrol car before they were driven to the county jail.

I found Cara relating our tale of wilderness survival to Lt. Johnson.

"I knew your wife was pretty and smart. What I didn't know was how tough she is," Johnson said. I was shocked at his attempt to be charming. "If you want to be a deputy, you've got my vote," he said to Cara, then turned to me. "From the sound of it, if it hadn't been for your wife, you'd still be wandering around in the wilderness."

"Maybe," I admitted. "Where's Althea?" I had noticed that both ambulances were gone.

"That woman is beyond crazy," Johnson said. "Because of her age, they were afraid to sedate her without a doctor present, so they had to strap her down to the gurney. She was still screaming about her grandson when they drove away."

"She'll have to be charged with the murder of her nurse, Ruby Banks."

Johnson was shaking his head in disbelief. "After this, I might be forced to believe you the next time you tell me things are a bit hinky. I'm not sure if I'm looking forward to or dreading reading your report."

"There are still a number of questions," I said, but now I knew how to find the answers.

CHAPTER TWENTY-SEVEN

Three days later, Darlene and I were on our way to the hospital in Tallahassee to interview and formally charge Andy with Cory's death. We also had conspiracy to kidnap and a few other random crimes we could book him for.

"So the only murder he's being charged with right now is the guy *you* killed?" Darlene asked.

"Perverse, isn't it? But Cory died while Andy was committing several felonies, therefore Andy can be charged for murder."

"How are you handling the shooting?"

"Better than I would have thought. Maybe because I felt like I was defending Cara at the time."

"You still need to go through the debriefing and see a counselor."

"Do you see a gun on me?" I said. I wouldn't get my service gun back until I was cleared by the review board, which Major Parks told me would happen before the weekend. At this point, it was just a matter of procedure.

"Have you finished your reports?"

"I'm still sorting it all out. I need Andy to clear up a few items. Motivation being the biggest. The sisters have clammed up on the advice of their lawyers, and Althea is crazy as a bed bug, so I'm counting on Andy."

"Didn't the boy fill in some of the details?"

"Marty? Yeah, he did. And to Paula's credit, she encouraged him to tell us everything he knows. Andy wasn't lying about Marty's drug use or his crush on Bridget. He used that to manipulate Marty into helping him. According to Marty, Andy talked Cory and the sisters into helping him to eliminate Bruce and Owen. Cory was motivated by his father's history. The family ostracized his father for years over an incident that happened when his father was fourteen. His dad still isn't over it, and his animosity got passed on to his son. Andy convinced Cory and the two women that, with a bunch of the family dead and Althea not long for the world herself, they'd be in line for an inheritance soon."

"They aren't even direct relations, are they?"

"No. They're grandchildren of Althea's sister, who's been dead for over a decade. But that side of the family has always believed they were entitled to a share of Althea's estate. That's why they came to all the family affairs. Althea encouraged the belief and teased them regularly about it."

"Honey child, in the parlance of the South, that woman is batshit crazy," Darlene said.

Althea had been admitted to the state mental hospital in Chattahoochee, where we'd attempted to interview her the day before. They weren't happy to have her, but no other hospital was willing to take her.

"What happened to the son, Jack, that she kept babbling about?" Darlene asked. "He's the one who supposedly drowned, right? But she made it sound like her husband killed him... if I interpreted her ravings correctly."

"I think that's possible, and would certainly explain her hatred. The father and son had never gotten along. They had a big fight and the son came out to the farm. He was found the next morning, floating in the pond. His blood alcohol level would have left him almost incapacitated. I think his father must have followed him to the house and found him drunk, or even passed out. To rid himself of a son who was rebellious and detrimental to his business, he might have dragged him into the pond and let him drown."

"What a lovely family," Darlene said with a sad laugh.

"And what about the death of Bruce Byrd?"

"That's easy. Well, sort of. Marty filled us in on that too. Seems that Bridget made exact copies of Percocet out of chalk. She's a very talented artist. Anyway, when they got here, they'd substituted the chalk pills for the real things in Bruce's prescription bottles. He'd been taking the fake pills and wasn't getting any relief. He kept upping the number of pills he was taking and, since the pain was excruciating, he resorted to drinking whiskey to cut it. On the day he died, Andy and the gang had put the real pills back in the bottle. Bruce took a handful and washed them down with the whiskey. Shortly after he laid down, his body couldn't take it and he stopped breathing."

"And Owen?"

"They just played the same phone hacking trick on him that they played on me. They let the dogs out of the pen and, when Owen went after them, Andy used his control of Owen's phone to lead him on a merry chase. At some point during the night, Owen had a major stroke. The gang found him, which was easy enough since he still had the phone with him at the time. Seeing that Owen was practically dead, if not actually dead, they decided to play heroes and bring him out of the woods."

"Talk about your bad seeds."

"I think there's a little of that. Actually, a lot of it in Andy's case. But with the others, I think Andy held a Manson-like sway over them. He was very good at knowing how to push people's buttons to get them to do his bidding. He had me fooled."

"You said Marty gave you Tracy's phone."

"Yes."

"I guess there was incriminating evidence on it."

"A whole series of fake text messages that Andy had put

on Tracy's phone, again using his favorite hacking program. I saw some of the messages. They were hot enough to make any spouse jealous. Let alone one as controlling as Austin."

"So the question is, why did Andy do all of this?"

"Let's ask him," I said, pulling into the hospital's parking garage.

Like most psychopaths, Andy craved attention and was more than willing to explain all about his crimes. Of course, in all of his stories, he was cast as the victim.

"They killed my father and disinherited me," he argued while trying to gesture with his hands, which were strapped to the hospital bed.

"Your father was Jack Byrd," I said.

"That's right. Jack and my mother were going to get married. She was pregnant with me. But his father wouldn't hear of it, which was rich since he'd been through the same thing before Owen was born. They fought and my grandfather followed my dad to the farm and drowned him."

"Your mother told you this?"

"No. She died two years after I was born. She died of a broken heart."

I'd already done a background check on his mother. "Rosie Calderon died of a drug overdose in 1994."

"She become an addict because of my father's death," Andy grumbled.

"She had a DUI in 1990," I said and let it drop. She'd also been picked up for possession of cocaine in 1991, but I didn't see the need to mention it.

"His brothers deserved to die. My mom's sister raised me and told me all about what they did to my mother. After my father died, no one in the family would talk to her or help her. His own brothers got the police to harass her and tried to get her to sign papers declaring that I wasn't Jack's son. They drove her to her death."

"So this was all about revenge?"

"Cory hated them as much as I did for what they'd done to his dad. He'd heard rumors about me and tracked me down, then introduced me to Roch. She and I really did kind of click. But don't let them lie to you. They all wanted to get the money I promised them. My grandmother was going to die soon anyway."

"You planned on killing her too?"

"No! She loved my father. Now that she knows who I am, she loves me!"

"When did you tell her?"

"When I knew you were going to make it back to the house. When I told her, she said that I was right to kill the others. The stupid nurse was going to call 911 and Grandma shot her." His voice was full of family pride.

I thought of Ma Barker. Just to have a piece of Jack back in her life, Althea had been willing to let Andy get away with murder.

"And Marty? You got him to hide Tracy's cell phone."

"He was weak. I knew that we'd have to kill him eventually. The only way I could control him was 'cause he had a thing for Bridget. Go figure. When I wanted to kill him that morning, Bridget pitched a fit. So we just tied him up."

"You would have killed him later."

"Absolutely. I knew he'd eventually talk." There was a pause. "I guess he *has* been talking."

We fingerprinted Andy and formally charged him.

"Sad and crazy," Darlene said when we were back in the car.

"Runs in some people's families," I said, then hesitated a minute before asking, "How'd the interview go?"

"I'm going to miss you," Darlene said with a smile.

"That good?"

"It's down to two candidates. Me and a guy from Tampa. The committee will decide next week and give the city commission their recommendation at the next commission meeting."

That night I came home to find Cara all smiles.

"Dr. Horvath liked the proposal and we're going to work out the details over the weekend."

"If that doesn't work out, remember that Lt. Johnson offered you a job as a deputy."

She came in for a kiss. "I think one deputy in the family is enough."

Larry Macklin returns in:

Autum's Curse
A Larry Macklin Mystery–Book 15
Coming Summer 2020

ACKNOWLEDGMENTS

As always, thanks to my wife, Melanie, for her editing skills and support; to H. Y. Hanna for her inspiration, assistance and encouragement; and to all the fans of the series. Larry never would have come this far without all of you!

Original Cover Concept by H. Y. Hanna
Cover Design by Robin Ludwig Design Inc.
www.gobookcoverdesign.com

ABOUT THE AUTHOR

A. E. Howe lives and writes on a farm in the wilds of north Florida with his wife, horses and more cats than he can count. He received a degree in English Education from the University of Georgia and is a produced screenwriter and playwright. His first published book was *Broken State*. The Larry Macklin Mysteries is his first series and he released a new series, the Baron Blasko Mysteries, in summer 2018. The first book in the Macklin series, *November's Past*, was awarded two silver medals in the 2017 President's Book Awards, presented by the Florida Authors & Publishers Association; the ninth book, *July's Trials*, was awarded two silver medals in 2018. Howe is a member of the Mystery Writers of America, and was co-host of the "Guns of Hollywood" podcast for four years on the Firearms Radio Network. When not writing Howe enjoys riding, competitive shooting and working on the farm.